It hit her then. Not like a ton of bricks, not a like a slap in the face, not like a cold shower.

This was a soft awareness, like picking up a sleeping kitten and cuddling it close.

He liked her. More than a boss usually liked his employee.

He liked her. Those mixed signals weren't all just self-preservation.

He liked her. A lot.

The proof was there. But what did it mean?

Nothing, her head said.

Everything, her heart said.

It could be a silly infatuation, created by the time they'd been spending together. Something that would fade.

Or it could be the beginning of a feeling that went down like a rich red wine. Something that expanded and lingered.

One thing she did know—she wanted to find out.

Dear Reader,

Welcome to Harmony Valley!

Things aren't as harmonious here as they once were. Jobs have dried up and almost everyone under the age of sixty has moved away in the past ten years, leaving the population...well, rather gray-haired and peaceful.

Enter three young men—Slade, Flynn and Will—friends, newly minted millionaires and hometown success stories. Slade Jennings is a former Wall Street whiz who can't seem to give up his ties, even though he's living in the wine country. This summer, he's running winery operations and hosting his twin girls.

Winemaker Christine Alexander is tired of wine with her name on it being changed by meddlesome winery owners. She's taken the job in Harmony Valley because she was promised autonomy. She hadn't counted on Slade being a control freak. If she's not careful, he's going to expand the winery's production before the quality is proven in the bottle. If she's not careful, her curiosity about Slade and his ties are going to change her priorities forever.

I hope you enjoy Slade and Christine's journey, as well as the other romances in the Harmony Valley series. I love to hear from readers. Check my website to learn more about upcoming books set in Harmony Valley and sign up for email book announcements. Or you can chat with me on Facebook (MelindaCurtisAuthor) or on Twitter (MelCurtisAuthor), and hear about my latest giveaways.

Melinda Curtis

HARLEQUIN HEARTWARMING

Melinda Curtis

Season of Change

HARLEQUIN® HEARTWARMING™

Recycling programs
for this product may
not exist in your area.

ISBN-13: 978-0-373-36677-4

SEASON OF CHANGE

Printed in U.S.A.

MELINDA CURTIS

has lived in humid Georgia and crazy-weather Texas. She prefers the possibility of California earthquakes. Her work experience prior to writing this book includes being an inventory-taker, a maid, a baseball announcer, a rodent wrangler, a copy writer, a focus group moderator and a cubicle wage-slave. She'll take romance writer and bare feet over suits and heels (or rodents) any day.

Melinda currently lives in California's arid central valley with her husband—her basketball-playing college sweetheart. With three kids, the couple has done the soccer thing, the karate thing, the dance thing, the Little League thing and, of course, the basketball thing. Now they're enjoying the quiet life of empty nesters before the grandparent thing.

Melinda writes sweet contemporary romances as Melinda Curtis and red-hot reads as Mel Curtis. She loves writing romances about women who don't realize how strong they are until a hero comes along to show them, while capturing the wry, humorous power struggle of falling in love. Because, really? What woman lets the man have the last word?

Nothing in my life would be possible without the love and support of my immediate family, extended family and close friends. A special thank you to my husband of thirty years for putting up with me and all the voices in my head clambering for a happy ending.

As always, special thanks to A.J. Stewart, Cari Lynn Webb and Anna Adams for their support throughout the writing of this book. Every writer needs a sounding board. You guys rock!

I spent sixteen years working at a winery. In writing the Harmony Valley books, I relied on my memory, as well as questions to friends and family who still work and own wineries. Think of Harmony Valley as you enjoy a glass of wine from The Iron Gate Winery in Cedar City or the Jordon Winery in Healdsburg, but know that all mistakes regarding wineries and winemaking are my own.

CHAPTER ONE

LIFE WAS A numbers game.

Count the years, count the money, count the marriages, count the mistakes.

Slade Jennings was thirty-two years old, had millions in the bank, one failed marriage, and one horrendous mistake.

He knew what he looked like walking down the street—success. Wrinkle-free khakis, wrinkle-free button down, Italian designer tie. Rolex. Titanium and onyx pinky ring. Dark-as-midnight hair, expensively cut. Eyes the color of money, always on the lookout for the next deal. Slade had come from humble beginnings and wasn't going back.

Except, he had. Gone back to his roots, that was, damaged though they may be.

That was what you did for friends who were also your business partners. You went with the flow, even if that meant returning to your hometown, to the house you'd grown up in, to the house where both your parents died, the scene of the horrendous mistake.

Harmony Valley's bridge club called the house at 1313 Harrison Street the Death and Divorce House. In Slade's lifetime there hadn't been any divorces. But there had been plenty of deaths. His mother gave in to melanoma in the master bedroom. His father hung himself six years later in the closet of the same room. It was the culmination of everything that was wrong with Slade's life—he'd lost his career, his bank account, and then his family. That was eight years ago. The house on Harrison represented failure, which was why it was vital Slade present only success to the world.

While in Harmony Valley, Slade was living in the Death and Divorce House. To stay elsewhere seemed like a betrayal. But stay in the master bedroom? No. He slept in the bedroom of his youth.

He'd returned to town earlier that year with Will Jackson and Flynn Harris, his childhood friends and the two programming geniuses behind a successful farming app. Slade was their sidekick and the partnership's money-man, the one who managed the bottom line, watched their backs, and made sure they didn't get screwed in any negotiations.

So, why weren't they back in Silicon Valley leveraging their achievement?

Because Will and Flynn burned out designing their first app. They were all local boys, if not best friends when they were growing up, as close as brothers now. When they showed up to decompress after five years of sharing a cramped apartment with the thinnest walls on the planet, they'd been asked by the town council to start a business to help save their hometown.

An explosion fourteen years ago at the grain mill had wiped out Harmony Valley's main employer. The ripple effect forced those too young to retire to move closer to jobs and all but a handful of businesses to shut down. Located in the northernmost corner of Sonoma County, Harmony Valley was becoming a remote retirement village. The population had dwindled below eighty, with the average age of residents above seventy-five.

Given that Slade preferred Harmony Valley become a ghost town when all the old-timers died, he'd voted against the partnership starting a business here. Then he'd protested their choice of business—a winery. They were three guys who drank beer. What did they know about making wine? Outvoted, he'd still stood by his friends through arguments with blustery octogenarians, a mountain of legal and financial paperwork, and the ups and downs of construction.

Today, the shell of the winery was finally completed. The winemaker they'd hired, Christine Alexander, granddaughter of a town-council member—would the nepotism never end?—was due to start work today and provide Slade with her input on the guts of the winery. Juice presses, tanks, barrels, and whatever else she needed to make great wine. Really great wine people would drop a C-note to drink. Because if they were going to make wine, it'd be the best wine around.

Slade checked his Rolex. Christine was late.

He sat on the porch of the old farmhouse they'd converted into an office and tasting room, and loosened the knot of his tie.

Summer was in full swing. The air was hot and dry. Barely a breeze swayed the palm trees lining the hundred-yard newly graveled drive. The sixty-foot-tall eucalyptus trees that marched along the river were silent, as well. Occasionally, a cricket offered complaint.

Something shook the house, a slight tremor that had Slade leaping up.

Eathquake!

The horse weathervane on top of the main winery building rocked, spun, then quieted. The ground settled and Slade drew a deep breath. As a native Californian, he was used to small, infrequent tremors. That didn't mean they didn't send his body humming with adrenaline faster than a shot of espresso.

His phone buzzed, announcing a text message from Flynn: Did you feel that?

His reply: Yes. Winery is fine.

A big black SUV turned into the driveway.

He'd thought Christine owned a small, newer-model Audi. At least, that was what she'd driven up in for her job interview last month. He shifted the tie-knot back into place and walked down the circular drive to meet her.

Only it wasn't Christine.

It was his ex-wife, Evangeline, a native New Yorker. Two shadows bobbed in the backseat, his twin ten year-old daughters, Faith and Grace. He was simultaneously overjoyed and overwhelmed. No one had told him they were coming. Not that it mattered. He practically flew down the drive to meet them.

Evangeline toggled down the window and gave him a scornful look. He hadn't seen her since Christmas, but she was as stylish as ever in a bold tiger-print blouse and chunky jewelry. Her black hair was short and blunt cut, framing her strikingly angular face, making her too-white smile seem fanglike. "I thought you'd be at the house. We saw Will in town and he told us you were here."

Slade was used to burying his emotions behind a facade of savvy sophistication. He hid them now, deep in his chest in a tight, burdensome lump.

Months ago, Evangeline had called and—amid a rant about how she resented the revised visitation agreement—had told him she would abide by it and let the girls stay with him while she and her new husband, provider of the four-carat monstrosity on her slender finger, took a delayed honeymoon to the South of France.

Evangeline didn't like sharing the girls, which was why when Slade agreed to increase child support, he also brought down the judge's gavel on enforcing his newly expanded parental rights. Evy was always agreeing to drop them off, but never following through. If she was here, husband number three must be something. And that something was spontaneous, because they weren't due to visit for another two weeks.

With effort, Slade shifted into "polite conversation" mode. "Did you feel that earthquake just now? It wasn't very big." When Evy shook her head, he leaned farther in the window to greet the twins. "Hey, girls. *Holy...*"

They looked like miniature, identical Gothic vampires. If his mother wasn't already dead, she'd have risen up and splashed them with holy water.

"Don't judge," Evangeline scolded sharply. "It's a phase. Today Goth. Tomorrow princesses."

He forced himself to smile. "Took me by surprise is all. Did you leave their things at my place?" The Death and Divorce House was dim and filled with bad memories. He slept there, but only because the past wouldn't let him bunk anywhere else. If he'd believed Evy would follow through this time and honor his visitation rights, he would have made other arrangements to stay in town or at the nearest hotel, thirty minutes away.

"Slade, we don't have a key. Not to *that house.*" Derision dripped from every syllable, bringing back too many memories of the hot-tempered, entitled woman he'd divorced.

Aren't whirlwind college romances swell?

But her contempt goaded him into a decision he'd most likely regret later—to have the girls stay at the house with him. "We don't lock the doors here, Evy."

"You know I don't like it when you call me that."

He did. He winked at the girls.

They didn't smile or laugh or give any indication that they appreciated being included in his inside joke. That was probably his punishment for only seeing them twice a year. When they were older, they'd understand why their mother kept them away and why Slade didn't press as hard as he should for visitation.

Slade opened the back door so the twins could get out.

Up close, it was even worse. Black lipstick, black eyeliner, black lace blouses over yellow-and-black-plaid capris. He hoped to heaven the short blond hair with thin black streaks were wigs.

Two silent strangers slid out. A far cry from the plump, happy babies he used to rock to sleep. Or the grinning, sturdy two-year olds that he used to push on swings.

Good thing he'd been hanging out with Flynn and his seven-year-old nephew the past month or he wouldn't have a clue how to deal with them. He tousled Faith's hair. She was the twin with a dimple that rarely disappeared on her cheek, even when she frowned at him and straightened her wig. Grace came to stand next to her. They stared at him in wordless retribution.

Ten. Crap. He'd thought teenage angst started at thirteen.

"You'll be all right, won't you, girls?" Evangeline waited for their nods before she commanded, "Get their things, Slade."

Her attitude was starting to cinch his collar, but it didn't make sense to argue.

Their things included four huge suitcases, three Nordstrom shopping bags, two identical backpacks with angry manga characters, and one stuffed lion the size of a large dog.

Slade dutifully loaded it all into the bed of his new black truck, giving himself and the girls a pep talk. "We're going to have a good time, aren't we?"

No one answered.

Evangeline reeled each girl in with one hand for fierce hugs. "You be good like I told you and you'll be safe." She gave Slade a sharp look that could have cut metal. "I'm trusting you with my babies." She named the date she wanted them back in New York, as if his daughters were on loan.

Since they'd separated eight years ago, he'd wanted to spend more time with the twins than his twice-a-year visits. The new settlement had given him hope. He'd pictured happy vacations to amusement parks and sunny beaches. He'd imagined laughter and enthusiasm and emotional hugs. He'd dreamed of having them for a day, a weekend, a week.

And here was reality: his girls had misplaced fashion limits, stared at him mutely, and there were nearly thirty days looming ahead like a prison sentence.

DAY ONE ON the job and Christine Alexander was late.

That didn't mean she expected to show up for work and see a glamorous-looking woman doing the tiptoe run around a black SUV in skyscraper heels, or a pair of identical little Goth girls. Not this far away from civilization. Not outside an anime film. Not at her place of employment.

Christine had thought she was escaping the high-drama, high-fashion, high-ego circus that was Napa wine making.

The queen bee in high heels gunned the SUV around the circular driveway. A relief.

Although the Goth girls were still a caution.

Christine parked her old bucket with its deceased air conditioner next to the big black truck that remained, turned off the ignition, and received a very brutal, vibrating massage as the engine fought and coughed and hiccuped trying to stay alive. It wasn't until it wheezed its last breath that Christine risked getting out.

Her boss, Slade, did a double take. The well-worn car. Christine in her red Keds, faded blue jean shorts, and black Useless Snobbery band T-shirt. Never mind that wine making was a hands-on, messy job. Her new boss didn't seem to understand that.

The little optimistic light inside her that placed such high hopes on this position—for loyalty, for legitimacy, and a nest egg for her future—faded.

She tossed her long blond ponytail over a shoulder, wishing she'd at least taken the time to put it in a French braid. The fancier hair-style made her look more serious and kept her hair off her neck, which was now hot and sweaty. It had to be ninety-five degrees today, if not pushing one hundred.

"Hey," she said to the two girls.

They didn't move or quit staring, which was kind of creepy. Goth mini-mannequins.

"Slade, good to see you again." Christine closed the distance between them and shook her boss's hand.

His handshake was perfect—not bone-crushing hard, not limp. Just the right amount of grip and shake. But then again, Slade was perfectly put together. He could have modeled for a living. He was tall and lean, with a hard chin, sculpted cheekbones, and black hair that was always tamed, always controlled. Seriously, the guy was so perfect, he almost didn't have a personality.

She wouldn't have fought for this job if she was only working for Slade. He was everything she was leaving behind—name-brand posturing and excess. It had been Flynn, one of Slade's business partners, who convinced Christine to accept the job. He'd taken one look at her suit and high heels the day of the interview and said, "You look nice, but if we hire you, I don't ever want to see you in a suit again. We're beyond casual around here."

Such was the joy of working for two millionaires who'd made their fortunes in the tech world. Will and Flynn didn't stand on ceremony like those in the wine industry. They shunned hosting black-tie, sequined events. And then there was her third boss—Slade.

"I'm sorry I didn't dress for the office." She gestured in the region of his fabulous tie. "I was trying to move the last of my things to town."

"That's all right." His accepting tone contradicted his disapproving expression. "Did you feel the earthquake a few minutes ago?"

"I'm assuming you're not talking about my car's unique way of shutting off." She gave him her best smile-and-laugh-with-me one-two combo, scoring a point when he smiled back, even though the Goth girls blanked her. "I may have felt something coming down Main. I thought it was bad gas knocking." Not hardly. She'd thought her old beater would suffice and had given up her lease on the Audi. She was in penny-pinching mode, living here with her grandmother, saving for a down payment on her own vineyard. She wouldn't have given up the Audi if she'd known her college car was in desperate need of a tune-up or a new engine or a trip to the scrapyard.

"It's a toss-up whether it was your car or the tremor," Slade deadpanned. He turned to the girls. "These are my daughters—"

His? Get out of town!

"Grace—" Slade gestured from one girl to the other "—and Faith."

"So that was your wife leaving?"

"Ex," he said curtly.

Immediately, Christine wished she could take the question back. Slade probably thought she was digging for information to see if he was single. What she really wanted was reassurance that Slade was more interested in the substance of the wine she made than the image he presented to the outside world. The wine industry attracted almost as many grandstanders as Hollywood. She didn't care if Slade wore a parka in this heat, as long as their vision for their wine meshed.

Slade smoothed his tangerine-colored paisley tie. "After our tour, we'll head over to El Rosal for a cool drink. Or some ice cream." This latter part she assumed was an offer for the twins. Little did Slade know Christine liked ice cream almost as much as she liked wine.

He led them into the tasting room, the girls trailing behind Christine like silent wraiths. How their quirkiness must upset the balance in Slade's otherwise balanced life.

Everything in the tasting room smelled of new construction, of sawed wood and fresh paint. The otherwise empty room had a large blue marble counter, behind which was a built-in oak buffet. And blessedly, they'd installed air-conditioning.

"Is that original?" Christine ran a hand over the buffet's polished wood. "It's beautiful."

"It is. We were able to save much of the

planked flooring, as well. This house was built over one hundred years ago by Jeremiah Henderson. The property remained in Henderson hands until we bought it earlier this year." He spoke as if he was behind a lectern, coolly enunciating every syllable. No awkward pauses, lisps, or stutters.

The poor man is so personality-free it's sad.

"It's been remodeled," he continued, "and had additions over the years, but this room is the original front parlor."

It wasn't every day a man used the word *parlor* in front of Christine. It drew her gaze to his perfectly formed lips. She licked her own, her gaze falling to his feet.

His loafers weren't knock-offs. The workmanship and shine practically screamed Italian. "We also have a bathroom and a full kitchen here." He led her to the rear of the house.

She passed through a doorway, dragged her gaze from the feet she was following, and fell in love. "I want to live here."

Baby-blue marble countertops, soft white cabinets, and a double-wide porcelain farm sink. They may have built this place out in the boonies, but they'd spared no expense. Christine could hardly wait to start talking about the wine-making equipment they'd be purchasing.

"It's nice, isn't it?" His smile was unexpectedly humble. She would have bet on chest-thumping pride. "The office space is upstairs." Slade led her up a narrow staircase. "We couldn't see a way to widen these without losing valuable space below. The footprint of the house is only one thousand square feet."

The office was open, empty space with front-facing dormers and soft blue walls. The windows had no coverings, allowing the sun to beat in and suck the life out of the air.

"We didn't think about desks until after the remodel was almost finished, so we're having furnishings custom-built. I hope you like them."

"Whatever you get will be fine." She'd work on a plywood desk held up by sawhorses in exchange for the power over all wine-making decisions. "What about the—"

Slade put a finger to his lips.

That was when she noticed they were alone.

Soft whispers drifted to them from downstairs.

Slade smiled broadly, like a papa bear finding joy in his cubs.

Whoa. Mr. Perfect loves his Goth girls.

It surprised Christine so much she was sure she reflected his grin right back at him. The humanness—so unexpected—explained why his everyday-guy business partners put up with him.

The whispers stopped.

"You'll get blinds or something up here, I assume." Christine quickly filled the void.

"Plantation shutters." He was still smiling at her, as if they'd shared a private moment and he wasn't ready to let the feeling go. "Let's check out the main winery."

Maybe he wasn't all staid ego and self-image. Maybe he'd had a business meeting earlier. Maybe he'd had a meeting before every time she'd met him previously. That would explain why she'd never seen him without a tie. But there was something about his rigid posture that negated that hypothesis.

From the farmhouse, they crossed the circular drive toward a barnlike structure on the same property. They'd only just broken ground on it when Christine first interviewed. She hadn't imagined it would look so welcoming and yet be so huge, nestled amid row after row of grapevines.

Untended, overgrown grapevines.

The road to harvest wouldn't be easy.

The heat pressed down on her once more,

like heavy hands on her shoulders. Christine didn't know how Slade could stand wearing a tie. The only concession he'd made to the heat was rolling up his shirtsleeves, revealing well-muscled, tan forearms.

Christine stepped through the forty-foot high double doors into the cavernous, blessedly cooler would-be winery. The new-construction smell was less noticeable here with the doors thrown open. It was empty, just metal support beams, concrete, and wood. But to her, it was paradise. She could easily visualize how to fill it with equipment.

"This was the site of the original barn, which we were unable to salvage." Was that a wistful note in his voice? "We built this to look like the original homestead, but big enough to accommodate processing up to eighty thousand cases of wine."

Eighty thousand cases?

Each case contained twelve bottles. He was talking close to a million bottles.

Red flag. Serious red flag.

"Slade." She carefully kept her voice even, her expression polite. "As I understand it, you only own forty acres of vineyard. That's enough to produce about five thousand cases." Seventy-five thousand less than his planned capacity.

Christine tried to ignore the alarm buzzing in her head. She'd been hired to produce boutique wine in small quantities, hired to obtain top ratings and reviews, hired to help build Harmony Valley Vineyards into something prestigious and rare. Eighty thousand cases crossed the border from rare territory into the gray zone, flirting with a fall into the quirky, quaffable territory occupied by wine costing less than ten bucks a bottle. Wines with cartoony icons and names like My Boyfriend's Favorite Red or Bow Tie Bordeaux.

"What's the use of starting a company if you don't plan for growth? It's where we need to be in five years." He stepped from the light into the shadows, his gaze on her intense. "Does success scare you?"

"No." Failure did. As her dad so often reminded Christine, her reputation was only as good as her last score in the bible of wine-review magazines. In just a few months, she'd find out in print if she was a scapegoat at Ippolito Cellars or if she'd dodged a bullet by leaving when her wine-making principles were undermined. "Fine wine can't be rushed."

Faith and Grace watched their exchange closely, holding hands as if they were in some kind of horror movie, ready to unleash deadly powers if Christine took this argument too far.

Yes, Christine had no social life. Yes, she watched too many scary films. Yes, she might have leaped into this job too quickly, since Slade seemed more interested in volume than quality.

"We should talk." A classic brush-off line from a boss who'd already made up his mind.

That alarm in her head buzzed louder.

"But let's get out of the heat before we discuss it further. You remember where El Rosal is? On the town square?" At her nod, he stepped out beneath the blazing sun, which painted silver-blue highlights in his black hair, as if he were a hunky rock star and she was just one of the little people in the audience dancing to the beat of his hypnotic drum.

Wilting in the heat, Christine trailed behind his two Goth girls, reluctantly contemplating her next job search.

CHAPTER TWO

WHEN HE'D HIRED Christine, everything about her had looked top-shelf, from her designer shoes to her carefully coiffed blond hair. She'd presented herself as the kind of woman Slade admired—beautiful, confident, someone he could count on, and with a genuineness that Evangeline lacked. He'd voted to hire Christine because she'd represent their winery to the world the way he would—with take-charge, bulletproof class.

Now he'd count her as…he'd count her as…

He wasn't sure how to classify Christine.

"What part of my five-year plan don't you like?" Slade waited to broach the subject until they were seated at an inside table at El Rosal and the girls had wordlessly withdrawn to the restroom. "Five thousand year one. Ten year two. Twenty. Forty. Eighty. In five years, we'll be the biggest employer around. And that's what this town needs, a big employer."

Christine's cheeks were flushed from the heat, making her look like a porcelain doll, one with sapphire-blue eyes and dark blond hair, similar to the dolls he'd given to the twins one Christmas. Sure, her mouth was a little bit too wide, but she had a friendly smile, which he hadn't seen since he'd talked about how much wine he wanted to make.

"It all looks good on paper." Christine slowly spun her water glass. "Like the way I thought giving up the lease on my Audi was a good idea, since I can walk to work here. Trust me when I say I miss my Audi."

Recalling how her current dented ride shook at shutoff, Slade nodded.

"But, Slade, no one's made high-quality wine with Harmony Valley grapes in decades. From what I gather, the few people who grow grapes here sell them to a bulk wine distributor, who sells them to a jug wine producer." Her shoulders shook slightly, as if she was containing a shudder.

"It doesn't mean fine wines can't be made here."

"It doesn't mean it'll be easy." The tension at the corners of her mouth hadn't been there ealier.

"Nothing about this winery has been easy." An understatement. Approvals, permits, and zoning had taken twice as long as planned. The barn conversion had turned into a demolition and full rebuild. Slade and his partners should have left Harmony Valley months ago. It was time to stop the budget hemorrhage on the winery, close the loop on this project, and get back to what they did best—designing game applications.

"One thing I didn't see today is your wine cave."

"Wine cave?" Slade echoed as if he was in a cavern.

"Yeah, the wine cave. Where you store wine." There was a tentative note in her voice, as if she was starting to doubt her decision to come work for them.

"There aren't any caves around here." And as far as Slade knew, it wasn't a prerequisite to having a winery.

"It doesn't have to be a cave. For energy efficiency, many wineries build their storage facilities belowground."

That sounded expensive. Slade's palms dampened. "Won't we be storing the wine in the winery?" Granted, he and his partners were beer guys, but they'd hired a consultant— a friend of a friend of Flynn's who worked for a winery in Monterey—for input on winery requirements.

The twins returned from the bathroom under scrutiny of Harmony Valley residents, who'd probably never seen preteens in wigs and Goth gear when it wasn't Halloween. Their Gothness stood out amid the myriad of bright primary colors that had been used to paint every chair, table, and wall in the Mexican restaurant.

Slade's next-door neighbor, who was the town's retired undertaker and former cemetery owner, sat two tables over. Hiro Takata had a perpetual hunch to his shoulders, a consistently rumpled wardrobe, and the kindly aging face of his Japanese ancestors. He'd been there the day of Slade's horrendous mistake, although he'd never said anything to anyone, not even Slade. "These your girls?"

"Yes." Slade hoped his smile said what a proud dad he was. He pictured them in conservative jeans shorts, pink T-shirts, with dark hair and no makeup. His smile came a little easier.

"What are they auditioning for?" Takata hiccup-belched.

Slade held on to his proud-dad-no-matter-what smile. "They're playing dress up." He hoped.

"In my day, you dressed up at home or in your backyard." Takata's scrutiny focused on Christine. "They look like those women on your T-shirt."

Christine held out her shirt at the waist, creating a rock-and-roll Useless Snobbery billboard of dark hair and black-on-white face paint. "The classics never go out of style." She winked at the girls, who didn't wink back.

The waitress arrived to take their order and Old Man Takata, as he'd been known to the kids of Harmony Valley for twenty-plus years, pushed himself to his feet, wobbled, then shuffled out the door wielding his cane like a third appendage.

The twins ordered ice cream by pointing to it on the menu, and sat without speaking, as if this was the most boring day of their lives but they'd power through it. Slade felt sorry for them, but he had a business to run. Amusement parks and sunny beaches would have to wait. Will had taken point on the permits and approvals. Flynn had taken point on structural construction. Slade was taking point on managing winery operations. Once it was up and running, he'd leave the day-to-day tasks to someone capable who shared his vision. He'd been hoping that person was Christine.

His winemaker scanned the wine on El Rosal's list, frowned, and ordered ice cream. Slade went for the fully-loaded nachos and a beer—late lunch of champions and comfort food of bad decision-makers. He wasn't sure where he was netting out today—champion or bad decision-maker. He hoped the jury was still out.

"Back to our storage needs." Her smile had a strained quality to it. "The winery you built will be used for initial grape crushing and fermentation. For the equipment we need, for the capacity you want long-term, I'll use up every inch of that place." She leaned closer and gave his hand a reassuring squeeze just once. "But we'll also need a wine cave."

"Why?" Slade closed his eyes and tilted his head to the ceiling, ignoring the fact that people didn't invade his personal space. Ever. All their plans. All that money. The tension in his chest unraveled into the familiar downward drag of failed expectations. "We paid someone to tell us what equipment we needed to start a winery. We based our budgets and our plans on his advice."

"A consultant?"

"Not exactly." Slade wasn't used to squirming. He knew they should have paid a legitimate consultant and not a friend of a friend of Flynn's. But at the time, it hadn't looked as if the winery would be approved by the town council. Failure tugged at him again. He wiped his palms on his slacks.

"Once fermentation is done, we'll be transferring wine into smaller barrels. That's where the magic happens. Our Cabernet Sauvignon may age in oak for three years, while the Chardonnay might only be a year." Her smile was patient when he probably didn't deserve patience. Overlooking proper storage was a stupid mistake. Slade hadn't made such a stupid mistake in eight years. "Why don't you show me your budget?"

He opened his laptop bag, retrieved a printed copy of their equipment-purchasing plan and operating budget, and woodenly handed it over. The twins watched wordlessly, their patience matching his winemaker's.

Christine spent a good deal of time reviewing it, making notes in the margin, crossing things out and drawing arrows. Finally, she moved his purchase plan and budget into the space between them and leaned close, so close he could smell the vanilla scent of her hair.

He'd admit she was exposing the partnership's mistakes a little too easily and was wreaking havoc with his confidence. And she hadn't shown up looking like an A-lister. But Christine was classy. She hadn't once looked at his daughters and broken into uncontrollable laughter. She smelled nice, and there was a friendly energy to her, a vitality that made him want to grin, as it had upstairs at the winery, when he'd been unable to stop grinning while listening to the twins whispering.

He measured success by the dollar—plus-minus, over-under. This project teetered on the brink of failure. And Slade had vowed never to fail again. Despite Christine's positives and negatives balancing out, the uneasy feeling of looming disaster spread, pooling in his gut. It wasn't the least bit reassuring.

"As I see it," Christine said, head bent over the budget, "you have three options. You can invest more money and build your own storage facility. But it's unlikely you'd be able to build one in time for our first harvest—you'd need town-council approvals, permits, an environmental study, water-table tests because of your proximity to the river, architectural plans, construction…" She was smiling again. "You get the idea."

Slade must have turned green at the idea of such a cost overrun, because his daughters' eyes grew wide. "Cross out option one." He took a deep drink of water, unable to wash away the partnership's goal of saving the town, even at such an expense. "But if it was an option…how many employees would you add?"

She traced her finger along a scar in the blue tabletop. "Maybe two at first. With your capacity goals, we might add one or two employees a year after that. A moot point, since you don't want to build."

"Option two?" His voice sounded muted and faraway.

"You budgeted for full-scale production. Cut back on equipment purchases and only buy when you're ready to expand. With those savings, we could convert part of the main winery into a climate-controlled storage area—for, say, five thousand cases?"

"Limiting overall production down the road," Slade pointed out. "This town needs the jobs ramped-up production will provide."

"We'll work through this…somehow." Christine's eyes flashed with an emotion he couldn't read. Disappointment? Determination? Her gaze cut too quickly to the twins, then returned to him, the chipper expression back on her face. "There are plenty of empty buildings on Main Street. You could convert some space there. I bet some of those buildings are historic landmarks and you could apply for a federal grant to pay for all or part of the refurbishment. The partnership could buy a building and lease it to the winery."

She had a good head for business. Not since he and Evangeline had spent their internships working at a Wall Street investment company

had a woman's situation analysis seemed…
well…almost sexy.

And look where that had gotten him. Unplanned pregnancy. Shotgun wedding. Nasty
divorce. Nastier custody battle.

Slade's grip on reality returned. Main Street
was almost exclusively owned by Mayor
Larry, who'd been the winery's biggest road-
block. The uneasy feeling in his gut intensi-
fied. "What's our third option?"

Her smile definitely dimmed. "You can
purchase all your wine-making equipment to
meet your five-year production plan and I'll
make cuts elsewhere to pay for storage-rental
fees. This makes the most sense to the bottom line, but I'll have to drive a minimum of
sixty minutes each way to check on our wine.
That takes a big chunk out of my workday."

Slade nodded. "Maybe we could hire a
fourth employee." It was, after all, why they
were building the winery. To bring people
back to town. And it seemed to have the least
impact on his budget.

"This shouldn't be about employees. It
should be about the wine." A warning of
boundaries about to be crossed.

"If you don't make good wine, I can't keep
people employed." He settled his elbows on the
table, setting boundaries of his own. "What if

the opportunity arose tomorrow to make more wine? Would you turn it down?" The town needed her to say no.

"It depends."

Unacceptable. She had to align with him. "I realize this is an unexpected and challenging situation. I want our wine to be of the highest quality, and at the same time employ as many people as we can. If the opportunity presents itself—"

"I'd have to know the quality of the grapes to assess the financial implications. Are you giving me grapes the quality of a five-dollar bottle of wine? Or fifty? And where would I store it while it ages?" Mexican pop filled the silence while she considered him with swimming-pool-blue eyes. "At this point, I can agree to consider it, but I can't promise you anything."

Several promises he'd welcome from her came to mind. None of them related to the business of wine making. Slade drummed his fingers on the table. The attraction to her was unexpected. He forced himself to look at her alternative-rock T-shirt. And then he looked at his daughters. This should be a no-attraction no-brainer. Business was business.

"How firm are you on this budget?" Christine asked.

"Concrete. The winery's already been a money suck."

She arched a brow. "Seriously? You didn't sock some away for a contingency?"

"We spent our contingency." And then some. A building collapse. Road improvements. Neither of which they'd budgeted for. He winked at the twins, trying to lighten the mood. "It's kind of like your mom's shoe budget—there were unexpected must-haves and then the contingency was gone."

The twins didn't so much as twitch. Not an eyebrow, not a lip, not a dimple. And Christine stared at him oddly. It wasn't fair. Slade was funny. In his own way. With his friends. And Flynn's nephew, Truman. Why was his humor falling flat?

It was of increasing concern that his daughters, who had at least spoken to him civilly at Christmas, weren't speaking to him at all. At first, he'd thought it was quirky, almost cute. It was starting to grate on his nerves.

Christine smiled slyly at the twins. "We ladies know that there's always room in the budget for another must-have pair of shoes." She gave the approaching waitress an encouraging wave. "Oh, good. Food's here."

Slade looked down in time to see a plate of nachos land in front of him and Christine's delicate fingers snatching a chip loaded with meat, cheese, sour cream, and guacamole. He glared at her. He was used to intimidating people with his glare.

Christine laughed, winked at the twins again, and positioned her bowl of ice cream for an assault. "This wine cave..." She filled her spoon with slightly melted ice cream. On its way to her mouth, a drip of vanilla landed on her chin. She swiped it off with her finger and sucked her finger clean.

The world narrowed to her mouth, her lips, the flick of her tongue.

Slade reminded himself he was Christine's employer, reminded himself she held the future of his investment in her hands, reminded himself that he hadn't been interested in a woman in a long, long time.

"This wine cave," she began again, swirling her spoon around the edges of her ice-cream bowl. "It isn't the only decision you need to face."

He made himself crunch a big bite of cheesy nachos before answering her. "What's your point?"

Christine put down her spoon, suddenly serious. "My point is that it might be better to scale back and understand the quality of wine we're dealing with before you invest more time and money. We can rent climate-controlled storage space with the small lots of wine we're producing this year if you can't afford something here in town." The word *afford* poked at Slade like someone questioning the legitimacy of his Rolex. "It's inconvenient, but I'll deal with it, because you may find after a year that you and your friends don't want to own a winery."

"We're committed to long-term success. I'd think you'd be interested in that, as well."

"I am." She patted his hand and then stole another nacho chip. "I signed a contract with you for a year. Where I come from, that's long-term."

Right now, a year was looking like a twelve-month tax season, one in which he was being audited.

"Now probably isn't the time to mention that there's some basic vineyard equipment I'll need, but I'm going to anyway." Christine pushed her empty bowl of ice cream to the center of the table and started in full-time on Slade's nachos. He arched a dark eyebrow at her, but she hadn't eaten anything that morning, since she'd been busy moving the last of her things to her grandmother's house. Ice cream wasn't cutting it. The man was a millionaire. He could afford to order another plate of nachos. "For starters, a tractor, a truck scale, a forklift, and harvest lugs."

Sighing, Slade moved the nachos closer to Christine, abdicating ownership. "We'll put together some estimates and new projections. You did mention something in your résumé about the ability to balance budgets?"

"I did." Christine decided she'd pushed the man enough for one day and merely grinned around the last bite of nachos. She wanted to make great wine, not a lot of wine that may or may not be great. And to do that, she needed to continually win the battle over Slade's well-intentioned but unrealistic production goals and his budget miscalculations.

He tossed cash onto the table. "I should get the twins home."

She followed him out the door. He sent the twins ahead to the truck.

"We'll work this out together, keeping in mind what our investment goals are and what goals you can deliver on," Slade said from between lips that barely smiled. "Can you bring me a revised purchasing plan and budget in two days?"

"Absolutely." Christine wasn't sure where she found the audacity to add, "But I'm going to make recommendations based on year-one output for the next few years."

Those perfect lips of his settled into a thin line.

The sad part was, it didn't diminish his perfection in any way.

"WELL? HOW'D IT GO?"

"Dad?" Christine shut her grandmother's front door behind her, taking a moment to enjoy the cool air, before processing her father was here. Forty-five minutes of back-road driving from his place of employ to Harmony Valley. Midafternoon on a Monday. *Uh-oh.* "What are you doing here?"

Brad Alexander stood in the living room wearing blue jeans, work boots, and a faded black L.A. Flash T-shirt. He looked at home amid the overstuffed leather furniture and big-screen television. He looked at home despite the white doilies and pink throw pillows Nana had scattered around the room after Grandpa left for the big man cave in the sky.

Standing in the doorway to the kitchen, Nana snapped a pink tea towel in her son-in-law's direction. "As usual, he's butting in where—"

"Agnes, I just wanted to see how my little girl did on her first day." Her father's smile was infectious, capable of smoothing over many an awkward situation. He closed the distance between them and gave her a hearty hug.

"It's a great opportunity, Dad. I think I'll like it here." If she could get things on track for a manageable launch.

She wasn't going to tell her dad about Slade's five-year production plan or their lack of quality wine storage. He'd worry. He'd stress. He'd show up one day ranting about Slade's plans to compromise the quality of her work or some other unforgivable action and insist it was time she moved on. As a lifelong veteran of the wine industry, her dad was always watching out for Christine's career and her brother's. It was what he lived for. It was his passion.

It had come to be her Achilles' heel.

"Now that you see Christine's happy, you can drive back to Napa." Nana tried to herd Brad out, shooing him away with her dish towel. Since Nana was barely five feet and her dad topped six feet, no amount of towel brandishing was going to work.

"We have to visit." Her dad pulled Christine over to the big leather couch.

Don't let this be one of those conversations.

"Tell me about the vineyards. I drove by, but you weren't there. The vines look—"

"Like they need tying off and cutting back. I know, Dad."

He walked my vineyards?

Her father was one of Northern California's best vineyard managers. He loved his vines almost as much as he loved his family, as proven by how well he groomed both his vineyards and his children's careers. Three times Christine had made the leap from one winery to another. Three times it had been because her father proved her wine-making values had been compromised.

There wouldn't be a fourth.

Too bad she hadn't told her father that.

No doubt recognizing the warning signs of a long conversation, Nana sank into the massive recliner with an annoyed huff. She was so short and petite, she practically disappeared into the cushions.

There's still time to cut him off.

Her father only had eyes for Christine. Or rather, Christine's latest challenge. "You should have some interesting Cab because—"

"The eucalyptus shades the southwestern corner in the afternoon. The grapes from those vines won't be as tannic." He stepped on her territory without an invitation. Primal instincts knotted between her shoulder blades, urging her to defend her turf. Instead, Christine patted his sunspotted hand and strove for peace. "That's perfect for small blocks of wine. I've got this, Dad."

"And I've got your back, like always." He grinned.

With effort, Christine held on to her smile. She had every reason to be happy—overseeing the final phase of a winery construction, producing small lots of high-quality wine. It was every winemaker's dream. She shoved aside the memory of Slade's quirking eyebrow. Held back knee-quaking concerns about wine storage. She'd make this place shine. Without her father's interference.

Nana folded the towel in her lap, patted it, and looked at Christine with raised silver brows.

"It means so much that you came by today," Christine said at the same time that her dad asked, "What about these bosses of yours? They're still committed to making the good stuff?"

"Yes." It wasn't a lie. Slade wanted to make fine wine. He just wanted to make too much too soon. If they'd spent their contingency budget, they were probably anxious for the winery to turn a profit. She just had to make sure they stayed patient. She had at least a year to convince Slade slow growth was the way to go.

"Because if they're not," her father said, "you need to keep your eyes open to other possibilities."

Christine plucked at the hem of her T-shirt. "Dad, it's my first day." And as with other first days—the fourth grade, college, an internship, her first full-time job—her dad was being overprotective.

"These boys are different," Nana said. "They promised this winery will turn things around here."

Brad rolled his eyes. "I have more experience with winery owners than you do, Agnes. Owners' principles are easily bent beneath the weight of budgets. You'd be surprised at how quickly the focus turns to case volume and profit margins."

Christine hoped this was one time her father was wrong. He respected profit goals, just not at the expense of wine quality. If Brad got wind of what he considered mistreatment of his grapes and vines, he was on to a new property quicker than you could say *You did what?* A phrase her mother had shrieked too often, followed by days of tears and tension.

Her dad knew when someone was cutting

corners or expanding too quickly, unable to uphold the promise of quality wine in the bottle. He knew before anything was confirmed, probably because he'd worked at so many different wineries his connections were tremendous. He was the one who'd told Christine that her boss had gone behind her back and disregarded their blending plan. He was the one who told Christine it was time to draw a line in the sand and leave the position as head winemaker at the prestigious Ippolito Cellars.

I knew I never should have hired an Alexander. Spiteful words from Cami Ippolito when Christine gave notice. *Your family isn't known for its loyalty.*

But they were known for their high-quality standards. And Christine did have her dad to thank for that, no matter how extreme he was at times.

Blame in the wine industry was like red wine stains on your clothing—impossible to remove. Christine didn't want to be the scapegoat for a disappointing wine she hadn't created or approved, even if it meant leaving the employer she'd thought of as her friend in a bind.

Nana waited until Brad left to ask, "Did you burn a bridge with Cami, dear?"

"I blew up the bridge as efficiently as the

one over the River Kwai." Her grandmother would understand the war-movie reference. There was no going back.

"You don't have to change a career every time your father says so." Nana began pulling out chicken and vegetables for dinner, setting ingredients on the kitchen's pink Formica countertop. The kitchen also boasted a pink tile backsplash and whitewashed cabinets with a tinge of pink. Being in Nana's kitchen was like being in a young girl's dream house, polar opposite of the modern, masculine living room her grandfather had loved. "I don't know how many times your mother and I have told you and your brother, but you don't seem to want to listen. This is your life, not your father's."

"I wouldn't make a career move just because Dad wants me to." No, Christine took lots of convincing, collected her facts, and corroborated Dad's theories. And then she leaped. "His career has been stellar. His reputation for quality unparalleled." She could only dream of such greatness. She'd chosen to dream big here while saving the majority of her salary so that her next move would be to her own winery.

"Have you ever thought that for all his high-and-mighty principles that just once your father may have done something wrong? Or perhaps he could have stayed and made it right?" Nana pulled a big knife out of a butcher block. "Most people don't run at the first sign of trouble. There's your personal honor and then there's loyalty. Honorable people stand by when things go haywire. Relationships are what make this life worth living, not your reputation."

"He never ran from Mom." Christine washed her hands, intending to help make dinner.

Nana shook her head. "Did you ever think that it was your mother who didn't run?"

Christine had. But she didn't like to.

Because what was she supposed to think of her dad if she did?

SLADE LOOKED AT the Death and Divorce House, trying to see it the way his girls did.

White peeling paint. Drapes closed across all the windows except the two upstairs. Lopsided green mailbox hanging by the front door. He watered the lawn, but it wasn't the green gem of Old Man Takata's next door.

"It's not Park Avenue." Inside or out. He led the girls up the front steps, opened the unlocked door, and turned on the light above the foyer. There was nothing charming about the place. It was hot and shadowy. Tomblike.

In three steps from the front door, you could be on the stairs, be in the hallway leading to the kitchen, or be in the living room, with its tan velour couch, the scarred coffee tables, an old television, and his father's brown leather wing chair. The best that could be said about the house was that it had dark planked wood floors.

"I've kept everything the way it was when your grandfather…left." Slade flipped on the oscillating fan in the living room and then pointed toward the television. "Don't count on anything other than basic cable."

He headed toward the kitchen, hesitating in the narrow doorway when he realized they'd paused at the stairwell. Both girls stared upstairs, trepidation in their gaze. Grace reached for Faith's hand as if they knew…

Impossible.

"You can eat anything you want in the kitchen. I warn you, I eat healthy." Not that his body was a temple, but he disliked stripping down to a tank top to work out, so he watched what he ate instead.

His brain registered what it hadn't wanted to for months—the kitchen was outdated and in need of some serious repair. A drawer had come off its glider. Cabinet hinges were loose, leaving cabinet doors lopsided. And the linoleum... Goldenrod polka dots had been fashionable during the swinging seventies.

Slade turned around. "We'll need to make a run into Cloverdale for groceries." He often ate at Flynn's. He supposed that would have to change while his daughters were here.

His daughters were here.

He'd tried for years to obtain unsupervised visitation. They were here and he was happy, wasn't he? Or he would've been happy if he could've arranged for the three of them to stay somewhere else. Somewhere without the memory of death and horrendous mistakes. He could still take them elsewhere.

But then he imagined Evy's smirk when he told her they hadn't stayed in the house. Where they slept shouldn't matter to the girls. They didn't know the house had a past. Or that he shared in it. Taking them to a hotel would mean Evy won.

Sticking with his decision, he led them upstairs, unable to shut out the memory of the last time the girls had been here when they were two years old. Evy's screams. The horror on her face. Her accusations that everything was his fault. He wouldn't make a mistake like that again.

"You'll be staying in the guest bedroom," he said. It had two single beds his mother had set up for when her twin sisters visited. He pointed out his room and the bathroom, ignoring the door to the master bedroom completely.

Silence wasn't golden.

The girls were mute as he carried their possessions upstairs. The girls sat wordlessly in the truck's backseat during the thirty-minute drive to and from Cloverdale to shop for groceries and pick up pizza. They played on a tablet after dinner without speaking while he sat in his father's chair, which always made him feel as if he didn't belong in the house. The back was too stiff. His legs were too long.

"How was school this year?"

Silence.

"Do you belong to any clubs? Girl Scouts? Sports teams?"

Silence.

"What's school going to be like next year?"

Silence.

And they moved like ninjas over the normally creaky floorboards.

The house was used to the quiet. Slade was used to the quiet. But he'd expected the girls to be chatty or fidgety or sighing with boredom, breaking the stillness, not adding to the taciturn hush.

He took out the kitchen trash, listening to the sounds of the night—crickets, the rustle of leaves in the poplar in back, a distant bullfrog by the river. Some nights he sat in an old chaise longue in the backyard until the stars faded, preferring to be where there was noise than in a stagnant house full of soured memories. He hoped he wouldn't add the twins' visit to his the list of disappointing recollections.

"That you, Jennings?" It was Old Man Takata sitting on his front porch.

There was just enough light from a streetlamp hidden behind a tree across the street to see smoke rising from Takata's porch. The man loved his cigars.

Slade crossed their parallel driveways, stopping on the edge of Takata's perfectly bladed weed-free lawn, because no one walked across that golf-course-worthy green without risking a tirade. "Enjoying the cool breeze?"

Takata scoffed and resumed puffing on his cigar.

Slade waited. He knew his neighbor was building up to something. He'd had enough dealings with the former undertaker to know when the old man had something on his mind.

Takata didn't disappoint. "It's not so bad out here, is it? Inside it's always too quiet, like

I'm waiting for Nancy to say something…"
Nancy being his deceased wife. "Only she
never does."

Air left Slade's lungs in a rush. The older
man nailed it. Slade always felt as if he was
listening for his father's voice, waiting for
him to say everything was going to be okay.

Before he could formulate a response,
Takata dismissed him. "Best get inside to
your girls. Old houses can be intimidating
at night."

Later, as Slade lay in the twin bed of his
youth, contemplating the ceiling and listening to his daughters' unintelligible whispers
through the shared bedroom wall, he thought
about Takata's words.

And tried not to listen.

CHAPTER THREE

SLADE MADE BREAKFAST early the next morning. Turkey bacon, scrambled eggs, whole-wheat toast. After breakfast he planned to update Flynn and Will on their need of a wine cave and recommend a course of action. His palms grew sweaty at the thought of admitting they needed more capital or a larger operating budget. The omission didn't rest completely on his shoulders, but it felt as if it did.

He was piling the eggs into a serving bowl when the back of his neck prickled. A glance over his shoulder revealed it was the girls, standing shoulder to shoulder in the doorway. Evangeline was right. Today the Goth was gone. Matching embroidered turquoise peasant blouses. Matching skinny jeans. Matching black cloth loafers. Their hair fell in single black braids down their backs.

"I can see your pretty eyes." Yesterday, he'd been happy to note beneath those blond bangs they were still green—no colored contacts. Today, he was relieved their hair was still black. He'd been afraid they'd hid hot-pink hair under their wigs. "You got your eye color from your grandmother Jennings."

They remained mute.

"What would you like to do after I get a little work done this morning?" He pretended they were as excited to be here as he was to be with them. "Go shopping? See a movie?"

The girls exchanged glances.

He'd read about twin speak, but he'd never seen his girls employ it before this visit.

It was as if Faith blinked and said, *Dad's such a loser.*

And Grace twitched her nose and said, *Tell me about it.*

Slade's cell phone rang. He answered, putting it on speaker while he ate. "What's up, Flynn?"

"Our new sheriff rolled into town last night." Slade could hear the smile in Flynn's voice. "I guess the mayor handed him the keys to the jail without checking it out first. A pipe must have busted during a winter freeze. The floors are ruined upstairs. The walls and ceiling are ruined downstairs. And the jail-cell bars are rusted."

"Sounds like the sheriff's in need of a

plumber." Slade buttered his toast, feeling the stirrings of interest.

A few months back, Flynn had started doing small repairs for some of the elderly town residents. After the requests morphed into a regular weekly to-do list, Flynn had recruited Slade and Will, and sometimes Flynn's father, who was a skilled construction worker, to help. As much as Slade wanted to leave town, fixing it up made it easier to stay.

"I put a call in, but the walls, floor, and ceiling need to be demolished so the plumber can see the damage." Flynn paused, then joked, "I'll lock you in the jail cell if you like, Slade, and we'll see just how rusted those bars are."

The twins blinked at Slade's phone.

"I'd rather lock up the mayor. Isn't that his building?" It was just like Mayor Larry to pinch pennies and lease the building to the county sheriff's office without checking its condition. Slade spooned some egg and a slice of bacon onto his toast and folded it over like a sandwich. "Where did our new sheriff sleep?"

"Nate was lucky. He spent the night at Mayor Larry's." Flynn's delivery was pitch-perfect deadpan. "Nate sent out his SOS this morning. If it was just Larry's building, I wouldn't jump in to help. I can't help feeling responsible for Nate. Before my grandfather passed away, he recruited him."

"Someday Mayor Larry will find out payback is indeed a cruel and itchy fleabag." Slade chuckled. "What else is on the list today?"

The girls ignored their food and looked at each other, as if to say, *There's more?*

In Harmony Valley, there was always more to do. The elderly population couldn't keep up on the maintenance of their older homes.

"That wind storm last week blew down a section of Sam's fence in the back. He said something fell into his Koi pond—"

"Sam has a koi pond? Snarky Sam? Sam who owns the pawnshop?" Slade couldn't believe it.

"It's an antiques shop, but business has been slow," Flynn corrected him, reciting what Sam himself had told them several times. "And Geraldine Durand's Saint Bernard saw a cat in her backyard and barreled through her screen door."

The girls' mouths hung open.

"It was one of Felix's cats, wasn't it?" Felix was a retired fireman who rescued felines.

"Yep. Those cats don't always stay where

they're supposed to." Flynn yawned. "I'll meet you in jail in fifteen minutes."

Slade disconnected and tried not to smile at the girls. "If you want to come help me this morning, you'll need to eat up. There aren't any fast-food restaurants or convenience stores in town. What you eat needs to last through jail cells, koi ponds, and large-dog damage."

They exchanged looks. He couldn't interpret what they meant. He was just happy he'd found something that might break their silence.

Slade finished his breakfast and rinsed out his dishes before they'd even started theirs. Whatever was going on with the girls, it was intimidating as hell. No wonder Evangeline had dumped them on him. He bet husband number three was spooked.

Slade liked to think he was made of sterner stuff.

"HAVE A GOOD DAY at work." Christine's grandmother waved to her from behind the screen door.

"Thanks." Christine reached the sidewalk in time to see Slade's truck take the turns in the town square, his daughters in the backseat.

He honked and raised a hand, presumably

to Christine, a house away from the corner, but it might have been for the small old man sitting on the bench below the oak tree with a cane. He waved, as well.

"What was that?" Nana asked, still in her violet chenille housecoat.

"Slade. Headed toward the winery." Drat. With the size of her to-do list and Slade's objectives, she'd need to stay one step ahead of him. She'd wanted to get to work before he did.

"Down Main?" her grandmother asked.

"Yes." Christine hefted her laptop bag higher on her shoulder and hurried off.

"He's going to jail."

Christine spun around. *What?*

"We have a new sheriff—well, not officially until the population tops eighty—but he arrived last night and found all kinds of water damage in the jail and the apartment above it."

It was a relief to know her boss wasn't being arrested or turning himself in for some heinous crime. "What's he going to do there? And how did you know about it?"

"Slade's partnership does minor repairs around town. I suppose they're going to see what they can do." Nana cinched her housecoat, looking slightly embarrassed. "As for how I heard, Rose called me this morning. Her granddaughter is engaged to Will, you know."

Oh, Christine knew, all right. It was one of the consistently repeated mantras in her grandmother's house: *Rose's granddaughter is marrying a millionaire.* As if Christine needed to realize a similar catch was at her fingertips.

She waved as she left, determined not to fish in that pond. Someone tall, dark, with the power to sign her paycheck had showed up in an early-morning dream. Sometimes you just had to let the big fish go, especially when you had plans to be a big fish someday.

The jail was on her way to the winery and was housed in a converted store, with the front office visible through a large plate-glass window. Behind the counter in the back of the space was the jail cell. Daylight came through a large hole in the ceiling. Next to it a large water stain bulged the drywall, threatening to burst. The wall near the stairs was in similar disrepair.

Slade's twins were sitting on a bench in the jail cell, looking SoHo cute and grinning like normal kids, while a smaller boy with ginger hair locked the door and said, "You're not getting out until you tell me where the bad guys are hiding."

"Hi." Christine stepped inside and rested her laptop bag on the floor.

The little boy turned, clutching the key to the door behind his back. "Who're you?"

She introduced herself, adding that she worked at the winery. "I'm looking for Slade."

"I'm Truman." He came forward to shake her hand, his expression suddenly too serious. "Uncle Slade and Uncle Flynn are upstairs with the sheriff. Do you want to be locked up with Grace and Faith and Abby?"

Christine double checked, but only Slade's daughters were in the jail cell. "Abby?"

"She's my dog," the little would-be sheriff said. A small, mostly black Australian shepherd barked from beneath a bench inside the cell.

"I think I'll pass, Sheriff Truman." She made her escape before the boy came up with a reason to lock her up, taking the creaky stairs to the second floor.

Upstairs was a studio apartment—kitchen counter, appliances, small bathroom. A small table and chairs rested haphazardly on top of a small bed in one corner.

Flynn knelt in front of the cupboard beneath the kitchen sink, poking his hammer inside as if trying to bust through a wall. A man she didn't know was next to him, ripping out floorboards with a crowbar. But it was her boss that Christine couldn't pull her eyes from. A sharply dressed man on his knees, wielding a big tool. Couldn't fulfill a woman's fantasies any better unless he brandished a vacuum.

Slade introduced her to Nate, the sheriff-in-waiting. No one spared more than a glance her way.

"Ma'am." Nate's nod was executed with military precision that didn't disturb the flow of his work. He had gentle eyes and a slow smile.

"Don't get up." Christine's gaze slid to the exposed framework beneath the floor. In one spot she could see through to the linoleum on the first floor below. Definitely not safe enough to cross and politely shake the new sheriff's hand. "I just stopped by to say hello en route to work."

"Nice shirt." Slade pried off another board without so much as looking twice at her navy Wilted Red Roses T-shirt.

"Nice tie," she shot back, smiling to take out the sting, because it was a truly excellent tie—complex geometric patterns amid bold greens with a silky smooth texture she could see from ten feet away. The man wasn't buying ties at a bargain store. "Just so you know, the T-shirt thing is a family tradition. My father, uncle, brother, and I all work in the wine industry. We get together at the end of harvest and count how many T-shirts we demolished during the year. I'm talking cracked designs, faded fabric, stains, rips, and tears. There's also a prize for the tackiest collection of T-shirts, although we made a rule a few years ago—T-shirts with nudity or that are politically incorrect don't count. My uncle favors political T-shirts. My dad and brother are sports fans. I tend to stick to rock bands and cartoon animals."

There. She'd explained her casual attire. Maybe now she wouldn't feel so intimidated by his ties. Her confession didn't get much of a rise from the men. In fact, they were ignoring her the way men did when they wanted to finish up a physically demanding project.

"I'm going to call around to see about hiring my support team." Since she was doing double duty as a vineyard manager, she'd need help in all aspects of wine growing and wine making.

"I won't be around the winery today." Slade wiped his arm across his forehead.

Christine hadn't known what she'd expected when she stopped by—an offer to chat over coffee, some last-minute instructions before Slade turned her loose in the vineyards and on his budget. What she got was nothing.

It was like being a kid again, when she'd been advanced into the fourth grade and still been ahead of her peers academically. To make friends in spite of her overachieving academic success among her classmates, she'd perfected her smile. A smile no one noticed today. "Well, the vines are calling."

The men mumbled goodbyes.

Truman was locked in the cell when she descended. The girls stuck their faces through the bars at him, making the little boy giggle. The children barely stopped playing to acknowledge her leaving.

She'd wanted to get away from Napa, someplace where people didn't schmooze her for favors, someplace where people didn't judge her by the price of her car. She'd landed someplace where people cared more about the jobs she was going to create than the job she was going to do in the vineyard.

Maybe she'd gone too far.

"WHERE'S WILL?" SLADE asked sometime after Christine stopped by. He and Flynn were downstairs sitting on the bench in the jail cell. As soon as Will arrived, Slade planned to have a frank discussion about money and the winery.

"You'll be happy." Flynn settled his baseball cap more firmly on his head. His grandfather had worn that hat the last week of his life. Flynn treated it as if it was made of solid gold. "Will started programming our new app. He said he'd work on some of the basics this morning and let me have at it this afternoon."

The perk of interest Slade had felt this morning over their Good Samaritan to-do list was nothing like the burst of excitement he felt at Flynn's news. "When do you think it'll be available for launch?"

Flynn gave Slade his best don't-rush-me look.

Slade held up his hands. "I'm just saying, I can't do a thing until we create a launch timeline."

Lately, he'd been worried his partners would never go back to designing. Will had fallen in love with his sister's best friend, Emma. Flynn had fallen in love and married his grandfather's caregiver, Becca. They'd made enough money that, if managed well by Slade, they'd never have to work again. Not that they planned to retire. The money gave them freedom. With this new app, they weren't bothering to ask for venture capital.

Slade flexed his fingers against damp palms. No investors to manage. And the winery situation a continuing drag on their bank accounts. How much longer would Slade be a vital part of the partnership? If he were Flynn and Will, he'd be preparing to give Slade the boot.

"I wanted to wait until the three of us were together to talk about the winery." Slade fiddled with the cuffs of his shirt. "Unfortunately—"

"There *is* earthquake damage." Flynn slapped a palm on his knee. "I knew it. How bad is it?"

"There's no damage," Slade said.

Flynn did a double take. "Is Mayor Larry causing more grief?"

"No."

"Then what's the problem?"

"We didn't build a wine cave," Slade blurted.

"A wine…a wine what?" Flynn stared at Slade as if he'd morphed into a puppy and misunderstood a command.

Slade wiped his damp forehead and proceeded to explain their need for climate-controlled storage and Christine's options. He ended with an apology.

"You're sorry?" Flynn resettled the ball cap on his head. "I should be apologizing to you. No one I asked about building ever mentioned a wine what's-it."

"Wine cave," Slade supplied. "Since your friend's friend works in Monterey, where the temperature never goes above seventy-five, they probably don't need wine caves."

"Oh, man. It sucks that we need to spend more money. We should get in touch with an architect right away."

"No." That came out more forcefully than Slade planned. "We're not going to become like those lottery winners who go bankrupt because they give all their money away." He felt sick just considering it. Flynn had a family to support. Will was just about to get married.

"This isn't *giving* it away," Flynn argued. "This is giving back."

Slade shook his head. The omission of proper wine storage combined with Christine's logical arguments about slow growth had shaken his confidence. "What if we *f-fail?*" The word stuck on his tongue. Financial failure meant emotional upheaval, like that he'd experienced at the Death and Divorce House.

"Think of your future. Think of Becca. As your moneyman—"

"You worry too much." Flynn's smile didn't often annoy Slade, but it did now as he slapped Slade on the back. "Build the wine cave. You know it's the right thing to do. Another building creates more jobs."

"But—"

"The farmer's market is open!" Truman ran in from the sidewalk, Abby at his heels. "Come on, everybody!" He spun around and ran away, the little dog still by his side. Truman was staying with Flynn while his mom was in rehab for alcohol addiction. In the past month, the little guy had gone from a shy, quiet boy to a talkaholic. Slade hoped Harmony Valley would have the same effect on his daughters.

The twins, who'd been twirling in office chairs, stood up and looked at Slade.

"Go on," Slade said. It wasn't much of a farmer's market. One vendor came in from Jimtown with baked goods. A few residents sold their extra fruits and vegetables. The tomatoes and corn were usually excellent. "We'll talk about this with Will later."

"You worry too much." Flynn stood.

"And you don't worry enough." Slade wasn't going to throw away a million dollars on the winery without seeing some kind of projection of return. It was irresponsible. He'd get Will on his side, and then the two of them would outvote Flynn.

"Thanks for the help. I think we're ready for the plumber." Nate came down the stairs, ending the partnership conversation. He studied the rusted bars. "These just need a good sanding and a coat of paint."

Nate had accepted the job of sheriff, which could only be funded when Harmony Valley's population topped eighty residents. They were currently at seventy-eight, not counting Slade. Having been put on paid administrative leave from his last job, where he'd lawfully arrested the mayor's son with good cause and refused to drop the charges, Nate was happy to prepare for his new position, despite burst pipes

Flynn loaded up his tools. "I say it's time for some of Olly Bingmire's ice-cold lemonade. She'll be out at the market about now." He carried his toolbox to his truck.

Olivia Bingmire had been making fresh-squeezed lemonade for the farmer's market for as long as Slade could remember. It wasn't a cure-all for the blues, but it came close on a hot day. Slade headed toward the door, pausing to look at Nate. "You coming?"

"What about the plumber?"

"He's got Flynn's cell-phone number on speed dial." Slade waited for Nate to join them. "It's time you started meeting the people you're going to swear to protect. Besides, we could use your hammer on our next few stops." They left the jail door open in case the plumber showed up.

"I thought you told Truman he could hammer the nails into Sam's fence?" Nate looked confused.

"I did." Slade fought to keep a straight face. "That's why we're going to need an extra hammer."

The three men walked toward the town square, leaving their trucks parked in front of the sheriff's office.

A slender woman with long dark hair came around the corner of El Rosal, a cloth bag tucked in the crook of her arm.

"Becs!" With a nod to the men, Flynn veered across the street to meet his wife, Becca, who'd wisely brought a cloth bag to make it easier to carry her purchases home.

Truman dragged the twins from table to table, his shrill, happy voice carrying down the street. "Make sure you always, always, always buy the brownies from the Jimtown table early. They go fast."

"Your daughters aren't very talkative." There was a hint of polite inquiry behind Nate's statement.

"They're shy." Slade watched his daughters, hoping it was true.

Nate had a long-legged amble that made him look as if he was walking slowly, when in fact he was covering more ground in fewer steps than Slade, who considered himself tall at six foot. And yet, there was something rigid about Nate's posture that contradicted his easy stride.

Wanting to change the subject, Slade, who didn't normally pry, found himself prying. "Did you serve in the military?"

"Two tours in Afghanistan. Army. You?" The sheriff was a man of few words.

Slade shook his head. "Four years at Harvard. Two years on Wall Street."

They exchanged respectful grins.

Flynn and Becca walked arm in arm in front of them.

For some reason, an image of Slade walking with a certain blonde came to mind. For the right reasons, Slade erased it. "You ever been married, Nate?"

"No...I... No." His stilted answer was out of character for the normally staid sheriff.

This time Slade chose not to pry.

About thirty residents clustered about the tables, many leaning on canes and walkers. The only residents under the age of sixty were Nate, the partners, Truman, and the twins.

They reached Olly's table. Slade bought a glass for himself, the sheriff, and the girls, who ran to him obediently when he called.

Nate was quickly snatched up by the locals, who circled him as if he was a celebrity.

Slade stood with the girls, drinking lemonade, wishing one of them would lean against him or hug him like they used to.

Grace looked at Slade's hand three times before gripping it and tugging him over to the Jimtown table to look at their baked goods. Faith skipped next to them.

Slade could hardly breathe, for fear of making the girls go back to their no-touching, somber silence. Grace pointed at the brownies and then looked up at him with big green eyes and a sweet little pout.

Slade nearly tossed his wallet to her, barely daring to ask, "Only if you say please."

Grace and Faith exchanged glances. Worry and determination flashed across their faces. Grace waved a hand as if swatting away a bug and faced Slade. *"Please."*

One word. Barely a whisper. His heart was lost.

Slade ordered two brownies, feeling like

the luckiest man in the world, so lucky that when he saw Old Man Takata sitting alone on the wrought-iron bench beneath the oak tree, he bought the man a glass of lemonade and sat with him.

"Weren't you sitting here this morning?" Slade asked.

"I was. I like watching the world go by."

"It's getting hot outside." The temperature was quickly climbing to uncomfortable. Slade knew all too well about uncomfortable summer days. He tugged at his tie.

"I have lemonade." Takata raised his glass.

Mae Gardner, president of the bridge club, flounced over in a flowered dress and brown orthopedic sandals. Her shoulder-length gray frizzy hair curled like a storm cloud about her lined face. "Slade, dear, when are you going to move out of that house?"

Takata, who was normally as slow and deliberate as a turtle on land, snapped to attention. "Ain't nothing wrong with his home."

Unwilling to give ground, Mae plopped a fist on her hip. "Why should such a fine young man live there after the shameful thing his father did?"

Shameful. The word spiraled up Slade's windpipe, closing it off to vital functions, like breathing and calls for help.

"Shameful?" Takata scoffed, sloshing his lemonade cup in Mae's direction. "You and that bridge club of yours know all about shame, don't you? Going down to Santa Rosa for those male dance reviews."

Air returned to Slade's lungs in a chuckle-suppressed gasp.

Mae's face turned pinker than the pink sapphires flanking the diamond Will had chosen for Emma's engagement ring. Mae spun and stomped away.

"Dang town gossips. Think they're better than everybody. Don't listen to her. What your father did was sad, not shameful." Takata drained his lemonade and handed his empty glass to Slade. "I've never met your daughters. Last time they were here, they were too young for a proper introduction."

Not to mention circumstances had Evy whisking their daughters away.

Slade called the girls over and introduced them, knowing Takata wouldn't be able to tell his identical twins apart as soon as they moved away. Slade handed the girls each a twenty and asked them to buy strawberries, tomatoes, and corn, and then run back to the house to put their purchases in the refrigerator. It was only a block and a half away, a safe errand in a small town.

"You gave them too much money," Takata complained after they'd skipped off.

"My ex-wife says I don't give them enough." It was a pleasure to give them something instead of writing a check to Evy every month.

"Kids who don't learn to work for things don't have a good work ethic." Takata eyed Slade. "Why do you think you're so successful?"

"Because I worked my butt off instead of living." From high school to his last job on Wall Street. He'd worked until he'd lost sight of what was important.

The old man scoffed and tilted closer, as if sharing a secret. "You're not living now."

Slade couldn't move more than his lips. "I live."

"You exist." Takata sat back, watching Grace stay just close enough to Truman, Becca, and Flynn that she could hear what they were saying, but far enough back that she wasn't part of their family unit.

Slade struggled to draw in air. He knew how it felt to be on the perimeter of relationships, to feel as if you'd never quite belong. He didn't expect to recognize the same thing in his daughter.

"Grace is an old soul," Takata was saying.

Lucky guess.

"And Faith looks before she leaps." Takata gestured to Faith, who was skipping by the Jimtown table, as if contemplating buying another sweet.

"You don't know that," Slade said gruffly.

The Jimtown clerk pointed at a plate of frosted cookies. Faith stopped and nodded enthusiastically, digging in her pocket for money.

Takata hammered his cane into the grass again. "As a funeral-home director and mortician, I've looked at a lot of faces and listened to a lot of stories. I think I know what someone's about when I look at them." He glared at Slade. "Your soul is wounded and trapped. Looks like it should be set free."

"Are you telling fortunes now?" Slade stood, tugging at his tie, feeling it tighten like a noose. The last thing he wanted was to rehash the past with the old man.

Takata caught his sleeve above the cuff. "I'm telling truths. You need to forgive, if not your father, then yourself."

Slade couldn't move. Not from the sudden unbridling of grief and guilt, or from the spot where his feet seemed to have taken root.

"Now," Takata stood unsteadily, "I'm ready to go home. If you let me lean on you, it'll go much quicker." When Slade didn't move,

he raised his voice. "Are you deaf? Lend me
your arm."

The twins ran by, heading for home with
their purchases. He could almost feel the air
move as they passed, feel grief and guilt re-
cede. They were his hope.

Slade stepped closer to the old man and
held out his arm.

"'Bout time."

CHAPTER FOUR

CHRISTINE HAD THE vineyards to walk and the morning sun was already hot, the air dry, her T-shirt damp with sweat.

Slade and his partners had bought forty acres, which wasn't even half a square mile. It was Christine's job to familiarize herself with the soil, vines, and fruit. The property wasn't large enough to justify hiring a full-time vineyard manager, full-time cellar manager, or full-time winemaker. She'd have to wear many hats and hire staff who could do the same.

Christine used a notebook and a stubby pencil to record the slope of each row, how it drained toward the river, the angle of the sun and where it was blocked by trees in the early morning or late afternoon. She recorded which blocks and rows of vines were lusher, which seemed almost scrabbling to survive. She sifted dirt through her fingers and checked that the vines had the proper support.

Grape clusters were developing nicely. She tried a bit of each fruit at different places in the vineyard. Most were tannic and promising in their complexity. The arid soil and growing conditions in Harmony Valley were influencing the taste of the grapes and would also influence the taste of the wine. Substance in the glass. Something Christine would be proud of. Something to finally prove without a doubt to her father and the world that she knew what she was doing.

She snapped pictures of a few grape clusters with her cell phone. The grapes on the Cabernet Sauvignon vines were still green, but soon the heat would begin veraison, when the sugars increased during ripening, reducing the acidity in the fruit and turning them a deep purple.

The vines were terribly overgrown. There was too much fruit, which meant as it ripened it wouldn't be as flavorful. And the fruit was becoming heavy, dragging tendrils down to the ground, which made the grapes available for any passing snail to take a nibble. Tomorrow she'd need to get out here with hand clippers and twist ties and sunscreen. It'd be nice to have helpers. Maybe she could put together a crew like the one she'd seen in the sheriff's office.

Christine paused, staring out over the vine-yard. Why not exactly like the one she'd seen in the sheriff's office?

She returned to the tasting room, where she'd left her laptop bag.

The partners had installed a communications tower on Parish Hill, a granite-faced mountain to the east. The tower provided Harmony Valley with free Wi-Fi and cell-phone service. Otherwise, they'd be too far out, in too deep a valley to receive any signal.

She called a few friends, putting feelers out for someone with diverse skill sets willing to relocate. She called some equipment suppliers on her cell phone and emailed a few more for bids. Slade had only collected ballpark estimates for equipment. They'd need companies to come out and measure their space, and provide a more detailed and precise bid, as well as timelines for installation. At this point, twelve or fewer weeks until harvest, she'd only approve purchases if they could guarantee delivery and setup.

She also got in touch with someone she knew who built wine caves to ask some initial questions. She was willing to make compromises to find wine-storage solutions locally, but long-term, she wanted a state-of-the-art facility in Harmony Valley.

She texted Slade: Who did you arrange to harvest the grapes?

If this heat wave lasted through July and into August, as it was projected to, they'd need to harvest earlier, rather than later.

His reply: Make arrangements with whoever you want.

"Are you kidding me?" Wineries arranged for harvesters up to a year in advance.

Christine made another round of calls and sent off more emails looking for a company available to harvest in their remote location. Initial response wasn't good. No one wanted to talk to her after learning where they were based.

For the second time that morning, Christine wondered if she'd strayed too far from traditional wine country.

She texted Slade again: Will need a work crew tomorrow at the vineyard.

His reply was predictably prompt: Hire however many bodies you need.

She laughed the kind of evil laugh that Slade would have known, had he been here, meant trouble for him: I choose you and Flynn and Nate and Grace and Faith and Truman and whoever else you can find. Bring pruning shears, hats, and sunblock. 6 a.m.

He didn't answer right away. And when he did, it was an anticlimactic Okay.

THE NEXT MORNING Slade and his crew reported for work, as Christine requested.

Slade knew the heat would make him miserable, but he still wore black slacks, a blue long-sleeved shirt, and tie.

Slade sought out his girls. At least the twins were dressed appropriately for the temperature in cutoffs and matching royal-blue tank tops. Each had her hair in a ponytail that swung through the hole in the back of a royal-blue baseball hat.

Christine was prepared for them with thermoses of coffee and hot chocolate, as well as a cooler full of water bottles, and her grandmother's banana-nut bread. She also had a box of old work gloves and pruning shears. She, too, was dressed for the heat in canvas shorts and a canary-yellow T-shirt featuring another rock band. Her hair was braided tightly so that only pigtails peeked out from either side of her floppy white hat.

Standing next to her, Slade felt more overdressed than he had in years. His tie felt too tight and heavy. Before he'd been able to talk to Will, he and his fiancée, Emma, had left for San Francisco a few days ago for a series of art-gallery openings featuring Emma's paintings. Slade was starting to think it'd be better to iron out the budget with Christine first. At least then he wouldn't be talking in generalities. He'd have hard figures to present. Will and Flynn were sentimental about Harmony Valley. They let it cloud their judgment.

"I know I asked you to, but you didn't have to bring the kids," Christine said to Slade as he poured himself a cup of coffee.

"I don't expect them to work much." Slade didn't expect them to do more than run around and have a good time. "It'd be nice if they felt useful before the real work starts."

Christine reached over and squeezed his shoulder, as if they were old chums. "That's so doable."

"I'm feeling guilty that we did nothing to the vines since we bought them." Flynn wandered over, tugging on a pair of gloves. "To Christine, it must be like ignoring your children."

Slade set down his coffee. It was too hot for what already promised to be a hot day. "It's not like that at all. We bought the property and didn't get rezoning approval for months. It wasn't as if we knew we'd be harvesting grapes this year."

"Are you going to be okay in this heat?" Christine pulled lightly on his sleeve. "Please go home and change."

"He won't be caught dead without the tie. I lived with the guy for five years. Trust me," Flynn said. "It's a fetish."

If there was a possibility Slade could ditch the shirt and tie, he would have. Instead, he unwisely took inventory of the rest of the crew. The guys wore shorts and T-shirts. Only Abby and Slade were overdressed. And Abby, being a dog, had no choice but to wear a fur coat. Soon, Slade would be panting just as loudly as she was.

Slade rolled up his shirtsleeves. "Don't worry about me."

"We've learned not to." Flynn grinned.

"Let's start before it gets unbearably hot." Christine stood next to a row of grapevines and shook a baggy full of what looked like short wires. "We're going to use twist ties— yes, just like from a loaf of bread. I know, highly technical stuff here. We'll use twist ties to fasten the load-bearing shoots to one of two support wires on the trellis system." She showed them how two wires were strung at two different heights from a post at one end of the row to the other end. "Too many clusters on the vine dilutes the flavor of all the grapes, so we'll want to thin the secondary clusters. That way, the primary clusters will be bursting with flavor."

Slade bent over for a closer look. There were a lot of clusters on the vine. "By thin you mean…"

"Cut back and toss in the bin." She gestured to two large containers with wheels. "You'll also be cutting back the tendrils that you can't tie, the ones that get in the way of the corridor between rows." At the group's blank looks, she added, "Imagine driving between the rows. If anything would brush your car's fender, cut it back."

"Shouldn't we hire experts to do this?" Slade would pay good money to be sitting in front of an air conditioner about now.

"Normally, I'd hire a crew." Christine gazed out over the vineyards. "But this should have been done months ago and I'm finding that no crews want to come out this far to work. Besides, it's not rocket science. These are plants. If you make a mistake, they'll grow back."

"But what if the cluster I cut off is the best cluster?" Slade's muscles knotted with stress. Anything he did, he wanted to exceed expectations. "What if we mess this up?"

Christine put a hand on his shoulder and

smiled up at him. It was a sparkly smile, one
that said, *Have no fear.* "At this point, there is
no best based on taste. The ripening process
hasn't shifted into full swing. We're doing
damage control, which means damage will
be done, but more good than harm." She
stepped closer, bringing the coconut smell
of sunscreen and the light scent of vanilla.
"Just think, this is only five thousand cases
worth of grapes. You want to bottle eighty."
And then, grinning, she pushed him forward
and they got down to business.

She paired them up—Flynn and Nate,
Slade and Christine—and they started down
two parallel rows. One person cut. The other
person tied off vines. She assigned the children to clean up. Faith and Truman with
Flynn. Grace with Slade.

The children pushed the bins, darting in to
grab cut vines and grape clusters and shoot
them into the bins like writhing basketballs.
Abby darted back and forth beneath the trellises to see how everyone was doing.

"Did I fail a test?" Slade grumbled, his
shirt clinging to his back, sweat trickling
down his spine.

Christine knelt a few feet ahead of him,
cutting clusters. She glanced back, her fur-

rowed brow barely visible beneath that floppy hat he was starting to envy.

"I got paired with teacher," he clarified.

That made her laugh. "You seemed stressed out about the work. I thought you needed reassurance. Go with the flow. Trust in nature."

"I do trust in nature. I just don't trust in me."

The gloves made his fingers clumsy. Grace watched him struggle to wrap a twist tie around a vine, undoubtedly thinking her father was a huge dork.

"You'll feel more comfortable when we get to the end of the row. Then we can switch."

Slade's twist tie dropped to the ground.

Grace darted in to retrieve it. "Can I?" she whispered.

Rescued by his daughter, Slade felt loved. He held the vine in place for her.

Her smaller fingers were more dexterous than his. In no time, she had the wire and paper tie wrapped around the vine.

"I'll hold the vine and you tie it up," he offered.

Grace nodded, grinning as if she'd just won the seventh game of the championship series.

They worked efficiently until about halfway through the row when Truman called, "Grace, break time!"

Grace didn't have to be asked twice. She whooped and scampered off.

"That brings back memories." Christine was twenty feet ahead of him, the snap of her clippers his cue to get back to work.

"Spent a lot of time in the vineyard as a kid, did you?"

"It was the only place I felt normal." He couldn't see her face, but knew she was smiling. It was there in her voice. He'd never met anyone who smiled as much as Christine, not even Flynn. "Kids running through a vineyard. You can't buy that experience at an amusement park."

Silently, he agreed. "Should I remind you I had to buy the vineyard?"

She chuckled, her enjoyment giving him respite from the hot sun. "Too bad days like that don't last."

"What? You grew up too soon?"

"No. My dad was always moving on. Somehow the kids I made friends with didn't stay friends when my dad no longer worked for their family." She paused in her cutting, her gaze wistful. "And I wasn't one to make friends easily in school."

"How could anyone resist that smile?"

"When you're younger than everyone else and earning scores that skew the grading curve, you have to develop survival skills. Like smiling. And when that failed, I became good at blending in with the crowd and being a good listener." Her customary sparkle didn't reach her eyes. She blinked and glanced away. "You'll have to master the twist tie now that you've lost your partner."

He tried, but his mind kept drifting to the image of a young blonde girl carrying a big stack of books while she walked the school halls alone. Soon he experienced misery of another kind. His shirtsleeves were streaked with juice from broken foliage. His face felt grimy. His loafers were encased in dirt and scuffed from when he slipped on some drainage rocks. The back of his shirt was wet and clung to him uncomfortably.

At the end of the row he gladly traded jobs with Christine.

She looked him up and down, an impersonal perusal that felt personal nonetheless. "Go home and change."

He shook his head.

"Not even blue jeans and sneakers? I'll let you keep your dress shirt and tie, although I'm telling you, even though you might win the best-dressed award, inside I'm crying over the certain loss of what looks like a fine Italian tie. Azure-blue basket weave." She removed one worn glove and reached over to stroke his tie. "It is Italian," she said reverently.

The image of her palm anywhere near the evidence of his horrendous mistake ignited a flash fire of fear in his gut. Could she see the truth? That his success was a facade? That his failures had sent his dad over the edge? Nearly dragging him into the chasm with him?

Her innocent blue eyes widened as if recognizing he was upset. She touched his biceps gently. "Have you always lived here?"

"No. I went to school on the East Coast and worked in New York until my dad died." He shifted closer to the bushy vine and the slim bit of shade it offered. "My marriage fell apart at the same time."

"You moved back then?"

He shook his head, surprising himself by admitting, "I kind of lost myself for a while. I drove cross-country from New York, intending to come here. It took longer than I planned." Three years. He'd worked odd jobs along the way, never staying in any one place too long. "The day I made it here—" he didn't say *home* "—I met up with Will and Flynn."

He and Christine stood there looking into each other's eyes—he fighting the need to confess more, she with a calm acceptance of whatever he chose to share. Telling his story would wipe that compassionate look from her eyes. He didn't need compassion from an employee, but he did need an employee. He had to keep expectations in his personal life low and his tie knot high.

He stepped back, tucking the end of his tie between two buttons. To speak, he had to drink some water and douse the fear. "My shoes might already be unsalvageable. Everything else I can clean." He desperately needed to change the mood. "Twenty bucks says my tie lives to see another day."

"You're on." She laughed, flashing that smile that said her wineglass was more than half-full, no matter what life threw her way. She moved on to the next row to check on Flynn and Nate.

And that was when he realized he didn't want her to walk away, he didn't want her to look at him the way Evy did. He wanted to be with someone—an acquaintance, a friend, a lover—and pretend the horrendous mistake hadn't happened, didn't matter.

Idiot.

Satisfied with everyone's progress and quality of work, Christine started down the next row. On leaden feet, Slade dragged himself after her.

It wasn't long before Christine was back to asking questions. "So, when did you develop a tie fetish?"

"At Harvard they taught us to live the leader look." Slade clipped away, taking out his frustrations on the vines. A tendril, a cluster, a branch holding a cluster. Looking back, he could see his progress. Finally, something was going right. "How did you know my tie was Italian?"

"I have an appreciation of everything Italian—wine, shoes, fashion, food." She was quicker than Grace with her twist ties, practically breathing down his back.

"I would never have guessed." He glanced briefly at the rock-band logo over her chest, forcing his gaze away to a safer zone. The sleeve of her T-shirt had a hole in it. He fingered the yellow cotton, then froze, staring at his clumsy, gloved fingers, before yanking them out of her personal space.

She didn't seem to notice. She kept on picking out vines and tying them up. "Come on, you couldn't tell I liked Italian? Not even when I interviewed in an Italian suit and heels?"

He'd almost forgotten that image. It came

thundering back, especially how her slender neck had been bare, the skin pale, smooth, and unmarred. "As your boss, I refuse to judge you by the clothes you wear."

She found that far too funny. "I don't see why not. Most people in Napa do."

"You're not in Napa anymore, Toto." Slade concentrated on trimming the vines back, trying to trim back his overactive imagination in the process.

Truman ran up to him, trailed by Abby and the girls. "I'm sorry."

"What happened?" Abby had her tail down and the girls were teary eyed. Slade dropped his clippers at the base of a grapevine and rushed to meet them. "Is anybody hurt?"

Faith drew a shuddering breath and shook her head. Grace clutched her sister's arm.

"Then what…" Slade nearly gagged, stopping and covering his nose. "What's that smell?"

Truman dug his toe in the dirt. "We found a skunk. In the barn. Abby cornered it and…" He sighed dramatically. "Everyone got sprayed but me."

THE APOLOGIES WERE wearing thin. The skunk smell was not.

Christine apologized to Slade for the skunk

spraying his daughters, to his daughters for
the skunk spraying them on winery property,
to Flynn and Truman for the skunk spraying their dog. Slade and Flynn apologized
to Christine for not being able to help in the
vineyard anymore, as they had to de-skunk
children and pets.

Nate was the only one who didn't apolo-
gize. Instead, he found a list of ingredients
for ridding skunk smell online and drove to
Cloverdale for supplies. Enough supplies to
rid the skunkiness from two girls, one dog,
and an empty winery.

In hindsight, Nate was the smartest of them
all for getting out of town.

While waiting for Nate to return, Flynn
and Truman took Abby down to the river,
planning to throw a stick for her until she
tired out and hopefully rolled in the mud.

Slade walked the girls home, planning to
have them sit in the bathtub until Nate returned. Christine hoped he trash-bagged their
cute outfits before they sat on anything.

After everyone had dispersed, Christine
tentatively entered the barn.

And then she backed quickly out.

Between the heat and the smell, it was
stifling inside. She whipped out her phone,
looked up the nearest pest-control company,

and gave them a call. They agreed to come out and set skunk traps two days from now.

Nothing left to do but continue the vineyard work.

Christine went back to it, falling into a rhythm. Ten feet of tying up, backtrack, ten feet of thinning.

Her cell buzzed: Taking the girls for some TLC after the remedy arrives.

She didn't answer Slade, maybe because she was thinking how nice some tender loving care would be for her. So the girls had been sprayed by a skunk and lost an outfit? She was sure they had outfits to spare. There was work here that needed to be done.

Way to show sympathy, Christine.

They were just kids, after all. Slade was being a good papa bear. And she was succumbing to stress.

Maybe having Flynn and Slade work in the vineyard this morning would make them realize that their growth plan was overly ambitious. Growing grapes and making wine was a meticulous business, and if they couldn't get field-workers, harvest companies, or other winemakers this far out, they couldn't possibly expand and uphold Christine's quality standards.

It was a shame. In some ways, Harmony Valley was just what she was looking for.

"SORRY IT TOOK me so long." Nate stood on Slade's front porch with a bag of supplies for skunk-odor removal. "I texted the recipe to you. Once you've made the paste, apply, let sit, remove."

"Thanks, man. The girls have been soaking in the bathtub since you left. I can smell them from the stairwell." Slade took the shopping bag from the sheriff with one hand, keeping his other hand on the doorknob, ensuring the front door didn't swing all the way open, which most people would take as an invitation to come inside. "How much do I owe you?"

"Nothing." Nate glanced toward the stairs behind Slade. "Not after what you did at the jail."

Slade glanced over his shoulder, too, feeling Nate's questions pressing on him. No one was there, of course. The girls were still upstairs in the bathroom. The ghosts of the house were memories only he could see. "It's not so bad," Slade surprised himself by admitting.

Nate held up his hands. "I wasn't asking."

"No, but you were wondering. I saw people in town talking to you yesterday at the farmer's market. They like to gossip, but…" Slade shifted the bag of supplies closer to his chest. The midday heat swirled in around him. "Whatever they told you is true."

"You don't know what they told me," Nate said gruffly, in a protective tone that told Slade the new sheriff didn't put much stock in hearsay.

"They told you two families that lived here experienced divorce. My family added death to the house's legacy." He shifted from one foot to the other. "They wonder how I can live here." They didn't understand why he had to live here. This house was a reminder of the consequences his financial missteps had on people. It was a reminder of the importance of responsibility and not letting people down.

Nate glanced up and down Harrison. "Do you have to live here? Seems like there's more than a few vacancies in town."

So logical. So impossible. "Where else would I go?"

"Anywhere. You can live in the apartment above the empty ice-cream parlor next door to me."

Slade shook his head. "I can't."

Something changed in Nate's gaze. His

dark eyes went from mild curiosity to gentle comprehension.

That can't be.

Whatever the sheriff took away from their conversation, Slade knew it wasn't understanding. No one could understand.

"Dad?" A meek plea from above.

"I better let you get to it." Instead of leaving, Nate hesitated. "If you ever need to talk about, you know…" He glanced at the staircase.

"I won't," Slade reassured him. He didn't talk to anyone about what had happened.

Nate gave him a sad look before turning to leave. "That's too bad."

As Slade closed the door, he felt something a lot like relief press against the back of his throat. Only it wasn't relief that he'd continued to keep the secret of his horrendous mistake. It was relief that someone was willing to listen.

AROUND NOON, CHRISTINE'S grandmother brought her a sandwich and some watermelon slices. "I thought you might need a break."

"You are a gem among grandmothers, Nana." Christine led her inside the air-conditioned tasting room. Lacking chairs, they sat in the window seats. Christine devoured the egg-salad sandwich and then moved on to the water-melon.

"You need a dog." Nana scanned the vine-yard, presumably for repeat offenders. "That'll help with the skunks."

"I'm adjusting to a new job. I can't add a dog to the mix yet." She stretched her legs and flexed her toes inside her boots. The balls of her feet were stiff and achy.

A blue older-model truck trundled down the driveway. Nate parked and lifted a power washer from the back.

Christine stepped out onto the porch to meet him. The heat reflected off the wooden porch steps with ovenlike intensity. "You can leave the equipment in the barn, Nate. I'll spray tonight." It was going to be a long day, and a longer, skunky night.

"You can't do everything on your own." Nate walked past, carrying everything into the barn. Soon the sounds of spray drifted out.

"Now, that man's a keeper," Nana said, holding the door for her. "Honestly, Chris-tine. You're thirty," Nana said, as if Christine needed reminding. "Pretty soon you'll be forty and I still won't have any great-grandkids."

"Not interested." And she wasn't. Nate was good-looking and had his quiet charm. But the only man she'd met in Harmony Valley who turned her crank was Slade. And perfectly handsome millionaires who signed her paycheck and never removed their tie were off-limits.

CHAPTER FIVE

LATER THAT AFTERNOON, Slade showed up at the vineyard wearing black work pants, a tan work shirt buttoned to the neck, spanking-new black work boots, and a plain black baseball cap. He would have looked perfect, like a millionaire vineyard owner who knew how to work the vineyards, if the temperature had been below seventy.

It was odd how a few days ago she'd been convinced Slade had no personality. Now she couldn't stop wondering what he was hiding behind all those buttons. An embarrassing tattoo? Burns?

"I owe you twenty bucks," he said. "Didn't protect the tie from eau de skunk when I gathered up the girls' clothes."

"When you get skunked, all bets are off." The heat was at its peak, somewhere in the mid-nineties, beating down on her shoulders. The back of her T-shirt was drenched with sweat. She'd been applying sunscreen religiously and was almost out.

Slade reached for the pruning shears, which she gladly handed over. "Flynn said he'd be back after dinner. He had to make a special trip to the vet for something stronger than a home remedy."

"That dog will smell like skunk for weeks." She started tying vines. "Did you buy yourself a new tie in town?"

"Nope. Those I custom order from Italy. I bought the girls a couple new outfits, though." He began clipping at a faster pace than he had in the morning.

"Are they that traumatized?" She hoped she managed to keep the sarcasm from her voice.

"I think it was more embarrassing than scary, although the more I think about skunks and rabies, the more scared I get."

Christine reassured Slade a pest-control service was coming. "So, were the twins laughing about it? Retelling their version? How big did the skunk finally get?"

He sighed. "They don't talk. Much. At least not to me."

"Do you visit them a lot in New York?"

"No." The word was as final as a door slam.

Christine took the hint and went about her work. Slade's pace slowed. She bent to work on tying a vine at his knee, brushing her shoulder against him with a muttered apology. The accidental touch created a flush of awareness she didn't need. How could that be? She'd touched his hand, his arm, his shoulder, and hadn't felt the rush of attraction before.

"Since we divorced, Evy allowed me to visit, but the girls weren't allowed to come here." He sounded weary and in need of a nonjudgmental ear. "We divorced when they were two. And now I feel like a stranger to them."

"I didn't ask. You don't have to tell me." That didn't mean Christine wasn't curious. She carefully backed out from beneath him.

He moved along the row quicker, talked faster. "When Evy found out we'd sold the app for millions, she had her lawyer request additional child support. I bargained for time with the girls and won."

Of course he'd won. She couldn't see Slade losing at anything he set his mind to. His intelligence and ability to wrap his head around the conceptual challenges of a winery had earned her respect.

"So you have summers with the girls." She had to stop herself from brushing a stray leaf off his shoulder. A second glance revealed it wasn't a stray leaf. She plucked a manufacturer's sticker from his shirt.

He brushed a hand over the spot absently. "I won four weeks a year. In total. Evy chose to lump my time all at once. I've already spoken to my lawyer about revising the clause to something like a week every quarter."

"Can you do that?"

The way he looked at her said he certainly could.

The way he looked at her said more about his other potential abilities.

Get a grip, girlfriend.

Christine needed a drink of water. Wouldn't do to get heatstroke and make a pass at her boss. It didn't help that he was turning out to have a very nice personality to complement his very nice looks. The buttoned-up shirt and tie mystery should have been a deal breaker. Instead, she was intrigued.

"I was hopeful that I could really connect with the girls this time, reestablish the father-daughter bond. Now I'm not so sure. Their silent treatment is killing me."

"The best way to prove you love them is to be patient and keep trying."

He stopped, pinning her with an intense stare. "What makes you say that?"

"I was a girl once."

He laughed.

She felt the need to defend herself. "My

dad was a vineyard manager. The only time we saw lots of him was during the Thanksgiving and Christmas holiday seasons. In between he'd occasionally remember he had kids and shower us with guilt gifts." It wasn't until she was older that she realized the gifts didn't make up for time with her dad.

"I spoiled the girls rotten at the mall, but they still didn't interact with me any more than they have been. It's hard to compete with Evy when she buys them everything."

"Don't compete." She removed a twist tie from her pocket, but paused before using it. "They'd rather spend time with you. I know that was really all I wanted from my dad. When I was a preteen, I followed him as often as he'd let me." By then she'd skipped another grade. In the vineyard, nobody cared how young she was or wanted to know how high her grades were. It was the only place she felt she fit in.

"You loved it." Slade's gaze connected with hers. "The same as you love what you do now."

"Yes, but I don't love the posturing and politics, or the decisions outside my control. Three times before this I've been hired to make great wine. Three times the rug has been pulled out from under me after my first few successes. In each case, someone—" she didn't say who "—went behind my back and made changes to my wine. Do you know what it's like to have someone you trust disappoint you like that?" She wiped at the sweat beneath the brim of her hat, juggling the feeling that she and Slade were kindred spirits against the feeling that she'd said too much. "I work long hours because I feel as if I can't let up or let my guard down."

"Work can be demanding and draining." He paused, a faraway look in his eyes. "But if you're lucky, it'll fill the empty spaces until you don't miss being in a relationship."

Christine, who had only started yearning to fill empty spaces since she'd arrived in Harmony Valley—drat Nana and her need for great-grandchildren—was surprised by Slade's comment. "It's all right to give yourself over to your work to build a career, but give up on getting married and having a family? I can't agree with you there. You want to get married again someday, don't you?"

The wavelength they'd shared snapped, as certainly as Slade's features hardened.

He never did answer her question.

BRAD ALEXANDER ROSE before dawn, chased sleep away with a double shot of espresso, and powered through his call list, regardless of the current hour.

Jolted awake by the ring of her cell phone, Christine answered with a muttered, "Somebody better be dead."

"I'm quitting my job."

"Dad." She sat up in bed. "Why?" Harvest was fast approaching.

"These owners just don't get it, honey. They've scheduled harvest early because a crew gave them a deep discount." The outrage in his voice was palpable. "I don't care how hot it is outside this week. What if the grapes aren't ready six weeks from now?"

"Can't you talk to them? Maybe if you and their winemaker combined forces they'd see reason."

"I wouldn't waste my breath." There was a sound in the background. An unpleasantly familiar sound of muffled sobs.

Christine could hardly bring herself to ask, "What's that noise?"

Her father lowered his voice. "Your mother. She isn't happy with me."

And just like that, Christine was a child again, sitting at the dinner table, chicken burning on the stove, her mother's face pale as her father told them he'd quit another job. Christine and her brother frozen in place, afraid to speak, afraid to move, afraid Mom would start crying.

Now it was Christine who lowered her voice. "Dad, you should go back and try to work something out. It's not too late."

"I thought you, of all people, would understand." He hung up.

Christine waited for her breath to calm, her ability to speak to return. She needed to be strong for her mother. But when she called the house, and then her mother's cell phone, Mom didn't answer. No one did.

SLADE WAS LEARNING that part of the joy of being Faith's and Grace's father was seeing what they chose to wear each day.

Today's fashion choice? Country chic.

Matching overalls, the length of shorts. Matching pink-and-white checkered blouses. Matching pink sneakers. Their black hair in pigtails at the base of each ear.

The good news was that they hardly smelled of skunk when he greeted them by sniffing their hair. Score one for Dad.

The bad news was that they didn't come down talking a mile a minute like morning deejays. Dad had a long way to go.

Despite their presence and their habit of scattering their possessions all over the house—dirty socks in the living room, pony-tail holders on the floor of the hall, dirty dishes everywhere—the house still seemed morose and quiet.

As usual, the first call of the day came from Flynn. Slade put his cell on speaker while he flipped whole-wheat pancakes onto each girl's plate. Yeah, he had kitchen skills. "What's on the agenda today? You're pro-gramming, right?"

Thankfully, they'd finished the vineyard work as the sun set around nine last night. Slade's body was aching as if he'd been to one of those hard-core boot camps people paid good money for. And despite the gloves, he had blisters on his palm and thumb from wielding the pruning shears.

But that wasn't the worst thing about work-ing in the vineyard. The worst discovery was that he couldn't stop thinking about Christine. They'd talked for hours while they worked. Oftentimes, she'd weave in and out of his space, trying to be efficient in tying up the vines. He'd wanted to grab on to the wire trel-lis on either side of her head and make her be still, with a touch, an embrace, a kiss.

Slade had spent a near-sleepless night ra-tionalizing his fascination with her and came to a conclusion. Christine was a captivating, compassionate woman who'd appeared just as his friends were pairing up. He'd been feeling left out. He hadn't had a serious relationship in the eight years since his divorce. It had nothing to do with Christine.

Realistically, he'd be interested in any attractive woman who came along. It was like being hungry while driving across the Nevada desert. The first sign of food and you stopped. Slade may have been hungry, but he didn't plan on stopping.

"Yes, I'll be working on the new app today," Flynn was saying, "after we get through our list. Roxie Knight says her chicken coop sprung a leak and there are chickens all over her yard."

Slade wasn't fond of Roxie's escape-artist chickens. "And…"

"And Mildred's stove isn't working. She wants to bake cookies for the kids."

"Chocolate chip, I hope." Mildred was a former race-car driver, now nearly legally blind and confined to a walker. Yet, she managed to make delicious chocolate-chip cookies. "And…"

"And Agnes says Christine needs some shelves in her bedroom."

Agnes? As in Christine's grandmother? Slade was about to say let Christine put up her own shelves, because he didn't need to be working anywhere near her bed, when he noticed the twins were sitting on the edge of their seats. "And…"

"Mr. Mionetti's antenna is out of whack again. Someone needs to climb up onto that roof. I did it last time."

"You are a cruel, cruel man." Slade smiled at his girls. They'd enjoy visiting Mr. Mionetti's sheep ranch. He might have been imagining things, but he thought their lips started curling upward.

"Uncle Slade!" Truman shouted into the phone with the enthusiasm only a seven-year-old boy could bring at this hour of the morning. "I caught a fish last night."

"You did? Did you eat it raw?" Boys liked things gross and Slade was happy to give it to the talkative boy.

The girls were definitely leaning forward now, their overall bibs almost sagging in pancake syrup.

Truman giggled. "No! Becca fried it for me. But Uncle Flynn had to pull its guts out first. It was *awesome*." And then he was on to a new topic. "Do Grace and Faith still smell like skunk? Abby does."

"I'm afraid they still have a slight aura of skunk about them."

Truman giggled again. "I'm going to smell them to see who smells worse—Abby or the girls."

The twins slumped back as one, grinning. Clearly, they didn't have this kind of action in New York City. Faith leaned over and sniffed Grace, who pushed her away.

"We'll meet you at Roxie's in fifteen minutes." Slade disconnected and dug into his pancakes.

HARMONY VALLEY WAS practically deserted in the early mornings.

Christine power walked up one street and down another, getting rid of the kinks from fifteen hours spent in the vineyard yesterday, and trying to shake her worry over her father's latest career move. He was running out of places to work in Napa. And her mother didn't seem to be taking his moves any better this time than the last.

Other than the occasional morning show being blasted out an open screen door as she passed, she didn't meet anyone. In Napa, she would have seen a dozen or more people she knew by now, exercising, gardening, or taking advantage of the cool breeze before it turned hot again.

She walked past the boarded-up elementary school and the vacant high school. She walked down a mostly vacant Main Street. In the distance, she saw Will jogging next to his fiancée on a bike. The only businesses she saw were El Rosal, a barbershop that may or may not be open, a two-pump gas station, and a pawnshop. It was a thirty-minute drive to good coffee, bad fast food, and any sort of a hair salon. The nearest shopping mall was an hour's drive.

There'd be no charity events requiring new sequined dresses and coiffed hair. No restaurant dinners with seven-course meals and decades-old wine, the bills for which siphoned money away from her savings. Christine wanted her own winery someday. Harmony Valley's low-key lifestyle—living with Nana, driving her clunker—would help her achieve that goal. She'd love to get her own place and offer her dad a job, and her mother peace of mind.

The only wild card was Slade and his aggressive business plans for the winery. But if she played her cards in just the right order over the next year, she hoped to bring Slade from the volume-producing, large-employee-roster dark side to the small-quantity, high-quality light side.

Christine turned down a side street that she vaguely remembered led to a small park along the river. She was walking at a good clip, breathing hard and enjoying the view as she took the path across the park.

She passed an ancient swing set, an old metal pushable merry-go-round, a few picnic tables, and lots of trees—poplar, oak, eucalyptus. There was so much shade the grass was sparse. Birds swooped from trees by the river, barnstorming the blackberry bushes that clung to the edge of the bluff. She reached the bluff overlooking the river and nearly tripped.

Immediately below her, on a narrow strip of dirt beach, a naked guy was doing yoga. She appreciated the male form as much as the next gal, but this man looked like someone's grandfather. Someone's shipshape, ponytailed grandfather.

"Good morning." He transitioned from a tree pose to a warrior's pose so smoothly he didn't startle the two ducks rooting in the shallows nearby.

"Good…uh…morning." Christine averted her eyes. She turned and started retracing her steps, hoping he hadn't gotten a good look at her.

"You must be the winemaker. Agnes' granddaughter."

So much for hoping for anonymity. Ettiquette dictated she not walk away. That didn't mean she had to face him, though. "That's me."

"I'm Mayor Finkelstein."

Oh, jeez. She'd heard stories about Mayor Larry. He was a die-hard hippy. But naked yoga in public? Did her grandmother know?

Christine took a tentative step away from further embarrassment. Wouldn't do to bolt when the mayor had her in his sights. "Nice to meet you."

"I'm digging your yoga pants. Are they for show or do you like yoga?"

"I do some yoga." With her clothes on.

"You can come down and join me anytime."

"Thanks, I'll think about it." *Not.*

"Oh." He chuckled. "I'd forgotten I was airing my laundry."

Not exactly the words Christine would have used. A few more steps and he wouldn't be able to see her anymore.

"Come down tomorrow morning at seven. I promise to bring my yoga shorts."

"I'll have to check my schedule. Have a good day." She glanced over her shoulder to make sure he couldn't see her before she raced out of the park. Halfway down Main

Street she started laughing and didn't stop until she burst into Nana's house.

"Whatever is the matter?" Nana glanced up from her coffee and newspaper spread across the kitchen table.

"Mayor Larry."

She didn't have to say more. Agnes sighed. "I should have called to let him know you liked to walk in the morning. He loves to commune with nature. We all stay away from that part of the river during his regular hour. He'll be dressed for a few weeks, at least."

"How can you be so sure?"

"He won't put his clothes on unless he feels he's made someone uncomfortable. But the clothes never stay on for long. And he does have a nice body."

"Madam Councilwoman! Did you peek?"

"I did no such thing." She folded her newspaper and tried to give Christine a playful swat with it, but her arms were too short to reach.

"You did!" Christine danced out of the way just in case. "I knew this town couldn't be that boring."

"You mean you thought *I* was boring," her grandmother grumbled.

Christine came back and pressed a kiss to her grandmother's soft cheek. "I'm beginning to think no one in Harmony Valley is boring."

CHAPTER SIX

"I HATE CHICKENS." At least, he hated live ones that raced away every time he tried herding them back into their repaired coop. Slade chased a blue speckled hen around Roxie Knight's large backyard.

"You've exhausted my hens." Roxie's voice was soprano smooth and belonged to a woman twice her petite size. She'd complimented the twins on their overalls, which was fitting, since the older woman wore a pair of blue coveralls the likes of which you'd find in a mechanic's garage. "I won't get any eggs out of them for a week."

A spreading oak tree shaded the chicken coop near the back of the yard. A strip of grass grew down in the middle, flanked on either side by a lush vegetable garden. The chickens were experts at darting in between snap-pea tepees and pepper trellises.

Slade gave up, sitting down next to Roxie on a redwood bench at the picnic table. "I hate chickens." He was frustrated enough that it bore repeating.

Behind Slade, Roxie had attached a fish net, abalone shells, and driftwood to the wall of the house. Roxie had worked most of her life as a fisherman…fisherwoman…a woman of the sea. And yet, she'd retired to the base of the mountains.

Flynn sank onto the bench across from Slade. "You know, Abby was bred to herd sheep. Maybe she could herd chickens." He'd left Truman's dog in the truck with the windows down, in case she decided she liked the taste of live chicken more than she liked chasing after live chickens.

Slade was ready to give Abby a try. They needed reinforcements.

Across from Slade, Truman swung his legs under the table with gleeful intensity. "We've never had to catch chickens before. Only over-the-hill poodles and stray kittens."

"Still haven't caught any," Roxie noted drily. "And I prefer you don't use the dog. Besides, I hear she smells like skunk. That'll put my hens off laying their eggs for days."

"Is that on top of the week from us exhausting them?" Flynn winked at his nephew.

The twins stood near a cherry-tomato bush.

A couple of times, Slade had stopped chasing chickens to watch his daughters break down in gasps of laughter.

"Huh." Truman looked at Faith and Grace. He seemed an honorary twin, so good was he at reading them. He communicated with them by using hand gestures and loud, broken English, as if they were deaf. To him, it was a game. To Slade, it was a weight he couldn't seem to lift from his chest.

Faith whispered to Grace. Grace whispered back. They approached the picnic table.

"We might as well try whatever idea the girls have come up with." Truman shrugged.

Flynn and Slade exchanged glances and then looked at the twins.

"Use the net," Faith said.

Grace pointed to the fishing net draped on the wall behind them.

Truman stared at the net. "You're brilliant."

"What took you so long?" Flynn resettled his baseball cap on his head and stood.

Slade couldn't stop grinning.

A few minutes later, holding the fishing net between them, with the kids flushing chickens out of the side yard, Flynn and Slade swept all the chickens back into the coop.

"Good idea, girls," Slade congratulated his

daughters as he drove to the next destination on their list—the Mionetti sheep ranch. Flynn was better at electrical and was going to Mildred's to work on her malfunctioning stove. "I bet you don't see many chickens in New York City. Or skunks."

They didn't answer him. Slade's grin faded, leaving his cheeks feeling worn-out.

When they got to Mionetti's, the twins petted the elderly man's half blind, half dead sheep dog. Slade climbed up onto the roof, turning the antenna in every possible direction, thanks to Mionetti yelling garbled instructions through the chimney. When they'd adjusted the picture to the old man's satisfaction, he gave the girls green pellets and let them hand feed a few lambs in his flock.

Which was a hit on the giggle meter, until Grace curled the pellets into her palm instead of flat-handing it and a lamb nipped her skin.

Grace opened her mouth in a silent wail, tears quickly spilling over.

"Well, I would have bet money that would happen," Mr. Mionetti said unhelpfully.

Quicker than Slade could get to her, Faith dumped her pellets to the ground, flung an arm over Grace's shoulder, and rocked her from side to side with unintelligible soothing noises.

"Grace, let me see it, baby," Slade said, kneeling and trying to pry the injured palm open.

The girls stilled.

"Faith, tell her it's all right." Slade didn't want to force his daughter to open her hand. "I need to be sure she's okay. Come on, Grace, open your hand."

Grace slowly unfurled her fingers. The pads on her palm were an angry red, but the lamb's teeth hadn't broken through skin.

Slade gently massaged her fingers and palm on either side of the bite. "You'll be fine." He took the opportunity to curl his arm around her waist. He hadn't hugged his daughters in years. It had just seemed too awkward for both them and him. But in that moment, he was pulled back in time to their smiling, gummy faces when he came home from work, chubby arms reaching for him. "Do you want some ice? It might help take away the sting."

Grace shook her head and sniffed, leaning into him. *Progress!*

He wanted to snatch Grace up and spin her around, followed by a similar spinning celebration with Faith. Instead, he gave his daughter an affectionate squeeze, before releasing her. "Time to move on to Christine's bedroom…er, Christine's house." Slade had to remain detached where his employee was concerned.

And he thought herding chickens was tough.

WHEN THEY ARRIVED at Christine's, Agnes was getting into her faded green Buick to drive a few members of her garden club to brunch and a flower exhibit in Santa Rosa. With a smile and a wave, the diminutive grandma directed them inside. "Christine's room is in front. She spent the morning working from home."

Agnes's house was compact, like the woman herself. Her living room still held the big manly sofa and recliner her husband had been fond of. No amount of doilies, frilly pillows, or colorful quilts could banish the feeling that this had been a man's domain.

Slade strolled past the pink kitchen with barely a glance, since he'd seen it before. Faith and Grace stopped to marvel at its pinkness. He continued into the narrow hall, just as Christine came out of her door.

The scent of vanilla immediately tantalized him.

"What are you doing here?" Christine's

surprised tone held just a hint of *Back off.*
Her legs looked incredibly long in gray jean
shorts. Her T-shirt was teal-blue with fluffy
cartoon rabbits and what looked like a dog
bite on the hem. Her long hair was down and
still a bit damp, making it seem more light
brown with blond highlights than blond.

"We're here…" He cleared his throat.
"We're here on the fix-it patrol per your grandmother's request." He gave her a jaunty salute
that said, *Your boss isn't stalking you.* To further prove his innocence, he gestured to the
girls he sensed coming up behind him.

Christine peeked around his shoulder. "I
like the country look you're rocking, ladies."
She tilted her head to look up at him. She was
a half-head shorter than he was. The perfect
height for kissing.

Not that he had kissing top of mind. *Oh,
no. No, sirree.*

"What is it you're here to fix?" she de-
manded.

"Your grandmother says you need shelves."

Her cheeks turned a soft pink. "You don't
have to help with my shelves. I can do a
Google search for a solution after work."

"A solution? So, it's a challenge? This I've
got to see." He reached for her doorknob.

Her hand got there first. His covered hers

for an instant, before he politely pulled back. He ignored the warmth of her skin, but not the flash of awareness in her eyes or the deepening blush on her cheeks. She'd felt something, too.

So much for a hungry man ignoring food in his path.

She frowned. "Shouldn't you be working? It's almost nine o'clock." She blinked, as if realizing she wasn't at work, either. "I've already made some phone calls and sent some emails. I was getting ready to leave to spray the main winery building again with anti-skunk-smell solution."

"The only thing I have on my work schedule today is a review of the equipment purchases you're proposing and a phone call to my broker." He planned on puttering around town spending time with the girls. But lurking on his mental agenda was Christine's agreement to his five-year growth plan. That required time spent together. Logical time. Businesslike time. Time to discuss where their differing points of view converged.

Building shelves in her bedroom while she left for the winery wasn't a good idea. Unless... "We can build the shelves together. An exercise in team building."

"Team building?" She mulled that over as slowly as a sip of fine wine.

"We need to learn to trust each other." His voice had dropped very low. He cleared his throat. "So we can agree on how we build and grow the winery, year after year."

He hadn't been tempted by her in an expensive business suit, but there was something about Christine in her work clothes that was a lawsuit waiting to happen. He couldn't let his guard down. This was about employee buy-in.

"Fine." She opened her bedroom door.

Her windows faced south. The sun bounced cheerfully off yellow walls, drawing him in. The room was brighter than his house had been in years. A small narrow bureau stood next to the bed, cluttered with framed pictures. Cardboard moving boxes were stacked in one corner. Slade would never have admitted to longing for a mere double bed, but hers, with its puffy golden comforter, was luxurious compared to the hard twin bed he'd been sleeping on for months.

She crossed the room and opened the closet, which was a smaller version of the master-bedroom closet in his house, the closet where his father hung himself.

Air left his lungs in a rush. Slade looked

away. Out of the corner of his eye, he saw her move boxes out of the closet, making a new stack in another corner. One box flap opened, revealing several designer shoe boxes.

Slade remained by the door, breathing fast and shallow. His hand drifted to his tie, traced the silk upward to the knot at his throat. "You don't…you don't want shelves on the wall?"

The twins peeked in around him.

"No. In the closet. On this side." She patted the closet wall.

He didn't do closets. Ever. But she'd drawn his gaze to this one, until he was fixated on the bare closet rod. Instead of seeing it smooth and empty, he saw a rod with a belt attached.

"In the closet," Slade repeated in a raspy voice he didn't recognize.

"That's where shoe racks go." Christine tossed her long hair over her shoulder, pulling his attention to safety, if staring at her as if he'd just seen a ghost could be called safe. The skin between her brows puckered. "We don't have to do this. Team building was your idea."

His palm pressed against the knot of his tie. He made a noncommittal sound. The kind of sound a man makes when he can't decide whether to stand his ground or flee.

Christine reached into the closet and pulled

out several plastic storage bags with colorful gowns. She tossed them onto the bed.

As if magnetized, the twins pushed past him and sped toward the dresses.

Christine noticed their interest. "You can try them on, if you like. This team building may take a while."

Faith and Grace exchanged glances. Slade ignored his light-headedness, ignored the closet, ignored the past, and focused on the twins. They were enjoying themselves. He had to pull himself together.

"The bathroom across the hall can be your dressing room." Christine turned on the sparkle, but not even Christine's joyful attitude elicited a response from the twins. "But since those are my dresses, you'll have to come out after each costume change and show us. Let's just stay away from the strapless gowns. Those are in the black bag."

While he tried to work up the courage to face the task ahead—thinking about Christine's elegant shoulders in a white strapless gown helped—the twins exchanged glances again and then dragged the heavy dresses out of the room.

Slade stepped aside so Christine could follow them across the hall. She hung the garment bags on the shower curtain and unzipped them. "Let me know if you need help." She closed the twins in the bathroom.

"That was very gracious of you." Slade leaned against the wall, trying to appear as if it wasn't holding him up. "I hope they won't ruin anything."

She shrugged. "I don't plan on wearing them again."

"You've converted to T-shirts permanently?" He could stand and talk so long as he kept his back to the closet.

Christine shoved boxes farther away from the closet. "Dresses like that can't be worn more than once or twice in social circles around the wine business, unlike shoes."

"That makes shoes a better investment." He couldn't seem to loosen his grip on his tie. Slade risked a glance at the closet and then away. He shored himself up against the wall.

"Don't ever say I'm not training you right for some lucky woman who loves shoes."

Ignoring where that comment led him, he moved to the bureau, ostensibly to look at her pictures. Reality was, he needed to put as much space as he could between himself and the open closet.

He picked up a framed photo. Christine smiled triumphantly with three blond men and stacks of what looked like T-shirts.

The scent of vanilla heralded Christine. She leaned closer. "That's my brother, my uncle, and my dad. I won the contest that year."

The next picture was of Christine holding a crystal trophy and a bottle of wine. Her smile seemed brighter than the crystal.

"Best in class that year at the World's."

He glanced at the clutter on the dresser. "Where's the trophy?"

"The winery gets to keep it." She added wistfully, "Not the winemaker."

That didn't seem fair. Neither did the way the closet seemed to be taunting him.

The last big picture was of Agnes with Christine and… "Is that your mom?"

"Yep."

If Christine aged as well as her mother, she'd still be a knockout thirty years from now. Not the train of thought he needed. "I can see you got your height from your father's side of the family tree."

There were other photos to check out, but the closet was six feet away. It felt like six inches. It felt like he was so close he could fall backward and… *Get a grip.*

Christine hadn't moved away from him. She had no idea how much he wanted to hold on to her to save him from the closet. He thrust a hand through his hair. "You don't want your own place?"

"Someday. My grandmother is lonely, although I hope she doesn't start imposing a curfew." She sent him a sideways look, the kind a woman sends a man when she's gauging his interest in the conversation. "Truth is, I want my own winery, so any chance I get to save money, I take it."

He understood goals and moving on. He gestured vaguely toward the corner where she'd stacked her shoes. "How many pairs of shoes are we talking about? Twenty? Thirty?" She could buy a rack for that many.

Christine glanced at the three large cardboard boxes she'd transferred from the closet. The ones guarding his back. "More like a hundred."

He must have made a manly noise of derision because she playfully punched his shoulder. "Hey, I thought you weren't the kind to judge."

"Maybe you need to donate a few pairs."

She was aghast. "Some of those shoes cost more than a car payment!"

"And now you're going to park them in a custom-built garage." One that she'd make herself, because he couldn't do it. He was 99 percent certain if he tried to so much as measure the closet for shelving, he'd pass out.

He didn't use the closet in his bedroom. He'd bought an antique wardrobe and hung his clothes in there. His closet doors were firmly closed. Had been for years.

"You don't want to build shelves for my shoes." Christine narrowed her eyes. "What do you have against shoes?"

"Nothing." Closets were his kryptonite.

And right now, he was too close to kryptonite.

CHAPTER SEVEN

"LET ME GET this straight." Keeping an eye on the bathroom door, Slade shifted sideways away from the closet.

Christine had never seen him look so rattled. Was it her? Her ego whispered yes. Or was it the girls? That was a more logical explanation.

One hand rested on his tobacco-brown designer tie. His other hand kept disturbing his normally perfect black hair. "You have the original box for each pair of shoes, yet you want to build shelves, take each pair out and put them on display, and store the empty boxes somewhere else?"

Feeling as if she was on trial with a weak defense, Christine nodded.

He reached the closet, slid the door closed, and then seemed to sag onto her stack of shoe boxes. He finally let go of his tie. "Are you going to wear any of these shoes while you're here?"

"You want me to give up my shoes?"

Slade looked at her is if she'd proclaimed she wanted to wear her patent-leather leopard-print Manolo Blahnik pumps to skip through the vineyard after a rain shower. "They're just shoes."

"I'll give up my shoes if you give up your ties." Her barb hit home. He huffed and puffed, his face reddening as he prepared to launch a counteroffensive.

Just then the bathroom door opened, and the twins lifted long skirts to promenade into the room.

One of the girls had chosen a ballet-pink ball gown. The fabric was gathered and criss-crossed over the bust, not that the little girl had one. It fell to the floor in a puddle of delicate chiffon. The other twin had chosen a bright red slinky satin floor-length sheath with a plunging back. The bodice was beaded with red sequins.

"You two look beautiful." Slade seemed to relax when he gazed upon his daughters.

Inspired, Christine dug into a box and found a pair of red sequined shoes worthy of Dorothy from *The Wizard of Oz*—if Dorothy was into high heels. Next she unearthed a pair of pale pink satin sandals. She handed the shoes to the girls.

"Did you just happen to open two boxes of

shoes that matched their dresses perfectly?" Slade asked softly. "Or did you know which boxes were which?"

"I catalog all my shoes by color, style, and level of formality." Christine pointed to the narrow ends of each shoe box, where a small label had been added. "I admit, I'm a little anal. But I'm a scientist, so it's okay." Was that uncertainty in her voice?

"All the more reason to keep your shoes organized and in their boxes."

"But they're so pretty." There was definitely a note of uncertainty in her voice, darn it. So what if she loved shoes? She said louder, "It makes me feel good to look at them."

"I'm just a guy," he mumbled. "What do I know?"

The twins wobbled in Christine's heels, holding on to each other and—yes indeedy— giggling. After spending several hours with his daughters yesterday in the vineyard, she was happy to hear normal-little-girl sounds from their lips.

Slade stopped short, his normally rigid features melting into that papa-bear expression Christine found so endearing. Something warm spread through her chest at the sight of a man head-over-heels in love with his daughters.

The rubber band holding the right ponytail of the girl in the red dress had slipped and was nearly falling off. Christine grabbed her hairbrush and touched the girl's loose lock of hair. "May I? A dress like this needs a more elegant hairstyle."

The twins fell silent, passing messages back and forth with their glances.

"It's okay, Faith," Slade said.

"Faith," Christine repeated. She was the twin with the dimple in her right cheek. "Did you know you have a big curl below your ear? My grandmother calls those cowlicks, because it would take a cow's big tongue licking it to get it under control."

Faith gave her a small smile.

Christine took that as permission to go to work. She moved behind Faith, freed all that long black hair, brushed it into an updo, with a few intricate twists and the ends sticking into the air like a rooster comb. Every once in a while she got a whiff of eau de skunk.

Grace craned her neck to examine Christine's work and then cleared her throat.

Slade butted in. "Grace, can't you ask like a—"

"Like Princess Grace." Christine cut Slade off before he could add *like a normal person* to the man-at-the-end-of-his-patience-with-silent-girls lament. "She conquered Hollywood, but left to marry the Prince of Monaco."

Christine then quickly produced a French braid from above one of Grace's ears to above the other, combining the extra length in a ponytail on the other side. She didn't notice Faith's surprised expression until she was through. "There. Two girls ready to party. Go put on another dress." She shooed them out of the bedroom.

The girls took turns admiring each other's hair and studying themselves in the bathroom mirror.

"Their hair's different." Slade frowned.

"They're twins, not clones."

"But we've always dressed them alike."

"That's a new form of torture." When Slade's gaze cut to her as if she'd accused him of wrongdoing—which she essentially had—she tried to remember he was her boss. And failed. "How would you like it if you had to dress like your brother every day?"

"A. I'm an only child. And B. They don't have to dress alike."

Faith and Grace were looking at him from across the hall, holding themselves very still.

Christine had a sickening thought. "Does your ex-wife agree with B?"

"She wouldn't be that—"

"Girls, time for a costume change." Christine waited for the bathroom door to close.

Slade held up a hand before she could say anything. "Don't. It's bad enough I'm an absentee father without pointing out the faults of the woman raising my children."

"What do you say we strike a deal? I don't question what's going on with them—" she gestured toward the bathroom "—and you don't question my love of shoes." She thrust out her hand. "Deal?"

"Deal." His grip didn't feel as coolly perfect as it had in the past. It was the warm handshake of a real man, one whose life wasn't perfect.

"You're right about my organizational system. I'm not going to put up the shelves, since I'm not going to wear the shoes." Christine chuckled when Slade looked relieved. "How about we sit down and watch the rest of the fashion show? After which you can go do something fun with the girls and I'll finish my purchasing proposal for you to review." She sat on the bed and patted a spot next to her.

Only to pop off her mattress a moment later. "Hold up. Hold up. I keep forgetting that you're my boss—"

"Really? I hadn't noticed." He grinned wryly.

She pointed at the pink shag carpet. "You sit on the floor."

He did. But he was grinning.

And when she was sure he couldn't see her, so was she.

AFTER SEVERAL DRESS CHANGES, Slade was feeling decidedly uncomfortable on Christine's bedroom floor, leaning against her bed, at her feet, which were bare, the toes painted an energetic orange. They had a business relationship, nothing more. It was time to get down to business.

And so they discussed projected timelines and her preferred equipment manufacturers. They discussed in depth her favorite methods of harvesting and wine making. He shared the partnership's views on the winery stimulating town growth. Interspersed between were oohs and aahs for the girls. It was hard to believe that one woman had that many evening gowns. Short ones, long ones, fitted ones, ones with slits and lace and shimmery trim.

Although he enjoyed seeing his daughters dress up, he couldn't help imagining what Christine would look like in each evening gown, until Grace came out in a black dress with a long feathered skirt. "Whoa. You did not wear that thing?" Slade glanced up at Christine. "It has feathers."

Christine stared down her elegant nose at him. "Feathers were in that year."

Slade chuckled. "Grace, you look beautiful, honey, but I can't see how that dress would look good on a full-grown woman." He pointed at the dress. "I mean...*feathers!*"

"I'm reminding myself you're my boss," Christine said through gritted teeth.

Grace exchanged a look with Faith, who was wearing a white beaded gown with flowing long sleeves. Both girls looked at Christine and nodded.

"Excuse me a minute, *boss*." Christine followed them into the bathroom.

Great. Add Christine to the growing list of people who understood his daughters' silent language.

Slade got up stiffly, stretched out the kinks, and sat on the bed. It was softly inviting. With effort, he kept from flopping onto his back and sneaking a power nap.

A few minutes later the girls came out dressed in their pink checks and overalls shorts. Their hair was still prom-queen grand. They bounced onto the bed next to him. Grace leaned on his shoulder.

He didn't dare move.

And then Christine stepped out of the bathroom in the black feathered gown. It fit her tight across the chest, with just a hint of cleavage, enough to catch a man's eye.

This man's eye.

She'd piled her hair above her head in a messy style that begged a man's hand to smooth it. And then she strode across the hall, revealing the dangerously high slit that exposed most of her leg with every step. A leg that ended in a bright red pump.

Slade's mouth went dry as his eyes traveled back up to her face.

Christine wouldn't release his gaze. Here was the classy, confident woman he'd interviewed. The woman who knew the power of her appearance and wasn't afraid to use it. Not that she had to wield her womanly power, given she was rocket-scientist smart when it came to her craft.

Faith and Grace leaned over to look at him. And giggled.

Christine burst out laughing. "That'll teach you to make fun of a woman's feathers."

The girls giggled some more, until Slade found himself chuckling, too.

"This has been fun," Christine said. "But

it's almost ten o'clock and I need to get out to the winery and spray for skunk again."

He patted Faith's knee. "Come on, girls. Let's find Flynn and Truman."

Because Slade was in need of some masculine grounding and space without high heels or feathers or closets.

THE LAST TIME Christine had hung out in her bedroom with a guy, she'd been thirteen and her father had just bought her a new video-game console. Her older brother and his friends had camped out on her bed for days.

Having Slade in her bedroom was extremely different. Often when she'd interacted with him before, he appeared stiff and standoffish, about to turn up his nose and dismiss her at any moment. This morning, his nervousness had been refreshing. His arguments for winery growth compelling. His warm papa-bear personality captivating.

And every once in a while—not often enough to be sure—she caught him eyeing her speculatively with a look of desire that spoke volumes. *I could be in deep trouble here.*

That zing of awareness made uncovering the layers beneath Slade's perfect veneer even more fascinating. A worried papa bear. She suppressed a sigh. There was nothing wrong with those girls a heavy dose of fatherly love wouldn't cure. They were testing him, plain as white bread. Grace and Faith would talk to him soon. No girl could hold her silence longer than a few days with such a good-hearted man.

When Christine arrived at the winery, she power washed the main building's floor again. The skunk smell was receding, although she suspected it wouldn't be the last time she had to spray the place down.

Later, using the tasting-room counter as a desk, Christine stood and shuffled through paperwork, playing with combinations of expensive tractors versus inexpensive tractors, new forklifts versus used forklifts, and different types of truck scales. Every time she added a column and compared it to Slade's original budget, she went back and changed something else. She ended up with two budgets—one that was her ideal, and one that was a compromise between her budget and Slade's original plan. Then she sent out more queries about the positions she had available.

She was flipping through a file of the winery's legal documents, just starting to read their application for bottling permits, when the tasting-room door opened, practically giving Christine a heart attack.

"Hello! Remember me? Mayor Larry Finkelstein."

She drew a breath, closed the folder, and put it on a stack of others she'd already gone through.

Thankfully, the mayor was fully clothed. He wore flip-flops and the kind of controlled smile that said he wanted something. "I thought we should discuss your little winery, since we're neighbors."

Christine invited him to sit on the window seat across the room. She really needed to find time to furnish the place. But more importantly, she had to find out what the mayor wanted.

"I know you still have much to do—set up the bottling facility, landscape the grounds, put up signage at the end of the driveway." Mayor Larry's smile hinged upward at *signage*.

"Whatever we decide to put up—" and she was a little surprised Slade hadn't installed a sign yet "—you can rest assured it will be sophisticated and in keeping with town ordinances."

His smile wound up into his cheeks until

it almost disappeared among his wrinkles. "We'll get along just fine. Just fine. You don't, by any chance, bowl?"

"No." Bowling was one skill she hadn't needed to perfect in Napa. "I golf." She chose not to add *poorly.*

He nodded his head as if that explained everything and moved on to uncovering which yoga studio she'd attended in Napa.

She, of course, had belonged to the most exclusive yoga studio in town, which earned her another invitation to do yoga with Larry the next morning at seven.

Call her gullible, but when she thought about the inspections and regulations that faced the winery, how could she refuse? She might need this politician on her side.

"So this is where you'll sell your wine." Mayor Larry studied the tasting room with a calculating eye. "Have you thought about offering other local goods? For example, I have my own line of T-shirts. Tie-dyed, like this one." He tugged a rolled-up T-shirt from a back pocket and shook it out. "I also knit sweaters from hand-woven wool."

Ah, the purpose of his visit revealed at last.

Tie-wearing Slade wasn't going to like Mayor Larry's business proposition.

But compromise-making Christine was going to consider it.

CHAPTER EIGHT

SLADE SAT ON an old rattan chair on Flynn's back porch overlooking the river. Beneath the railing, plump blackberries hung from thick brambles. He was too hot and tired to pick any.

To his left, Faith and Grace ran around the front yard with Truman and Abby. The dog had won Truman's most-smelly-skunk award, but that didn't stop the kids from playing with her.

Flynn sat nearby. Nate leaned on the porch railing watching the slow-moving river pass.

"Do your girls have speech impediments?" Flynn asked, more direct in his questioning than Nate had been.

"I don't think so. Evy hasn't said anything. They may have been like this for months or just decided to torture *me*." And Slade felt tortured. He should know what was going on with his kids. Evy wasn't answering her phone or email or texting him back. Husband number three must have been too cheap to spring for an international-calling or data plan.

"It's just a phase." Flynn's wife, Becca, came out the back door with cold beer, repeating his ex's claim. "Kids enjoy testing limits. Kind of like the elderly when their independence is threatened." She distributed a bottle to each of them. "They play pranks. They hide chocolate and sneak out of the house. You should keep your truck keys safe."

"How was your day, Becs?" Flynn accepted his beer with a kiss, and a lingering hand on her hip. They'd been married less than a month. The honeymoon was far from over.

"Busy. I picked up two more new clients today. Found a stash of chocolate and a spare set of car keys." Becca swung her dark braid over her shoulder and sat on Flynn's lap, making the ancient rattan chair they were in gasp and groan. "One thing about being the only elderly caregiver in a town of elderly people, I don't lack for clients. I had to run into Cloverdale twice for groceries and prescriptions. When are you going to attract a grocer to town?"

"You work too hard for being the wife of a millionaire," Nate observed.

Slade plucked at his tie. "If I ever get married again, which I don't plan on, I wouldn't want my wife working."

Becca laughed, sinking against Flynn's chest so she could look out toward the river. "What would I do with myself if I was home all day? Eat bonbons and clog my arteries?" Becca kissed Flynn's chin. "Besides, I have bills to pay. House rule number ten—debts acquired prior to marriage are my own."

"I told you I'd pay Gary off." Flynn sounded annoyed, as if this was an old argument.

"And I told you—"

"Children, please." Slade slouched farther into his chair. "I just want to enjoy some peace and quiet."

"How's your new winemaker doing?" Becca politely changed the subject. "I haven't had time to meet her."

Slade angled his head toward them. "Unlike you, she wants to spend our money."

Nate looked around the porch, taking in the aged furniture and perhaps reconciling it with them being millionaires, but said nothing.

"This house was my grandfather's." Flynn interpreted the sheriff's wary gaze and explained, "I grew up here, and since Grandpa Ed only recently passed on, I'm not ready to change anything."

"Because he wouldn't let you change anything when he was alive." Becca gave Flynn an affectionate squeeze.

"Getting back to Christine," Flynn said. "Has she convinced you to build a wine cave? If it creates more job opportunities, I say let's do it."

Slade stared toward the river, but all he saw was his father's suicide note. "At this stage, this investment is capped out."

Flynn wouldn't let it go. "We promised the town—"

"And I promised you," Slade snapped. "I promised if we never sold another app that we'd have money in our old age. I can't keep my promise if you keep dipping into the coffers. Let me do my job." He drew a breath, trying to calm down. "We agreed the winery was going to be a tax write-off, at least at first. I don't expect the winery to make monstrous profits. But I draw the line at subsidizing the town."

He'd learned a lot in the past few days about running a winery. It made what he thought he knew look like kindergarten material. At the rate Christine wanted to grow the winery, they'd never create enough jobs to save the town. And at the rate Slade had hoped to grow the winery, they risked failure by producing an inferior product, which in turn would decrease the value of their portfolio. The same portfolio they were basing their retirement off of. The last time he'd managed a retirement portfolio, it'd belonged to his dad. He'd bankrupted his old man, who'd hung himself after hearing the news.

Yeah, he was nervous. He didn't trust himself to predict how people were going to react to monetary loss. Suicide? Divorce? An end to a valued friendship? He didn't want to find out.

Slade rubbed a hand over his face. Another change of subject was in order. "How's the progress on the new app?"

"Slow. Hit a snag today when the programming script kept crashing everything." Flynn's voice welled with frustration. "I can't wait for Will to get back from the city."

"You'll figure it out, Flynn." Becca reassured him with both words and a kiss, if Slade's hearing was correct.

Nate drained his beer and shot the happy couple a significant look that said they didn't need to be making out in front of guests. "Thanks for the beer. I'm outta here." He looked at Slade. "You coming?"

"In a minute." Slade kept his gaze carefully on the river, finishing his beer more slowly.

He'd never been jealous of the love his friends had found.

All the same, he felt a twinge of what felt like jealousy for a love like theirs. A love that didn't count his past against him. It was dangerous thinking. Dangerous because what woman could find it in her heart to love him—scars and all?

CHRISTINE TRACKED SLADE down at his home after dinner that night. He lived on the north end of the town square just a block and a half away from Nana's house.

His house was a narrow, white-planked two-story home with a small porch out front and a driveway that led to a small detached garage in back. Although the lights were on, the drapes were shut tight, giving the house a neglected look.

Slade opened the door and frowned at her. "Did we have a meeting?"

"No, but I need one. Can I come in?" She hitched her laptop bag, loaded down with papers, higher on her shoulder. "I have my budget and purchasing proposal. I would have brought them earlier, but the mayor came by, and then the town council, and then…" She noticed he wasn't speaking. And still had his tie on.

"Oh, shoot. You have company, don't you?" She backed away from the door. "A date? I'm sorry. I just assumed—"

"There's no one here but the twins and me. I just don't..." His voice dropped almost to a whisper as he smoothed his tie. "I don't let people inside the house."

Grace appeared behind him, a small smile on her face. She touched her hair and looked sideways, presumably at her sister, who came to join her.

"Is it haunted?" Christine meant it as a joke, but Slade stiffened.

His eyes glazed with pain. "If you must know—" the confession fell reluctantly from his perfectly chiseled lips "—my parents died here."

"I'm so sorry," Christine said, automatically modulating her smile. She had a vague memory of someone telling her that once. "Did they die recently? Like, is it safe to be inside? Is that why you keep people out?" She was only half joking.

"They didn't die of anything you could catch," he snapped.

She was learning that his bark was brief and usually territorial. "So it's okay to come in? You just don't want anyone to feel uncomfortable?"

The twins drifted away from the foyer.

Sighing, he opened the door wider. "The bridge club calls this the Death and Divorce House. Death being my family's contribution."

"Wow. I've never lived in a house that has a name." She said it lightly to prove to him the house didn't bother her. Then she stepped inside and the claustrophobic atmosphere of the place closed around her as firmly as the door shutting behind her.

"Don't say I didn't warn you," Slade grumbled. "I'm used to it and the girls don't seem to mind."

"Hi, girls," Christine called, cheerfully waving a red flag in the house's face, because, dang, there was a weird sensation skimming up and down the back of her neck.

Or it could have been Slade's breath. He was right behind her. But that would have been a pleasurable skim.

The house was poorly lit, leaving shadows in the hall and up the stairwell.

The twins stared at her. They sat on the couch sharing an iPad. Dirty dinner dishes staked out space on the cluttered coffee table, surrounded by a line of cups with various levels of different beverages in them, as if the twins had changed their mind several times about what they wanted to drink.

There was a stack of business magazines next to a brown leather wing-backed chair, the kind of chair you saw in pictures of exclusive men's clubs, places where they smoked cigars and drank bourbon straight. A stuffed lion the size of a Great Dane sat in a corner, the one spot of energy in an otherwise drained room.

Oh, boy. He'd let her inside. She had to follow through. But that didn't mean she had to give the depressing house power. "Girls, if this house ever seems too creepy, you'll have to tell your dad. None of that subtle twin speak. I want full-on hand waving, moonlight-madness screaming. Are you on board?"

They nodded their heads solemnly.

"First off, let's open the windows and get some air in here. It's cooled off outside and there's a breeze blowing." She dumped her bag on an empty corner of the curved-legged, low coffee table and made for the front windows. She had to walk behind the tan velour couch to reach them. Cobwebs brushed over her bare calves. She yanked open the rose-colored drapes, dousing herself in a shower of dust.

"I'm sorry. Do you live here?" Slade. Angry.

Christine chuckled, but she was pretty darn desperate to get some fresh air into the house and not be bitten by a spider. She struggled with the first window. "When was the last time these windows were open?"

"Eight years ago."

That creeped-out feeling made way for a bit of sadness. What had happened here that Slade knew how long the windows had been shut? "Okay, girls, raise your hands with me. Your dad's freaking me out. How about you?"

That too-brief stereo sound was definitely a contained couple of giggles.

The twins raised their hands.

Slade came to stand next to her. His hip gently bumping her out of the way so he could open the window.

One window up and the breeze rushed in. It might have been Christine's imagination, but the house seemed to sigh in relief.

Soon Slade had all four windows in the front room open. A cool breeze was lifting the curtains gently, as if even the wind knew change had to come slowly.

"WE GOT A LOT done tonight," Christine said to Slade as he walked her home. "With the cuts we came up with, we can afford to arrange for storage in town. And the way you recalculated those columns in your head got us there that much quicker. Thanks for letting me in."

Slade made a noncommittal sound. He hated that Christine had been in the house, hated more that she'd opened the windows. That house was his penance. He didn't want anyone, including Christine and the girls, coming in and making it seem livable.

"It's kind of odd." Christine could talk nonstop, and generally did, punctuating her words with smiles and a swing of her hair as she twisted to look at him, "I feel as if I've known you forever."

He resented her thinking she knew him. She didn't. She didn't know about the long nights of his youth spent watching his mother, afraid she'd stop breathing before his father came home from the graveyard shift at the grain mill. Afraid she wouldn't be breathing when Slade returned from school. She didn't know about the promises he'd made his father when Slade invested the last of his dad's retirement funds. She didn't know—

Christine laughed, a sound that crooned about the possibility of smoothing over unknown hurts and old grievances. "I guess sitting in my bedroom discussing what to do with my shoe collection was a good idea after all."

The morning seemed so long ago.

She'd opened up his windows. He couldn't wait to get home and shut them.

They rounded the corner to Taylor Street. Two houses down was her grandmother's place.

Christine had sat in his living room and tried several times to talk him out of what she saw as unnecessary expenses in year one of the business. She'd been convincing, even in the face of him totaling up columns and presenting his arguments. But that wasn't all she'd talked about.

The things that needed to be done before they got through the next twelve months were mind-boggling. And yet, Christine had distilled it down to a very long list, with approval dates, and action dates, and dates she'd need funding by. She'd gotten what she wanted— a compromise on the budget and wine storage in town.

"I know I can make good wine for you." She stopped at the end of her grandmother's driveway at her clunker's fender.

Even her grandmother's Buick was newer than Christine's rust heap.

She was conscious of the money she needed to make good on her promise. He liked that. What he didn't like was uncertainty about future productivity.

"I can run things by myself until harvest, when I'll need those two other hires we talked about." She blinked up at him, as shiny and optimistic as a newly minted dime. "I haven't found anyone yet who's willing to work for us, but I will."

So many obstacles.

The street was blessedly silent. Every street in Harmony Valley was generally quiet after eight o'clock. Most people in town were comfortably ensconced in their recliners, remote in hand, or on their porch or backyard swing escaping the heat. A dove cooed from the eaves of Agnes's house. A cricket chirped in response.

He wondered what rock-band T-shirt Christine would show up for work in tomorrow. Maybe a throwback, like Darlings Deluxe. Maybe something with attitude, like Mercy Becomes Dust. Although, the all-girl band Cococats seemed like a better bet.

Christine had stopped talking. Her lips, a gentle pink he couldn't appreciate when they were moving, were still.

"What?"

"I said I was sorry about barging into your house. I can tell it threw you for a loop." She fiddled with the strap of her laptop bag. "I get really into my work. I can get overly excited. I'll try to do a better job at respecting your boundaries."

He doubted that. She was too touchy-feely. Invading someone else's personal space was as natural to her as smiling, despite her developing the skill to wield the expression as a survival tool.

She smiled at him now, as close to a purely happy expression as he'd seen in a long time. "Thank you for this opportunity. I'm so very grateful."

Fool that he was, he wasn't ready to say good-night. "Are you going to work at the winery tomorrow? Or from home?" It wasn't as if there was a pressing need for her to be on-site yet.

"May do a bit of both." She turned and crossed the lawn. "I've got an early-morning yoga date with Mayor Larry. See you." She disappeared into the house.

Leaving Slade worried, because he knew Mayor Larry practiced naked yoga.

The question was, did Christine know?

Still wondering, Slade retraced his footsteps. He turned the corner at Harrison and caught sight of his house. Or rather, he heard it.

Laughter.

Drifting out the open windows. Chasing away his efforts to keep the place a somber reminder of his horrendous mistake.

Something in Slade's chest shifted, tried to lighten. He promptly ignored it.

"Nice to hear some life in there again." A disembodied voice drifted from the house on the corner and had Slade's pulse pounding double time until he realized it wasn't a ghost who spoke. It was Old Man Takata.

He had to add tree trimming to Flynn's list of improvements needed around town. The too-tall, too-bushy trees blocked streetlights.

Slade moved up the walk to Takata's front porch. The old man was smoking a cigar. He'd been Slade's neighbor since forever and the town's undertaker until recently. Crummy time to retire. People in Harmony Valley were in need of a good undertaker.

Takata puffed on his cigar, the deep scent of peppery wood enveloping Slade. His knobby knees stuck out of his cargo shorts like tooth-picks out of a sausage. "Are your girls home to stay?"

"No." Heaven help him if he had to raise those girls in that house.

"When it's cool, I can sit out here all night." Takata's voice was smoke roughened and oddly hypnotic. "That's when I miss your dad most."

The old man was one of the few people in town who talked about Slade's father without speculating aloud why he'd committed suicide, or, worse, avoided mention of him at all. Takata treated what happened with an acceptance that was oddly similar to Nate's reaction when he'd dropped off the skunk-removal supplies.

"Your father would sneak out the back after you and your mother went to bed, and we'd sit out here smoking cigars. He liked people and he liked to talk." Takata took a big drag off the cigar. "He came less frequently after your mom passed. And then not at all after the explosion at the mill. Daniel didn't want anything to do with a match after that…or people."

The novelty of the smoke wore off. Slade felt nauseous. He shoved his hands into his pockets. "You seem to be the only one who remembers him." It was the way Slade tried to remember him.

Growing up, Slade and his father had been close. His dad coached his Little League team, and later, his school baseball and basketball teams up until his mother died. Like

Slade's twins, he and his dad had been able to look at each other across the room and know what the other was thinking. They'd fished together and watched sports together, sharing a special bond that Slade hadn't seen his friends have with their dads.

Until his mother died. Until the mill exploded.

At sixteen, his dad became a stranger, a man who had little interest in Slade other than to warn him of impending doom. Their relationship disintegrated. Back then, it'd been a relief to be accepted to Harvard, a reprieve to land a job on Wall Street four years later. For the first time in years, Slade had money to spare and no one bringing him down.

Guilt pierced his chest. When Slade looked into his father's eyes that last time, he'd had no hint of what was coming. Failure drove the shard deeper. Slade rubbed a spot over his heart and tried not to feel anything. "I should never have left. I could have saved him."

"How? By arguing with his certainty that he was going to die soon? Or that civilization was going to collapse? Or that whatever you loved or were excited about was short-lived?" Takata scoffed.

"But I—"

"You couldn't have done anything," Takata

spat. And then his tone softened. "You might have fallen under his spell eventually. He had charisma, even when his life drifted off the rails. Your father could convince a tiger he didn't need his stripes."

Slade took an instinctive step back.

How much does Takata know?

"It still bothers you, doesn't it?" Takata's eyes were in shadow, but Slade felt the man's gaze upon him. "That your father checked out the way he did."

Slade looked at his house, but said nothing, because the house ate away at him, like an angry ulcer. Even now, his gut was churning.

"I expected you to sell the house after it happened. Sell or set the place on fire." He paused for a quick puff-puff. "I didn't expect you to hold on to it. Or move back in."

"I can't sell." The words were wrenched out of him against his better judgment.

"Means there's unfinished business there." He took a long drag from the cigar, then another. The end faded in and out like a beacon on a remote airport runway. "Never see the light on in his room at night."

As if hypnotized, Slade's gaze went to the master-bedroom windows. He clenched his fists. "I don't go in there. No one goes in there."

"I was a mortician for sixty years. I've seen grief in all its stages. And guilt in several more." The hand holding the cigar drifted downward, hanging over the arm of his chair. "You're still grieving. And you've got an unhealthy dose of guilt, as well."

Slade's hand drifted up to the knot at his throat, but he said nothing.

Takata's eyes were dark, shadowy holes that sunk deep into his scowling face. "I was there that day, you know, working in the yard. I heard the screams. One of grief. One of horror."

How much does the old man know?

Slade wanted to cover his ears with his hands, but it wouldn't have done any good. His voice, Evy's cry. He couldn't erase them. Even if he closed his eyes, he couldn't shut out the image of what he'd seen, of what he'd done afterward. But some wounds never healed.

He had to swallow twice before he could speak. And then the words sounded so inane. "Are you bowling tomorrow?"

Takata didn't answer right away. He played on the mayor's league team, which also had a weekly bowling date with Slade, his partners, and whoever they could pick up to round out their team. Slade's preference was

Will's fiancée, Emma. That woman bowled near-perfect games every time. But she didn't always have someone to stay with her grand-mother at night.

"I expect I will play. It's our turn to wipe the floor with you." Takata chuckled. "You'd be a lot harder to beat if you opened that door upstairs. Just once. Downstairs windows don't count."

Several retorts came to mind, several dis-respectful ones laced with a few choice cuss words about Takata minding his own busi-ness. Slade dismissed them all and headed for his house. Not directly, as that would have taken him across Takata's lawn. He'd had his butt chewed out enough times as a kid to know you didn't cut across Takata's lawn unless someone had died.

He continued along the sidewalk, listening to the murmur of the twins' voices drifting out the window. He felt as if he'd made more progress with them today. A few words. Some carefully guarded smiles. Half a hug.

He opened the front door. The living room was empty. The girls stood at the top of the stairs, each holding a short, glittering chain of gold. Their baby bracelets.

"Those are yours." He kept them on his dresser, draped around the neck of a black

Labrador figurine, one that looked like Chief, the dog he'd had as a kid. He wasn't angry they'd found them. He didn't lock his bedroom door and there was nothing in his room he had that he didn't want them to see. It was natural for kids to poke around, and the master bedroom was locked up tight. "I bought them the day you were born so we could tell you apart." The bright hospital lights. Evy's happy, exhausted face. The future had seemed uncomplicated and bright. "It didn't take long for us to be able to tell you apart."

Faith draped hers across her wrist. It was far too short to circle around and close.

He smiled. "You've grown quite a bit since then. I like to look at those bracelets every morning when I wake up." While he wondered what his daughters were doing. If they ever thought of him. If they missed him. The father they barely knew.

What a dreamer. The answer to that was clearly no, based on their behavior here.

"Why don't we drive to the jewelry store tomorrow and get some new links put on them, so you can wear them...if you want?"

After a moment, Faith nodded.

And Grace smiled.

CHAPTER NINE

SLADE WAS UP with the summer sun—long before civilized people got out of bed. Coming downstairs, he faced a truth—maybe not the one Takata wanted him to face, but a truth nonetheless. His girls were slobs.

Dirty dishes littered the living room, dirty dishes crowded the center of the kitchen table, dirty dishes formed a pyramid along the kitchen counter, ready to tumble into the sink.

How could two little girls have created so much food-encrusted chaos? It wasn't as if he had that much food in the house. He should have cleaned up last night instead of dragging his butt to bed after being confronted by Takata and his philosophical words of wisdom. No matter what Takata said, he wasn't opening the door upstairs. Ever.

But he was taking the girls shopping. And Grace had smiled. It made cleaning up their mess downstairs easier.

Slade picked up dish after dish and set them to soak in the sink. He wiped down the coffee tables and the kitchen table. He scrubbed at some kind of spill on the kitchen floor.

And every time he paused, he checked the time.

Six-fifteen.

Six-thirty.

Six forty-five.

Christine would be heading out toward the town's river park for her yoga session with Mayor Larry. Was she aware he'd be naked? Was she going to be naked?

He didn't want to know.

Really.

Because discovery meant risking an image he didn't want burned into his memory again.

The worst way to start a man's day was to round the bend on the river path and see Mayor Larry doing a yoga pose in the buff.

But if Christine was in the buff...

She wouldn't.

But she might be unknowing, ambushed and flustered.

That would be worth seeing. The thought made him grin. Other than his daughters, not so many things did lately.

"I'll be back in an hour," Slade called upstairs as he went out the door.

He could see the town square from his front porch. The large, noble oak spread its branches in the center of the square. A few months ago, it had been diseased. Its prognosis grim. Will had brought in a specialist, who swore the tree wasn't a lost cause. All the residents who'd received marriage proposals beneath the tree were relieved.

Slade couldn't understand what all the fuss was about. It was just a tree. Trees died, like everything else.

"Morning." Takata sat out on his front porch on his lounge chair, his greeting just as startling as it had been last night.

Slade paused. "Did you sleep out here?" It looked as if he was wearing the same cargo shorts.

"Young people always leap to conclusions." Takata gestured he come closer. "Give me a hand up, will you?"

In the morning light, Slade could see the dirt-filled planter he used as an ashtray and how his gray hair had that bed-head quality in back. "You did sleep out here last night."

"As if I haven't seen you sleeping on your chaise longue." The old man grunted as he tried to leverage himself to a standing position.

Slade steadied Takata and helped him to the front door. "The difference is that I can go in at any time. Can you?"

"You don't know squat."

Slade was afraid the two of them knew far too much about each other.

"You didn't turn on the light in Daniel's bedroom last night. I watched."

"Like I need to." Just the thought sent a shiver up his spine.

"You do." Takata closed the screen door and locked it behind him. "Don't come in. I've got it."

"You're welcome," Slade said under his breath as he hustled down the walk.

He hurried through the town square and along Main Street. Years ago he'd worked as a stock boy at the now-empty grocery store. He gazed in as he passed the crumbling brick front. He'd learned valuable lessons about life in that store. You had to constantly put the effort in to get ahead, and even then, something would happen to set you back.

He turned a corner and crossed over to Adams. Flocks of birds lived by the river, swooping and singing to one another, a chirpy good-morning chorus. He'd never understood what birds were so happy about all the time.

He entered the park. There was the bench where he'd stolen his first kiss. There was the merry-go-round his mother pushed him on until he was dizzy and couldn't stop laugh-

ing. There was the path that led down to the
river. The same one he and his father used to
take to go fly-fishing every spring.

Slade's feet stopped moving. He didn't want
to be in the park. Not with the memories or
the images or the inevitable feeling of failure.

Then he heard Christine's laugh and a
throaty male voice ask, "Can we try that
again?"

With only a heartbeat of hesitation, Slade's
feet moved. In twenty paces, he'd be able to
see them.

Christine's voice and laughter grew louder.
"This is twisted."

Ten feet.

"Be like the eagle." Mayor Larry's voice.

And there they were. Both fully clothed.

Tension Slade hadn't realized was between
his shoulder blades loosened.

Larry wore short-shorts and no shirt. For
a guy in his seventies, he was healthy and
toned. Christine wore long black yoga pants
and a pink clingy tank top. Her hair was in a
high ponytail, straight blond tresses hanging
down her back.

They both stood on one leg with their free
leg wrapped around the standing leg and their
arms entwined in front of their chests. It sort

of looked as if they had to go to the bathroom and were trying to hold it.

Slade chuckled.

They hardly wavered as their bare feet hit the dirt.

"Slade, come join us." Despite blocking the winery, Mayor Larry was always friendly, hence his eight terms in office.

Christine shot Slade a look that seemed to say, *Really? You're checking up on me?*

He hadn't been worried about her. It was pure curiosity. "I don't have the flexibility for yoga."

"What are you doing out here so early?" Christine didn't pull her punches. "Where are the girls?"

"Probably eating cereal in front of the television in their pajamas." *Think fast, man. Why am I here?* "I was wondering if you had time in your schedule to go pick out furniture for the farmhouse. Tables and chairs for the tasting room and patio." *Nice save.* She'd had those items on the purchasing proposal he'd signed off on last night.

Christine's expression brightened. "That would be great. I'd love to get that taken care of before the bigger equipment is delivered."

Slade arranged to pick her up after lunch and made his retreat, dignity still intact.

It wasn't until he was strolling past the empty grocery store, replaying Christine's laughter in his head, that he realized he was grinning.

And realized he had no right to be.

"FABULOUS DRESSES, GIRLS," Christine said as she climbed into the passenger seat of Slade's truck.

And they were fabulous, smacking of designer chic—soft pink ruffled bodices, lemon-green skirts with pockets, black headbands in their straight black hair, pink sequined Mary Janes with lemon-green bows.

Christine's gaze turned to Slade and his loud blue polka-dot tie. "Fabulous tie." He'd been wearing it that morning.

His gaze landed on her neon green plastic flip-flops. He was unsuccessful at concealing a smile. "You couldn't liberate a pair of Italian sandals from a box?"

"I sealed up the boxes and put them in the garage, next to my grandfather's fishing gear." She extended her toes closer to the floor fan that blew out cold air. "It's rather sad putting them away like that, but it's for the best."

He gave her an indecipherable sideways look that said volumes about her keeping her shoes.

It was definitely time to lighten the mood. "You brought your platinum credit card, right? I had fantasies about spending your money all morning long." Her overactive imagination had tried to fantasize about other things, like Slade's perfect lips test-driving her own, but thoughts like that were career ending, so she'd stuck with the thrill of a cash register beeping.

Clearly bored with the conversation, the girls put on headphones and started watching a movie from a screen that came down from the ceiling just behind Christine's seat.

"I know why you came to the park this morning," Christine said. What a bluff that was. First thought when she saw him, instantly rejected? A bit of male possessiveness. *Me, Tarzan. You, Jane.* She couldn't shake the expression on his face when he saw her in her black swan evening gown. But who was she kidding? Slade was her boss. To him, she was an investment of his time and money.

Second thought, instantly accepted? He knew Mayor Larry did naked yoga and wanted to see if she bared herself. Not that he wanted a peep show. It was more likely that sly sense of humor Slade had was looking for an opening, questioning whether or not she knew

Mayor Larry did naked yoga, guessing she'd be embarrassed and he'd bear witness.

"Really?" He pulled onto the two-lane highway leading to civilization.

"Yep. When you're a female winemaker in a mostly male wine-making world, you learn quickly how to spot a setup." She poked his shoulder with one finger. "You knew about Mayor Larry's naked yoga and you were hoping I didn't."

Slade's stoic expression was almost unreadable. He'd be a deadly competitor in a poker game. His face gave little away—anger, disappointment, and, sadly for her, male interest. But there was a crack, a lightning flash of a dimple like Faith's—here, then gone.

She laughed. "You are so busted."

"I admit nothing."

They didn't speak for several miles. Christine looked out the window at the fields of golden wild oats, tall corn, and the occasional untended vineyard. Plenty of land to buy if you had some extra millions lying around. "If you guys are all millionaires, why do you even have a budget?"

"We could be saving up to buy an island in the Caribbean."

"Really?" Grace whispered from the backseat.

"No," Slade said. "Go back to your movie, honey."

When Slade didn't explain, Christine prodded, "Aren't you going to tell me why?"

He was paying far too much attention to the road, which was straight and empty. It took him too long to begrudgingly admit, "It's a matter of principle."

"Not telling me or the whole budget thing?" She liked ribbing him. He tried so hard to pretend she was an annoyance. Mostly, he failed.

But the topic must have been a sore spot, since Slade shot her a dark look. "A budget is a promise. People's emotions get all tied up in their money. That's why they go crazy when they get overcharged five bucks on their cable bill."

"Or jump off the Golden Gate Bridge when they lose everything."

His lips were sealed tighter than she'd ever seen before, making her wonder what she'd said wrong.

He didn't speak again until they reached Highway 101 and headed south. "How did you know Mayor Larry does naked yoga? He had on clothes today."

Points to Slade for putting that together. "Okay, I'll admit I stumbled upon Larry in the buff yesterday morning."

"I would have paid money to see that." He let a smile slip. It was gone as fast as it came.

"I knew it! You are so busted."

CHRISTINE STOOD IN the middle of a high-end jewelry store trying not to huff. She had a gazillion things to do and shopping for baubles for little girls wasn't on her list.

How had Slade sidetracked her?

The twins flanked Slade as a sales clerk showed them lengths of chain. Faith was fingering a rapper-thick chain and Grace was looking at a more delicate one. Slade was looking as if he'd let them choose whatever they wanted, just because he wanted them to be happy. Neither choice was appropriate for a baby bracelet.

With a reluctant sigh, Christine crossed the plush carpet. "I hate to interrupt this shop-apalooza, but if you choose a chain that's thicker than the original, all anyone will look at is the chain. And if you choose anything thinner than the original chain, it'll break and you'll lose it."

Her observation earned her a shadow of a scowl from each of the twins and a definite frown from the salesclerk, who had undoubtedly been looking for a heavy commission on Faith's choice of a heavy chain.

Slade blinked at her, as if blinking helped him process her words. Or maybe he'd been hypnotized by having his daughters so near and was just now coming back to reality. "You're right."

"Great." Christine clapped her hands together. "Let's measure and pay and move along."

Shoulders drooping, Faith let go of the thick chain.

Ten minutes later they were out the door, slogging through the heat to reach Slade's truck.

"Come on. I know a place where we can get some fantastic dining sets." The thin soles of Christine's flip-flops did little to keep her feet cool on the hot pavement.

Grace took Slade's hand. "But…"

Faith took the other. "Clothes…"

Christine sighed, recognizing the woe-is-me tactic, having used it on her own father countless times growing up. "They must have packed their bathing suits. Spend time with them floating down the river."

He looked horrified.

She couldn't imagine why. "Buying them things every time they ask won't help them manage money when they're older."

"So I've been told," he quipped. "My girls

won't need to worry about money. Ever. Especially if we stick to a budget on the winery."

"I don't have time to be your shopping buddy." She dug her phone from her purse. "I'll get a taxi."

"Wait. I promised you we'd buy furniture for the winery." Points to Slade. He didn't cave when his daughters released his hands and pouted.

Twenty minutes later, it was Slade who was pouting.

"*This* is where you want to buy tables for the tasting room?" Although he'd pulled into a parking space in front of the warehouse Christine had directed him to, he didn't turn off the engine.

"Everything here is top quality. It only made it here because it didn't sell last season or…" Christine hopped out of the truck and shut the door, not wanting to tell him the other reason for furniture making it to this warehouse.

Heat shimmered from the asphalt with a parched, desertlike intensity that immediately drained her.

She was relieved when she got to the warehouse doors and found Slade and the girls following her. More relieved when the doors slid open and bathed her in cool air.

"This is crazy," Slade said as he entered. "We're not buying anything here. I told you I wanted top quality."

"Give it a chance." Her words echoed through the expansive space.

A man in dusty blue jeans and a tan polo shirt approached and asked if he could help. Christine explained what she was looking for—eight tables for two with chairs to match, six barstools. High-end, primo condition.

He nodded and led them to a back room where tables were stacked on top of each other, floor to ceiling. "This is our return room. What style are you looking for?"

"Return room?" Slade murmured, practically in her ear. "As in *used?*" He tugged at her arm, but she shrugged him off.

"Hepplewhite or mission. Nothing too modern," Christine said.

"I like modern," Slade said.

"Modern doesn't fit the farmhouse," Christine argued.

"Modern says success." He fingered his tie.

"Weren't you the one insisting we stick to a budget?" Christine wasn't backing down. Every day it seemed she came up with a new need. Buying used was the best solution to stretch their funds.

"I think we have just what you're looking for," the salesman said. "A lot of wine-country businesses have gone under recently."

"Let's hope we aren't buying their bad luck," Slade whispered.

The twins sat at a table, sharing a pair of earphones.

Christine did a double take, but couldn't see what they were plugged into. "Do they have smartphones?"

Slade shrugged. "Probably."

"You don't know?"

He put his hands in his pockets and started to whistle.

She had to give him the look—the one that said, *Dude, go find out*—before he made a move in their direction.

"It's their tablet." He lifted the device from Faith's hand so Christine could see it. "Harmless."

Christine shook her head. He had no idea the extent of trouble he'd be in when those girls got to high school. Limits? They had none.

It took the salesman three tries to find a mission-style set of tables and chairs that satisfied both Slade and Christine. None of the barstools were in good enough condition.

Slade was ready to whip out his credit card, but Christine haggled the price down further.

"You're killing me." Slade paced while their order was written up and a delivery scheduled.

Christine patted his arm. "I'll never understand why men think paying full retail adds to their image. It only makes you look gullible."

"It reassures us of the thickness of our wallets." He noticed the girls were looking at him and grumbled, "I'm kidding. I like a good deal as much as the next guy."

"Liar," Christine said under her breath, but loud enough for him to hear.

He checked his watch. "Jeez, look at the time. How about we skip buying the patio furniture? It's not as if anyone will be sitting outside on our patio until next year."

"Not true. We'll have to invite critics and reviewers for barrel tastings next spring. They need to experience the quality of work we're doing while they enjoy the outdoor view. It's all part of the ambience of Harmony Valley." They stepped outside into the summer heat.

Slade fiddled with his key fob, and his truck started from halfway across the parking lot.

Her clunker couldn't compete with that. When she had time, she'd sell it and buy a more practical truck. "And this fall we'll need a place for the crush workers to take a break. Treat your seasonal workers well and they'll make sure to return every year as promised. Besides, if we put in the fantastic landscaping you approved, they'll tell two friends how wonderful it is out here, and they'll tell two friends. And—"

"Fine." He opened the rear truck door for the girls, releasing a precious burst of cool air. "Take me to your thrift store."

She hurriedly climbed into her own seat in front, which had air-conditioning vents in it, waiting until Slade was sitting beside her to say, "And with the money I save, you can buy me a forklift."

Diamonds may be a girl's best friend, but during harvest time a dependable forklift was a close runner-up.

When they arrived at the next warehouse, Christine pulled the girls aside. "Fashionistas, I'm looking for three or four outdoor tables made of black iron—no glass tops. They need to be in good shape and classy, like you'd see at a New York sidewalk café. You shop the right side of the store, we'll shop the left."

The twins nodded and skipped off.

"That was nice to include them, but you

know they'll lose interest twenty paces in," Slade said.

"Don't be so sure. I bet those girls love to shop."

It was the twins who found three square tables and twelve chairs in great shape at a real bargain. Slade paid and arranged to have them delivered.

"Maybe we can fit in a trip to a clothing store," he said to Christine as he stuffed the receipt into his wallet.

"Quit trying to buy their affection." Christine touched his arm. "Do I sound like a broken record?"

He nodded.

"Tough. I love my dad, but he made me happier letting me hang out with him in the vineyards than with any material gift he gave me."

Faith and Grace watched Slade closely. He didn't seem to notice.

"I bet you never turned down any of his gifts." Slade led their entourage out to the parking lot and hit the magic starter button that ensured the air conditioner would be humming when they got in.

The girls gave up on him or were just too hot, and raced to the truck.

"He gives me the gift of advice to this day." Sometimes she even turned it down.

"I'm going to let that slide." He opened her door this time. "How does dinner and bowling sound?"

"Excuse me?"

"The partnership has a team. We're playing the mayor's team tonight and there's not enough time to take you home before our game."

"Oh, Larry asked me if I bowled." She climbed into the front seat.

Slade continued holding the door open, watching her. "And what did you tell him?"

"The truth. That I suck at bowling. Now, what are you feeding us?"

Slade took them to what she would have called a hole-in-the-wall and her dad would have called a joint with character. When they were seated, Christine did a double take at the menu. "These burgers are twenty dollars. You picked this place to prove the thickness of your wallet, didn't you?"

He had a subtle grin. Sly.

She liked it more than she should.

The twins didn't notice. Their heads were together as they reviewed the menu.

Christine set hers down. "Okay, come clean.

Why the aversion to buying used? It has nothing to do with your wallet, does it?"

He shrugged, visibly uncomfortable. "I struggled a long time. Made money. Made some bad decisions. Went broke." There was a catch to his voice that seemed to surprise even him. Slade's hand drifted to the Windsor knot at his throat. He swallowed, dropped his gaze to the menu, and dropped his hand. "I vowed never to be broke again."

She winked at the twins, who were now an avid audience. "You mean you don't have money to burn?"

His smile was sad, touching her heart for no reason other than she hated to see him look so defeated. "I appreciate your efforts to save money today."

"A gracious recovery." Christine grinned. "Now, if I order the thirty-dollar walnut, cranberry, and chicken salad, will you think I'm crass?"

CHAPTER TEN

WHEN THEY ARRIVED at the bowling alley, Slade was a fifth wheel on his own team. Will had returned from San Francisco and was there with his fiancée and bowling ringer, Emma. Flynn had brought Nate. His friends encouraged him to bowl with Faith, Grace, and Christine. Even Takata shooed him off.

"Guys are so competitive. Chill out." Christine gave him an affectionate shove. "You'll have more fun bowling with your daughters."

Slade knew she was right, but the feeling that he was outliving his usefulness to the partnership wouldn't go away.

While they put on their bowling shoes, Mayor Larry approached Christine. "You say your logo is a horse on a weathervane? I can silk-screen that on my shirts." He unbuttoned his purple tie-dyed bowling shirt and flashed them a look at the T-shirt with a weathervane logo beneath.

"What?" Slade tied his shoe too tight.

"Next I'm going to make samples of knitted sweaters for your tasting room." Mayor Larry beamed. "If Christine approves them, we'll be doing business together."

Slade stared at Christine's face, trying to find signs that she'd lost her mind. There were none. He waited until Larry returned to his lane, several lanes over, before confronting her. "Are you kidding me? I don't want to sell anything as ordinary as tie-dyed T-shirts or homemade knitted sweaters. The next thing you'll be doing is getting Mrs. Mionetti to knit you some lampshades for the tasting room. And don't forget about Snarky Sam." He gestured to Mayor Larry's bowling team. "He does taxidermy. You like skunks? I think he still has one dressed as Sherlock Holmes for sale."

"I was—"

"I haven't seen any tie-dyed T-shirts at any wineries I've visited."

"I think—"

"I want this to be a high-end experience, not a trip to the flea market."

"It's not—"

"What were you thinking? Don't tell me. I know." He knew he was working himself up over something that was small in the big scheme of things, but his team had abandoned him and he was still smarting. "You were thinking of trying to add character to the experience. Something friendly. Well, I don't want friendly. I want people to come in and drop twenty-five to fifty dollars for a taste of your wine and more than a hundred dollars for a bottle to take home. How is that supposed to happen if we've got homemade junk for sale on the counter?"

Christine waited until he'd run out of breath. "Are you through?"

Slade noticed the twins were watching him. The bluster drained out of him, and he nodded.

"Forget about image in the tasting room for a moment because with only five thousand cases to sell, we won't be having hundreds of excited customers making the pilgrimage to our door every week. Most of our sales are going to come through an online wine club, with supplemental sales through trendy bars and restaurants." She patted his hand. "I was looking at the available land for a wine cave nearby and Larry has undeveloped acreage right across the street. What harm does it do to *consider* letting him sell his merchandise in the tasting room? You've got to have some type of souvenir for folks who made the long drive to take home. Branded corkscrews, magnets, local recipe booklets, and so on."

Slade bit his lip to keep his mouth closed. On some level, Christine's arguments made sense. It was just going to be easier to create a classy experience for their customers, something that reaffirmed he was a success, something that made his partners realize he was indispensable. "We'll talk about this some other time."

A few lanes over, Emma bowled a strike and the team leaped up to give her a group high five.

Slade slumped in his plastic chair.

Christine nudged him. "Hey, Boss Man. Big Daddy-O. How about you quit sulking and teach your daughters how to bowl?"

Oblivious to his mini meltdown, Grace and Faith were trying to tap-dance in their hard-soled bowling shoes. He hadn't even known they took dance lessons.

"I stink at being a dad," he mumbled.

"Only if you give up." Christine got to her feet and pulled him to his.

Instead of moving away, he stood inches from her, gazing down into those amazing blue eyes and wondering how different his life would have been if he'd had a woman like her by his side years ago, instead of Evy.

Christine dropped her gaze and patted

both his shoulders, before stepping back. "Soldier on."

Slade felt as if he'd been doing that for far too long. Or maybe Takata was finally getting to him. "Ladies, the first thing we need to bowl is a ball. We'll be looking for lighter ones, not pretty ones." He led the twins to the ball racks, showing them how to find a ball that was small enough for the spread of their fingers and wasn't too heavy.

With their bowling balls chosen, they trouped back to their lane. He taught them how to swing and release the ball, how to keep from crossing the line, and how to aim, just as his father had taught him. And then he put up the lane bumpers so they wouldn't throw any gutter balls.

Faith took to it like a pigeon to Central Park. Grace struggled, although not as much as Christine. For all his winemaker did physical labor in the vineyard, she was completely honest when she said she wasn't a good bowler.

Finally, in desperation, Christine swung the ball between her legs with both hands, granny-style. Perfectly centered, the ball rolled slowly down the lane and tumbled into the pins.

"A strike!" Christine jumped up and down. "I've never made one before." She kept on jumping.

The twins joined her, holding her hands and leaping and laughing, as if they'd just won a gold medal.

Grace held a hand out toward him. "Come on, Dad."

Those words, so few and far between, made being left off his own bowling team seem inconsequential.

If Christine's ball had seemed to move in slow-motion, Slade's approach to inclusion in their bouncing, celebratory circle seemed just as surreal. And then he, too, was jumping up and down, clinging to his daughters' hands and laughing as if he'd made his first strike ever.

In the afterglow of Christine's triumph, Takata ambled over wearing his team's purple tie-dyed bowling shirt. He sat next to Slade, landing with a grunt on the plastic seat. "Grace, you're twisting your wrist on your release."

Grace, who was hefting her ball as she readied her approach, glanced back at the old man.

"Like this. Wrist to the ceiling the entire time, even after you let the ball go." Takata swung his arm up. "Not like this." He swung his arm up again, twisting it this time.

Grace nodded and stepped forward. She

wound up and released the ball, freezing in place long enough to look at her wrist, which was facing the ceiling. Her ball had more velocity than Christine's and hit the front pin hard enough to knock them all down.

This time, Slade led the leaping. His tie flew up and down so often he tossed it over his shoulder.

Grace ran on her tiptoes to the old man and gave him a hug.

"Eh? I can't hear you." Takata cupped a hand to his ear.

"Thank you. Thank you. Thank you." Grace planted a kiss on his cheek.

"You're welcome. Come by the house sometime and I'll teach you jujitsu. You'll be dating soon and you need to know how to keep boys in line." Takata, who never smiled, was grinning as Grace told him she'd love to kick boy-butt. "Help me up, Slade. It's almost my turn to bowl again."

"Thank you." Slade helped Takata stand.

"It's what family does, prodding you forward, giving advice even if you don't want it."

Slade didn't comment. They weren't family. They were just neighbors.

But Takata, in typical Takata style, seemed to read his mind. "For people like us, who are otherwise alone in the world, your friends become your family."

A few years ago, Slade would have denied the old man any claim to him. But he couldn't, since his words rang true. Will and Flynn were like brothers to him.

With Takata's statement still ringing in his ears, Slade couldn't stop staring at Christine laughing with his daughters, and wondering if she'd still be his friend if she knew the truth.

"TELL ME YOU convinced Slade to build the wine cave," Flynn said to Christine as they turned in their bowling shoes.

He was so earnest, Christine chuckled. "I have other things I'd rather spend your money on right now."

"I hear this wine cave will create jobs." Will, the third partner, extended his hand to shake Christine's. "I didn't get a chance to welcome you properly. Or throw in my support to build whatever you need."

Carte blanche. It was every winemaker's dream.

Slade stood at the corner of the shoe counter, frowning.

"I'm sure a wine cave would need a custodian or a groundskeeper," Flynn was saying.

"Maintenance man," Will added.

Christine's toes should have felt as light as air. She should be dancing.

Slade's frown deepened.

"Receptionist." Flynn was on a roll.

"Tech support." Will wasn't far behind.

Balls struck pins. Someone hooted. A pinball machine played a techno tune.

And Slade? He turned away, gathered up the girls, and made for the door.

Christine knew it was financially irresponsible to sink too much money into a winery in the middle of nowhere. She knew, but the feeling of power was a rush all the same.

CHRISTINE'S NEXT WEEK was filled with phone calls, emails, visiting suppliers, deliveries, and workers installing various items, including desks on the second floor. The skunk smell was finally eradicated. Two skunks were trapped and removed, with a promise to relocate them to a state park many miles away, since they seemed rabies-free. The signs for the driveway and tasting room were put in place. They were, of course, very grand and sophisticated—Harmony Valley Vineyards with their logo, a horse on a weathervane. Mayor Larry, who was busy knitting and tie-dying samples, stopped by to compliment Christine on them.

Most of their equipment to crush the wine and put it in barrels was either on-site or on-order. Her biggest concern remained finding a company willing to book them for harvest. Secondarily, they still hadn't received their bottling permits from the government, although they wouldn't be ready to bottle until sometime next year.

With Slade's approval, she hired a young assistant winemaker who'd apprenticed with a small winemaker in nearby Healdsburg the year before, had returned to UC Davis to finish up his enology degree, and was looking for a permanent position that started immediately.

Ryan Phillips was tall, gangly, and claimed to be calm as a rock in a crisis. He was willing to work the bench, testing and recording the sugar levels in the fruit that would determine when they harvested, sending soil in for analysis, and researching the heritage of their vines, since no one knew their lineage or when they'd been planted. His presence allowed Christine to focus on the installation of equipment and the continued search for a harvesting crew.

Her father hadn't found another job. To

ease her mother's mind, Christine would have offered him a position working in Harmony Valley, except she couldn't afford his salary.

Of Slade, she'd seen very little since they'd been bowling, which was for the best. For a while there, they'd seemed like one big, happy family. The joy on Slade's face while they'd bowled went beyond papa-bear adorable. She hoped he continued making progress with the girls, but for the sake of her career, she was glad he was keeping his distance. She liked him, but she didn't want anything between them to go beyond liking him as a boss and a friend.

One day, after listening to Christine complain one time too many about how much hotter it was up in the office than downstairs, Nana showed up with bolts of fabric, curtain rods, and a portable sewing machine. Her machine was old, but it did the job and sent mild vibrations through the floor all afternoon.

Christine had been going at such a fast pace and her grandmother had such a busy social life that she hadn't had a moment to ask her grandmother about Slade's parents. She hung up the phone, saw a sticky note Slade had left her about finalizing their design for the website, and turned to her grandmother.

"So heartbreaking." Nana carefully cut the

lining for the curtains on a card table she'd set up in a corner. "His mother died of skin cancer years ago, right before the mill fire. She hung on a lot longer than they thought she would. Died at home in her own bed, which is really the best place to go. That's how I want to do it. Don't let anyone take me away."

Ryan very carefully did not look up from his computer screen.

"I'll do my best to let you die at home, like Grandpa did." Christine prayed that was a long time away. "And Slade's dad?"

"Daniel...Daniel is a more complicated story." Her grandmother paused again, clearly not of the generation able to multitask. She finished cutting and folded the panel before saying any more. "He was a foreman at the grain mill and a volunteer fireman. He was one of the first on the scene when the grain mill exploded. Four people died. The condition of the bodies was said to be quite horrific. And they were his friends, his employees. He told me once he felt responsible for their deaths." She tsked.

"Slade said he hadn't opened any windows in the house in eight years."

"That would be about the time Daniel hung himself." Nana looked out the window, her face drawn, as if she couldn't bear to think of the tragedy. "Slade was home visiting. I think he was the one who found his father upstairs. Daniel did it in the bedroom closet, although I never could figure out how. I suppose it'd be rude to ask Slade."

"Nana." Christine recalled how unsettled Slade had seemed in her bedroom after she'd opened her closet. And here she'd fantasized his discomfort was due to an attraction between them. That misconception had spawned some smarmy dreams involving lace and wedding dresses. Who was she kidding? They were polar opposites. She was cutoffs and flip-flops. He was leather loafers and ties.

Nana smoothed the already smooth fabric. "I would've thought Slade would sell that house long ago, not that any of us would buy it." She met Christine's gaze. "Something binds him here. We all have our reasons for staying places, I suppose."

But in Slade's case, Christine didn't think it was happy memories that rooted him in Harmony Valley. She'd felt the sadness in his home. Slade was a strong man to live there.

Sometime later, Slade came upstairs as Agnes was finishing tying a bow on the last fancy swag window treatment she'd sewn. As usual, he looked like he'd stepped off the pages of a men's fashion magazine, instead of out of the afternoon heat. "What's this? I thought we agreed on plantation shutters up here, the same as downstairs."

He was lucky the drapes were blue, not pink. "I can't get the installer to come out and measure again. He said he's booked up until October. Nana decided to take pity on us." Christine handed Slade a stack of invoices. "Those need checks written. Where are the girls?"

"Over at Flynn's." Slade stared at the invoices and then looked at her. Stared at the invoices again and took a deep breath. "Would you like to have dinner at my house tonight?" He hurried to add, "With the girls and me?"

Nana exchanged glances with Christine. Nana's look seemed to say, *Don't turn down a millionaire's offer for dinner.*

Christine resisted rolling her eyes. She didn't believe in polite offers of dinner. Not from her boss. "There's an agenda behind this invitation, isn't there? What is it?"

He hesitated too long before answering. "You've been busy. I've been busy. It'd be nice to get an update."

Easy-peasy. She had everything organized in her action file.

Except Slade wasn't looking at her, which

implied the possibility of a different agenda. "And…"

He didn't move, and yet he appeared as if he was squirming in his Italian loafers. "Could you bring…your hair stuff?"

Christine smiled. "Do the twins want me to do their hair again?"

"No. I do." He smiled sheepishly, his gaze bouncing around the room. "They're still barely talking to me, and the last time you did their hair, they seemed happier."

Poor papa bear. Christine sympathized. "Girls can be brutal. I once succeeded in avoiding conversations with my dad for three weeks."

That caught his interest enough that he met her gaze. "What made you stop?"

"Dad took me with him to the vineyard."

"I tried that." He managed a hint of a smile. "They got skunked."

His wry humor and clear desire to win his girls over made it impossible to refuse. She sighed. "What time?"

Slade had barely left when her grandmother started in. "He's attractive, wealthy, and good-looking. I won't lie to you, I'd love to see you finally settle down, but then I realized as he was leaving…he's also your boss. Things haven't changed so much since I was young. You can't date your boss."

Ryan slumped behind his computer monitor. Hard to do when it was a laptop and you were over six feet tall.

"You're embarrassing Ryan," Christine pointed out. "Not to mention me."

"You young people just don't get it." Nana frowned, clearly exasperated with the scene.

Christine couldn't resist pushing her. "Nana, first you want me to get a life, and then you don't. Slade and I are friends. Don't go looking for romance where there is none." Advice she'd best heed herself.

"I need to check something outside." Ryan escaped down the stairs. The back door slammed.

"Honey, men don't ask women over because they're good with their daughters. They ask women over because they want to give them a test run." Agnes crossed the room, took Christine by the arms, and gently shook her. "This is the perfect job for you. You're in charge of everything for the first time. Don't mess it up by kissing your boss."

"Hey, no one said anything about kissing. This isn't a date. We'll talk business and I'll help him with his girls. Consider it a pity mission. Poor things, they don't seem to get enough attention. And Slade keeps throwing gifts at them. When I was at his house I saw they had an unlimited account online and they were ordering whatever they wanted on the internet. Without limits, they're going to be uncontrollable in high school. What'll it be like when they turn eighteen?"

The door below slammed again. No footsteps sounded on the stairs.

"Ryan?" Christine called out.

No answer.

With a sinking feeling in the pit of her stomach, Christine moved aside the curtains and saw Slade disappear down the path toward the river.

"Crap." Christine smoothed her hair away from her face. "What did I say just now? I think Slade heard every word."

"Nothing really." Her grandmother packed up her sewing machine. "Only that you were paying your boss a pity visit tonight and his daughters were heathens-in-waiting."

Christine thunked herself on the head.

SLADE WAS PRETTY good at barbecuing. He wasn't so good at taking criticism, especially when criticism involved his parenting skills. But he was willing to swallow his pride and learn, if it was good for his girls.

After asking Christine to dinner, he'd stopped in the tasting room to answer some emails and text messages before heading back out into the heat. Voices carried in the small house. It was impossible to miss Agnes's opinion about his intentions for dinner, or Christine's pity comment.

He stewed about dinner all afternoon. Should he text Christine and cancel? Should he take her aside when she arrived and admit he'd heard what she thought of his parenting skills? Should he blow her off and drive the girls into Cloverdale for dinner? Should he pretend he'd heard nothing?

It was hard waffling between cowardice and anger, stomping on his pride.

He took out his frustrations on the food he cooked. It was guy food. Salad he chopped himself. Baked potatoes he poked within inches of their lives. Seasoned tri-tip he pierced as he grilled. He'd put the twins in charge of the garlic bread, appropriate since they were wearing the colors of Italy—red-and-white striped blouses and green shorts.

A mistake, as it turned out. They burned the bread and set off the smoke alarm while he was in the backyard with the barbecue. Windows and doors were flung open. The bread came to rest in a severely singed lump on the stove, next to some deflated baked potatoes.

That was it. He was canceling their ramshackle dinner.

And that was when Christine appeared, in blue jeans, pink ballet slippers, and a flowery blouse, a far cry from the black Protect the Bears T-shirt and jean shorts she'd had on earlier. The sight of her in casual date clothes brightened up the drab, outdated kitchen and rendered him speechless.

"Let me give you this peace offering before we have to call the fire department in Cloverdale." Christine thrust a bottle of wine into his chest and took over the situation, calmly explaining to the girls why it was important to set the timer every time they left something in the oven or on the stove. She took an oven mitt, put it on, and lifted the loaf of garlic bread over the sink. "Here's how you salvage the bread." She scraped off the black, burned parts with a knife.

"I'd throw it away." Slade set the wine on the counter and rummaged in a drawer for a corkscrew.

"Spoken like a man who'd rather drive through somewhere than salvage his meal." She finished scraping. "See? Almost perfect." She put the bread back on the baking sheet.

It looked battered but edible. She glanced around the kitchen. "What else are we having?"

"The meat!" Slade ran out the back door, down the steps, and into the small backyard.

The tri-tip was sizzling and only a little blackened on one side. He shut off the grill, put the meat on a plate, and brought it inside to rest.

Christine poured the wine. It was one of hers from Ippolito Cellars. A deep red Zinfandel. She handed him a glass. "There are days when life gets to me and my mouth filter goes on the fritz. And then there are days when nothing goes right and you just have to start over. I'm afraid both describe my day. I'm sorry. My grandmother was being her usual meddlesome, yet good-natured self and I cracked. I know you mean well with the girls. It's just…" She swirled her wine gracefully. "It's so easy to take things for granted when your parents make a good living and give you things. Before you know it, you end up in the middle of nowhere with a hundred boxes of designer shoes you'll never wear."

He hadn't played out his gifting scenario in those terms before. "And a feathered dress in your closet you only wore once."

"Touché."

"Did I catch an apology in there somewhere?" Slade didn't want to admit how relieved he was to hear it.

"Yes. Let's make a toast." She raised her glass. "To burned toast and apologies."

Slade studied the burned loaf of garlic bread. Christine wasn't one to throw something out just because it was burned around the edges.

"Yes, even burned toast can be fixed." Her blue eyes sparkled. At him.

He couldn't remember the last time a woman had sparkled at him.

They clinked glasses and drank. The red wine coated his mouth with dry, subtle hits of something fruity. Slade was no wine connoisseur, but he was willing to learn with something that tasted this good.

Grace dug in the refrigerator. She came out with a juice container. Faith got down two more wineglasses. Grace poured. They clinked glasses and drank, giggling. Their golden baby bracelets glinted in the light.

"What flavors should I be tasting in here?" Slade tried to swirl his wine as Christine had done without spilling. His wine sloshed dangerously close to the lip of the glass.

"Do you want the layman's terms or the wine-snob terms?"

"Both?"

She took a sip and closed her eyes. "If I was writing a wine review or back label copy, I'd say that it opens with aromas of bright raspberry, followed by the taste of dried berries and plums, with a hint of pepper in the finish."

"And if you were just someone drinking the wine with dinner?"

"I'd say it tastes good." She grinned.

It wasn't beer, but it wasn't bad, either. He took another sip, then started carving meat, while the girls set the table.

"Grace. Faith." Christine crossed her arms as she regarded them. "I haven't seen you for days. You're my pulse on fashion. What did you wear the past few days? Goth girls again? Punk rockers?"

They giggled again. The sound filled Slade's heart until he thought it might burst.

"And I want a fashion show, complete with an announcer. If you don't talk, I may fall asleep." Christine gave Faith's hair a gentle tug. "Seriously, after dinner, I want to see what you've been wearing and not as a unit. We'll cover more ground if you each wear something different. If I get my fashion show and if your dad takes his tie off, I'll show you how to French braid hair. Deal?"

Slade held himself very still. Christine didn't know what she was asking.

The twins exchanged glances, and then Grace looked at Christine and said, "Deal."

Slade didn't dare look at Christine or either of the twins.

Maybe he was pitiful as a dad, maybe he was spoiling them, but there was a chance that he could improve. In order to do so, he'd have to bare his soul to Christine.

And, if they were observant, his girls.

CHAPTER ELEVEN

"WHY AM I taking my tie off?" It was after dinner. Slade's hands were shaking. He didn't want to take his tie off. He was her boss. He shouldn't have to take his tie off.

Christine sat next to him on the small couch. She slowly wound a strand of hair between her fingers. "It's after 7:00 p.m. You're at home. This shouldn't be a big deal. You still had your tie on the other night when I came by. Don't you ever let your hair down?" She tilted her head and glanced at his crown. "Besides, you can show the girls they can break out of their mold by example. What's wrong? Take the tie off. It's not like I've never seen a man without a tie on before. I'm not going to stuff dollar bills down your collar."

The twins were upstairs changing. It was just the two of them in the somber living room. A breeze ruffled the curtains. He should tell Christine no. He should tell her she'd overstepped the bounds of the employer-employee relationship, that it wasn't appropriate to undress him.

Slade swallowed. "Uh…"

"It's not that hard." Christine, who knew nothing of personal, or apparently professional, boundaries, reached over and loosened his tie.

Slade couldn't breathe, couldn't stop looking at her, noting the slight flush to her cheeks. He couldn't help himself from feeling the warmth of her hands so near his secret. So near the reason Evangeline had given the court as to why their marriage wasn't salvageable.

Christine glanced up at him, a hint of a smile on her face, probably about to give him grief about something else. The horror he was feeling must have been mirrored in his expression, because she froze. "I'm sorry. I shouldn't be touching you like this."

He captured her hands. "It's not you." Three rasped words. He was as hoarse as if he'd been shouting for days.

The twins bounded down the stairs.

Slade dropped her hands. Christine continued to stare at him. When Faith said, "Ahem," she snapped out of it, taking in the girls' latest outfits with an avalanche of appreciation. "Awesome, unique, fabulous, wonderful, sweet-sweet-sweet."

"I like this one," Faith said when Christine stopped babbling. She wore a black ballerina tutu over a red-and-black striped body suit. Her black biker boots clunked across the floor. Sunday's outfit.

"And I like this better," Grace said. She wore a pretty pink sundress with white sandals. Saturday's outfit.

They spoke!

Christine continued to muster a smile and general enthusiasm for their ensembles. "I like it when you wear different things. I can see your two personalities."

"Grace is the girlier of the two. Faith likes to make a bold statement," Slade said, marveling at the change in his daughters when Christine was around.

The twins stared at him as if he was a lion escaped from the zoo. Then they blinked and ran back upstairs. Their voices drifted down, excited but unintelligible.

Slade slumped against the sofa. "Please don't push them." *Or me,* he wanted to add, but he couldn't. He liked it when he and Christine joked back and forth. But the tie… the tie was off-limits.

Except he wanted her to touch him. He wanted to know if he was salvageable, like the loaf of burned garlic bread.

Stupid. So very stupid. He knew the answer to that question.

"You could make it easy on me and ask them if they feel like they have to dress alike all the time. Then we could forget the tie."

"They wouldn't answer." Slade focused on a crack in the ceiling, wishing, wanting, knowing nothing he wanted or wished for was going to come true. She'd see. And she'd leave, just like Evy.

"How do you know if you don't try?" Stubborn. She was so stubborn. "What are you afraid of?"

"Nothing." *Everything.* He was afraid she'd remove his tie and his arms would close around her, drawing her to him, close enough to kiss. "What are we doing here?" Slade's gaze snared hers.

She looked like a rabbit caught in a trap, one who was only now realizing that the carrot she was pursuing wasn't the carrot she'd originally been drawn to.

"Christine—"

"You take things too seriously. The tie, the shoes, the ring." She pointed at the titanium ring on his finger. "Why can't you just be yourself? Get out from behind this facade you work so hard at perpetuating."

"Because I don't think people would like

what they see." Understatement of the millennium. Underneath it all, he was a disappointment.

"You've got your guinea pig right here." She was close enough that he could see her out of the corner of his eye. "What are you hiding under your collar? Tattoos? Burns? A third nipple?"

"You don't want to know." His was a relationship-killing secret. Not that they were in a relationship. But he needed her. He needed her to run the winery and to make fine wine. Anything else—he swallowed—anything else was off-limits.

But he didn't move to stop her.

Christine's hands were at his neck again. Gentle. Skilled. She did more than loosen the knot this time. She slid the black silk free of his collar.

"Italian. Why did it have to be Italian?" There was a hint of soft, inviting humor in her voice. She ran her hands slowly over the silk. "Now I know why you're always smoothing your ties. They're so soft."

He knew she wouldn't leave him alone, not until she'd seen. She was curious and she had guts. Her playing with his tie was only a reprieve. She was like a horse whisperer, soothing with words, before moving in to uncover the real damage.

"How about unbuttoning a button?" That smile. That sparkle. Ten days ago he'd known neither. "Just one. You look uncomfortable."

Uncomfortable? He was dying. He wanted her to touch him. Badly. And yet, the last woman to see his neck had left him. Slade swallowed and shook his head. Or he tried to. In reality, his head barely moved.

Her hands reached for him once more.

Slade didn't think he could hold still, remain sitting, let this woman *see*. His breath came in labored chunks now. The breeze coming through the window behind him sent goose bumps down his spine.

He imagined in one quick burst what the next few seconds would be like. She'd free the top button of his shirt, maybe two. She'd see. She'd recognize. And she'd recoil. Because she'd realize he wasn't as put together and in control as he appeared. She'd see his cool exterior of success was a lie.

He couldn't produce enough saliva to swallow this time.

Her fingers worked at the first button. Worked at the second. Worked at the third.

She was killing him.

Only after the third button was free did she

spread the Egyptian cotton apart. Only then did she gasp and draw away.

But not for long. "Oh, Slade." She leaned in closer, using her finger to trace the tight scar that wound halfway around his neck.

CHRISTINE KNEW SLADE'S mother had died at home of cancer. She knew his father had hung himself. No one said anything about Slade's scar.

Was it from an attempted murder by his father? A mugging from when he lived in New York? Or had Slade attempted suicide?

Little footsteps hammered down the stairs, almost as loud as the hammering in her heart.

Slade's green eyes revealed remorse, regret, guilt.

Someone cleared their throat.

Christine assembled a disjointed smile and focused on the twins.

Grace in a floor-length blue flowered dress. "I like flowers."

Faith in jeans and a black tank top, leather cuffs on her wrists. "I don't."

Christine needed to say something to Faith, to Grace, to Slade. She needed to be light and supportive and charming. But it was Slade who needed her most. She wanted to draw him close and hug him, hug him tight.

So tight that he'd realize it was okay. Whatever had happened. Because clearly, by the anguish in those eyes, he thought she'd run away in disgust.

And her not saying anything was stretching the awkward chord near snapping.

"These looks are…expected." Christine put a hand on top of Slade's.

He nearly jerked off the couch.

She squeezed his hand reassuringly. "I'm not saying they're bad looks, but tame by what I've come to expect from you two. What else have you got? Can you shock me?" She tried smiling again. It was no easier this time.

What was Slade thinking? Did he realize she was talking to him as well as to the girls?

The shadows around his eyes said, *I'm sorry. It's true. I tried to commit suicide.*

Christine's arms tingled with shock. Something in Slade's life had been so bad he'd tried to kill himself. He kept it hidden. And yet he'd let her unbutton those buttons.

Why?

The girls ran enthusiastically up the stairs with their assignment.

Slade loosened Christine's fingers, which had been digging into his knuckles. "You can go now."

"Is that what she did?" Somehow, Christine

knew his ex-wife had left him because of this. "Your wife left you because she couldn't trust you to...you know...not try again."

Instead of releasing her, his hand closed around hers. "It doesn't matter."

"It does." Christine turned to him in wonder. "You haven't told anyone. At least not anyone here in town. No one over the age of sixty in this place can keep a secret." With her free hand, Christine reached for the collar of his shirt to get another look. "No. She left you."

Slade pulled away.

"But you showed me."

He released her hand and rebuttoned his shirt.

Her mind raced, that scientific mind that had made her an outcast when she was little, because she understood too much, leaped ahead of conversations in class. "You want me to leave," she stated matter-of-factly. "You think this will disgust me. You must..."

It hit her then. Not like a ton of bricks, or a slap in the face, or a cold shower. This was a gradual awareness of something truly special. Once-in-a-lifetime special. He was...he was great. She liked him. A lot.

And he liked her. More than a boss should like his employee.

He liked her. Those mixed signals weren't all just self-preservation on his part.

He liked her. A lot.

The proof was there. But what did it mean?

Nothing, her head said.

Everything, her heart said.

It could be a silly infatuation, spawned by all the time they'd been spending together. Something that would fade. Or it could be the beginning of feelings that went down like a rich red wine. Something that expanded and lingered. That filled up the empty places.

But which was it? Science required she test out her theories.

"I need to kiss you," she said, surprising both of them.

He stared at her. Shocked.

Somewhere above them a floorboard creaked and a girl giggled. Outside, a dog barked in the distance. Then everything fell silent.

"It's not like that." Christine wasn't even sure what *that* was. "There's this…whatever it is between us. And I need to conduct an experiment." To determine if he was worth risking her dreams for.

No man was worth compromising her dreams for.

Except…maybe…this one.

She wasn't going to get caught up in any silly fling, not when everyone in this small town would take note. Not when everyone she knew in the wine industry would talk and speculate.

"I'm not a lab specimen." He crossed his arms over his chest, clearly ruffled.

"No. You're a man. A very attractive man. With a dark past." She grinned at him. "Don't tell me you were brave enough to show me your scar and you're too chicken to kiss me."

"Why?" he rasped, still bound up tight behind those crossed arms.

"Because I don't care about the scar. But I care about why you showed me. What if you showed me for nothing? What if we kiss and there are no sparks? You know how it is. Sometimes you see someone or you talk to them for a few minutes and you wonder, *Are they for me?*" She risked a hand on his forearm. He tensed, but didn't jerk away. "If we kiss and it falls flat, there's no harm. This tension between us will settle into something… different."

They could finally be more comfortable at work. She wouldn't dream about him at night or admire his physique as he walked away. She'd laugh at the idea of them as a couple.

She'd prod him to stop wearing those beautiful ties. At least not every day.

He was looking at her as if she'd just landed on Mars and asked him to return with her to Venus.

She moved her hand to his knee. "You're afraid."

"You don't know what you're asking." His voice lacked his usual self-confidence. "It freaked Evy out. She couldn't take not knowing if I'd crack again and hurt myself. Or hurt Faith and Grace."

"You won't try it again." She knew that with a certainty. He kept talking about the future—for the winery, for his budget, for the town, and the girls, and a dozen other things she couldn't remember right now. Because she was looking into those green eyes in wonder. "You'd never hurt the twins. I don't know what she was thinking or why you believed her."

He may not have believed he'd try again or hurt the girls, but he put a lot of stock in the lack of trust a woman was willing to give him. He couldn't take being rejected again, that much was clear in his rigid spine and folded arms.

The girls pounded back down the stairs.

"You're not off the hook," Christine whispered to him, telling herself this was just a test, telling herself it was the fastest way to clear the air.

She could prove she was good friend material and a great employee with a simple kiss that fizzled.

She just had to make sure it fizzled.

DRESS-UP TIME was over.

While Slade cleaned up the kitchen, Christine showed the girls different hairstyles they could try. Although their conversation wasn't racing, they'd progressed beyond one- or two-word sentences. Slade's ability to speak seemed to have regressed. His racing mind seemed to have put his speech function on mute.

What had he been thinking?

He'd shown Christine his scar. She was nosier than any Harmony Valley resident he'd encountered so far and she could easily weasel the truth out of him. Given time. And her easy smile.

He'd opened up his house to her. The house that was his penance and his refuge. An error in judgment.

He hadn't told her a kiss was a monumentally stupid idea. Because…because…

He wanted that kiss. How he wanted that kiss.

It had snuck up on him, this wanting. As if

he'd held himself back from everyone, even his closest friends, for too long. As if he'd ignored emotion until it rebelled and had to find a target.

And Christine was the one unlucky enough to cross his path. He wanted to hold her and stroke that golden hair, as if stroking it would give him some of her optimistic, sunny attitude. He wanted to learn the feel of her lips on his, experience the gentle caress of her breath against his skin.

He finished doing the dishes and went down the hall to the living room, leaning against the doorframe to watch the girls with Christine and try to find perspective.

His daughters had changed into their pajamas and were sitting patiently as Christine played hairdresser. Even their pajamas matched—pink bunnies with sunglasses on lime-green cotton. Was Evy suppressing their individuality? The wrongness of it was a sour taste in his mouth.

Christine was braiding Grace's hair and entwining it with his black tie. She looked up and met his gaze with an accepting smile. She seemed so certain there would be no passion in their shared kiss.

Slade was equally certain there would be more passion than he could handle.

"Girls, time for bed. Thank Christine for doing your hair." *Thank Christine for not running screaming out into the night when Daddy showed her his Frankenstein-like scar.*

"Thank you," the twins said, before racing up to bed.

"Lights out in ten minutes." Slade was envious of their energy. He felt drained. He turned back to Christine. "I'll see you home."

"Yep." She stood. "I'm ready."

He wasn't.

She held out her hand. "Come on. I promise not to put my theory to the test until we're at my house."

He had a block-and-a-half reprieve. He charged past her, ignoring her hand, ignoring Takata smoking on his porch. You'd think he'd slow down—like a man headed toward the firing squad, determined to do anything to avoid the end. But no, he charged ahead, until he reached her house and looked down to see her panting beside him. His heart was pounding hopefully, his head hoping for rejection.

Slade dragged her against him—without suave moves, without gentleness—and claimed her lips. He swallowed her gasp of surprise and kissed her with a fierceness and intensity that should have scared her away.

She didn't run for Granny's house.

And so his hands—*the hands that should have stayed on her arms?*—wrapped around her, drawing her closer, until he couldn't tell where he ended and she began.

This wasn't a chaste I'll-see-you-home kiss.

This wasn't a simple first-date peck on the lips.

This was a heart-racing, blood-pumping, you're-the-one-for-me kiss.

As quickly as he'd latched on to her, Slade let her go. This was madness. He knew better. No woman could ever love him again. His only hope was that he'd shocked her with his zeal.

She staggered back, a dazed look in her eyes, if the fading light of summer was any indication.

"There," he said, forcing the word past a too-tight throat. "It's done, then."

He left her there in the gathering darkness.

Left her knowing he'd scared her away for good.

CHAPTER TWELVE

HUGE MISTAKE.

Christine had assumed that Slade would kiss with methodical control. It was how he approached everything. Like adding up a column of numbers in his head. Or creating a graph of growth rates. Predictably ho-hum.

Huge, huge mistake.

The passion in his kiss had been methodical in its heart-stopping assault, but there was nothing controlled about it.

What she'd hoped would be a brief moment of embarrassment, closing the door on any niggle of attraction between them, had opened the door to possibilities and complications.

Worse. Slade's kiss left her hungry for more.

He was her boss. She couldn't quit. Her career would be blindsided if she left before bottling even one vintage. Slade thought Harmony Valley residents were gossips? Try winemakers.

He was her boss. If word got out, her path
to starting her own winery would have a foot-
note. The wine wouldn't stand on its mer-
its as much as the feet of a romantic liaison.
She had to set her feelings aside and focus on
her dreams. When she had her own winery,
she'd give Slade a call. They'd laugh about
this night over a glass of wine.

She wasn't in the mood to laugh now. How
could she look at Slade again without reliv-
ing the urgency with which his hands had
touched her? How could she look at his necktie and not recall the thin scar that curved
around part of his neck?

He'd tried to do something terrible to himself. When and why had he done something
so desperate?

She wanted to comfort, to question, to hide.
She understood why his ex-wife had left. What
he tried was horrifying. But his ex-wife was
a coward for not standing by Slade. Christine
liked to think she wouldn't have dumped him
had she been in the same situation, but she
didn't know. She didn't know. Who was she
to judge Slade's ex-wife's choice?

And how could she ignore these feelings?
Even now, instead of going to sleep, she
wanted to talk to someone about them. She

wanted to talk about it with Slade. He'd think it meant she wanted to date him.

It wasn't just Slade she'd have to deal with if they started something. Slade's was the kind of secret you didn't keep from family if you were in a relationship with him. Her grandmother would try to reason with her about her safety—ridiculous, since she didn't see Slade hurting anyone. Her brother, Jake, would tell her she was crazy to stay with him—not that he had a track record of success in the romance department. Her father would insist she leave Slade and the winery—although whether he would advise her to quit before or after her first vintage was hard to predict.

She tossed and turned all night, eventually dragging herself out of bed for coffee as dawn broke over Parish Hill. She had no answers. She couldn't run from this. And she sure as heck couldn't tell her grandmother. Nana sat in the control room at Gossip Central.

The only person she could talk to about this was Slade.

But first, she needed caffeine. Christine fixed herself a coffee in a large travel mug, doctoring it up with cream and sugar. She headed toward the river, choosing to sit on top of a picnic table at the park. The river flowing slowly past was almost calming, almost as much as realizing it was too early for Mayor Larry to be doing yoga.

"Thought I'd either find you here or at the winery." Slade's deep voice resonated right through her. He sat on the bench near her feet, not looking at her. There were dark circles beneath his eyes. And despite the fact that it was only six o'clock in the morning, he had on a button-down, slacks, and a beautiful mossy-green tie. Her fingers longed to touch it.

"I'm sorry," they both said at once. Their glances collided and shot back toward the river.

"I never should have made the suggestion," Christine said. "I got carried away. I never imagined…"

"I knew," he stated glumly.

"At least we know now. And we can…you know…work together, right? Ignore whatever that was." Christine wasn't sure what she'd do if Slade said no. "Because we know." That their attraction ran too deep. That the timing was wrong.

He glanced at her again, only this time his gaze held as firm as that kiss. "You're okay with that?"

"I am." That sounded weak. She said it again, stronger. "I have to work long hours and stay focused. Anything between us would be a distraction, not just at the winery, but here." She tapped her chest. "You've seen how I get when I'm working. I lose track of time. I push myself to the brink of exhaustion. But if I don't take that shot now, if I screw up something here, I may never get a chance again."

His nod was far too curt. "What about the, uh…?" He touched the knot hiding the scar.

"It's your past, your story to tell. I won't share it with anyone. But…could you tell me what happened?" She bent over, her elbows between her knees, so she could look him directly in the eye.

His eyes, such a beautiful green, shuttered.

Levity was called for. "You don't have to, but…I mean, you weren't successful at it for whatever reason, and I can't imagine you failing at anything."

He blinked. "Are you teasing me? *About this?*"

"I suppose I am." She shared just a hint of a smile. "Does it help?"

"You confound me." He stared back at the river, but didn't leave. "Every time I try to add things up about you…things never add up."

"I'm trying to be straightforward." The

urge to sit on the bench next to him and put her head on his shoulder was powerful. She straightened and blew out a breath.

"I've never met anyone who says exactly what they think when they think it." He said it as if it was a character flaw.

"You'd rather I didn't say anything." It was school all over again. She didn't conform, so she didn't fit in.

He didn't deny it.

So she didn't say anything. For several minutes.

He sighed. "Just say it. Tell me what you're thinking."

"Fine. I was thinking I really miss a good coffee shop. A vanilla scone would hit the spot about now." She finger combed her ponytail over one shoulder. "And I was thinking that my list of things to do is getting smaller at the winery, but that I still can't find a company to help with the harvest." She tossed the ponytail onto her back. "Then I thought about how your house seems different since you opened up the windows, and how the twins are slowly opening up and letting you in, even if you don't see it."

She sucked in a breath. "Oh, and then I couldn't help but think about how it would be really cool to date you if you weren't my boss. Then I could give you a hug whenever I thought you needed it. And make you smile when you took yourself too seriously." That might have been an over-share. She tried for a quick recovery. "But mostly…I was thinking about that vanilla scone."

SLADE WANTED TO kiss Christine again.

If he turned toward her and drew her down, he could kiss her. Maybe in her kiss he'd lose himself, as he had last night. She didn't look to be his type in her raggedy pink T-shirt and sweatpants cut off at the knees. She didn't act like his type in the way she butted gently into everyone's business, as if she knew how to listen, if not how to remedy.

But she felt like his type. His antidote. The person who'd make it seem as if his past wasn't made up of one huge mistake. He knew it from the way she'd touched his scar—so gentle. From the way she'd stared deep into his eyes, and instead of trying to dredge up all his secrets, she'd tried to test what kind of man he was today. With a litmus test. A kiss.

He'd hoped that kiss would scare her, had half hoped she'd turn in her resignation. It would be easier than being her boss, her coworker, her *friend*. But a woman like Christine—who saw past scars—deserved her wishes respected. Because she'd drawn the same conclusion he had from that test. There was something beneath the surface between them, below appearances, below ties and ratty T-shirts, below roles of boss and employee. It was something that could heal and understand and forgive, something he wasn't going to name, because no matter how much he'd believed he'd never find it, it would forever be out of reach.

Christine wants to be friends.

His friends had never seen his scar. He'd thought if they saw it they'd lose respect for him. What with budgets constantly being revised and the winery costing more than they'd ever planned on spending, respect seemed a precious commodity.

Christine sipped her coffee, waiting for him to say something.

He wasn't going to turn toward her. He *wouldn't* turn toward her.

He turned toward her and rested his arm on her knee, surprising even himself with an invasion of her personal space. "You honestly think I'm making progress with the twins?"

Other than the initial jolt when his body touched hers, she played along. "Oh, totally. They want to please you. They must have said a handful of words to you last night while I was there."

"Twenty-five."

Her eyes sparkled. "Twenty-five is better than five."

"But who's counting?" He was. Counting was what he did. He counted money and opportunities. He'd tally this moment under the missed-opportunities column.

"So what is my millionaire boss doing today?"

It didn't escape him how she subtly put a stake in the ground. He was invading her space and she felt threatened enough to remind him of the boundaries of their relationship, although with Christine, there were no boundaries. Such a cute little hypocrite.

"Flynn has me on hammer patrol again this morning. The girls enjoy going." And Slade wanted their time with him to be fun. "I caught them whispering in Truman's ear yesterday. I wish they'd whisper in mine."

"Someday." Christine smiled at him. "You'll see."

Her optimism never wavered. He admired that about her. "I've got less than two weeks left with them." He'd checked the calendar yesterday and realized it wasn't enough time.

"You can do anything in two weeks." She made it sound like a vacation.

There it was again—her belief in him. His chest seemed to swell with confidence and pride. He'd regained his confidence long ago. But pride? It was a newly rediscovered emotion, partially attributed to her.

"I should be getting my day started." The awkward tone was back in her voice. With gentle fingers, she edged his arm off her leg. "Lots to do."

They stood. She, conveniently within reach.

Suppressing a sigh, he stepped back.

Something in her eyes shifted, narrowed. "Seriously? You're scared of a girl?" She gave him a one-armed hug, as her other hand held her coffee mug.

It was a quick embrace, a jolting tease of what might have been. And then she was marching across the grass toward Main Street.

Leaving his arms as empty as his heart.

"CHRISTINE!" A FEW days after the unforgettable kiss, Ryan ran down the winery's gravel drive, whooping and shouting at Christine. "We got it! We got it!"

Christine had been monitoring the installation of the fermentation tanks along the far wall of the barn, but was drawn outside when Ryan didn't stop hollering.

"The government bottling permits." Ryan stopped in front of her, bending over and putting his gangly arms on his gangly legs. He clutched the mail in one hand. "We were approved. Eighty thousand cases."

"Eighty?" Christine swiped the certificate and scanned it. "That's got to be wrong. We've only got fruit for five thousand." And that was only if it ripened to a consistency Christine approved of.

But it wasn't a mistake. Whoever put in the request—and let's be serious, it was Slade—had thought ahead to winery expansion. Despite knowing he'd applied for the permit months ago, Christine felt oddly betrayed. They'd agreed to be conservative and move forward slowly. He'd never mentioned submitting an application for year-five production. Her mind jammed with implications and possibilities.

She'd been unable to talk him out of buying enough equipment to make eighty thousand cases a year. She kept telling him the idle equipment was too much overhead, but he'd insisted. Twelve bottles to a case—that was nearly a million bottles of wine. Not that he could have known if the entire eighty thousand would be approved.

Did he have plans for the excess capacity? She couldn't believe he did, but she couldn't believe he hadn't told her about this.

Was he going to buy bulk wine? Did he expect her to make it?

Doubt warred with the reality of black ink on paper. Eighty thousand cases. You just didn't obtain a permit like that and let it sit idle.

Unless… Unless he'd decided to extricate the partnership from the winery business altogether. He could sell the permit to another winery. He could sell the facility and the permit to another winery. Some big, impersonal winery that wouldn't appreciate all the love and attention to detail Christine was putting into this one. Her wine. Her reputation.

She whipped out her phone: Where are you?

Slade's reply: Phil's barbershop.

Christine sprinted to her car, clutching the permit in her hand. She'd left the keys on the center console. The old car started up with only a few coughs of protest. And then she was driving into town.

She barreled into the barbershop on Main Street a few minutes later, the edges of the permit crumpling in her grip. "We need to talk."

"Hey, Christine," the twins greeted her. They sat together in a barber chair, spinning it around. They had on matching white capri pants and filmy orange blouses over tank tops. Orange headbands held their dark hair away from their faces.

"Hullo, Christine." Phil, the old barber, sat in the other chair reading a newspaper.

She managed a breathy, "Hey."

Slade wielded a drill, screwing in hinges on a storage cabinet. He hadn't abandoned the button-down-and-tie look. Today's tie was a bright red with darker red pinstripes. Snazzy. "Can I help you?"

"What is this?" She came forward, shaking so badly she could hardly walk. "Are you selling?"

"No." He put another screw on the drill bit and fitted it into a hinge hole. "Why?"

The whine of the drill filled the air, making it impossible to speak without shouting. Since their kiss several days ago, he'd treated her as if the kiss never happened. They had a good working relationship. Or so she'd thought. He'd never said a word about the permit.

When the drill quieted, she struggled to catch her breath. "You submitted an application to bottle eighty thousand cases and you were approved. That's year-five production, not year one."

"They approved eighty thousand cases?" Slade sent another screw smoothly into the wood. He still hadn't looked at her. "I wasn't expecting that. The government sent someone out to inspect us last month before you started, but it was more about record keeping than capacity. I only put the big number in on the request form on a whim."

"You aren't whimsical." She leaned against the wall. "You can't just leave capacity like that idle. You either use it or you sell."

He frowned. "What would we sell?"

"The permits. The permits and the winery. Either. Both." Her ponytail had fallen over her shoulder. She tossed it back. "I should have seen this coming. We're not making any wine this year, are we?"

"I'm not sure I see what your problem is." He stood, maddeningly calm. "I told you. Eighty thousand was an end goal for me. We agreed on your bottling figures for this year."

"You don't understand." Christine stared out the front window at a lonely Main Street. "You don't know what this permit is worth. I'm going to have to give notice. Reputation is everything in this business. Who knows what the new owners will want to make here."

Slade put down his drill and took her by the shoulders. "Christine, none of those things are happening."

"But a permit this size is too valuable to sit idle. If we're not filling capacity ourselves, whether you want to sell or not, companies will start to call and offer to buy it. Do you know how much this permit is worth?"

"No." He looked surprised that he didn't know. "Don't worry. Someone would have to offer us an obscene sum of money. And I don't mean what I would consider obscene, but a dirty, obscene amount of money that the partnership would be foolish to refuse."

"That doesn't reassure me." She stared at the permit, trying not to think about how reassuring it felt to be held by him, trying to focus on what this meant to her career. If… if…if…

She didn't want to think about it anymore.

"Touch my tie," he said softly.

"I don't wanna." She'd started to read a copy of his application the day the mayor surprised her in the tasting room. She should never have set it aside. She wouldn't have felt so betrayed. She wouldn't have kissed him.

"You should have told me you'd submitted it for this amount."

"I didn't even tell my business partners I changed the number on the application. Christine, it was a gamble, designed to position us for growth." He sighed and pulled her close. "Now, touch my tie. It's Italian. You'll feel better."

Christine touched the red silk, just below the knot, and ran her hands down its length. It was simply smooth, nothing like the man it kept locked in.

"Feel better?" He stroked her hair.

"Yes." But she was still convinced he'd sell something.

As if reading her mind, he said, "We're not selling the permit. We're not selling the winery." He pressed a sweet kiss to her forehead. "Now, get back to work. We want our first five thousand cases to be fantastic."

It was a dream come true—building a winery exactly how she wanted, making high-end, limited-quantity wine with the possibility to grow.

But experience had taught Christine how easily dreams became nightmares.

CHAPTER THIRTEEN

"YOU LIKE HER." Faith's dimple accented her smile.

"We like her," Grace seconded.

Slade tried not to grin and failed. He couldn't get used to the girls easily smiling and talking to him. And he did like Christine. A lot. When he wasn't focusing on the girls, he thought of little else but Christine. About how lucky he was that she hadn't quit and didn't run away every time he tentatively touched her hand, her shoulder, her bright blond hair. He'd settle for friendship if that was what she wanted. Who was he to ask for more?

"You girls are right. Look at your dad, smiling like it's Christmas morning." Phil peered in Slade's direction from over the edge of his newspaper. The hands that held the paper shook. He may have been the town barber, but you'd risk your ears requesting a cut. "I like the way you operate, Slade. And your girls are cute as plums, but your partnership promised the town you wouldn't sell.

And just now, you promised that little wine-maker the same thing. Wouldn't do to lie to the woman you love."

Love?

It was too soon for that, not to mention too optimistic. Between having his daughters with him, the support of his friends in town, and Christine, he'd been thinking this was about as good as life got. Why swing for the fences and strike out?

"We're not selling." Slade leaned on the back of the barber chair the twins occupied. "Thank you for telling me you like Christine."

"Are you going to marry her?" Grace unwound the orange headband she was wearing and wrapped it triple around Faith's wrist. She angled her back toward Faith. "French braid, please."

"We approve." Faith started finger combing Grace's hair.

Grace put her small palms on either side of Slade's cheeks. "You need someone nice."

"To make you smile." Faith didn't take her eyes off her work.

Grace wobbled his head ever so gently. "Because you don't smile enough."

"And we should know. Our newest step-dad…" Faith stopped braiding to look at him.

She rolled her eyes. "He says we don't smile enough."

"And Mom always says we got your smile." Grace removed her hands from his face and folded them in her lap. "And that our smile is pretty."

It was the longest conversation they'd had to date. Slade imagined his grin stretched from ear to ear.

"Well?" Grace said, staring pointedly at him.

"Well, what?" Slade was confused.

"Are you going to marry Christine?" Faith repeated her sister's question.

Phil angled forward, aiming his good ear in Slade's direction.

That was all Slade needed—for the local rumor mill to go off half-cocked about him and Christine. He'd be lying if he said he wasn't interested in her, but that was nowhere close to marriage. For anyone to be in a relationship with him long-term, they had to trust he could hold it together. That was a whole lotta trust to ask of someone, even if Slade was convinced suicide wasn't the answer to overwhelming problems.

"Dad," Grace whispered.

"We'll see," Slade said quickly, because he

feared the whispers would deteriorate to twin speak once more.

"That means no." Faith shrugged when he looked at her. "That's what it means when Mom says it."

"Those girls are smart." Phil raised his paper in front of his face.

Slade's cell phone rang. It was a number he didn't recognize.

"Mr. Jennings, I'm Tom Bartlett." The man's tone was so perfectly pitched, Slade could see him sitting at a large mahogany desk in a heavily carpeted room. "I represent several firms that are interested in bottling permits in Sonoma County."

The hair on the back of Slade's neck went up, exactly how it did when he noticed a big opportunity to make money.

"We hear that you've just received a moderate bottling permit, but that you haven't completed your winery yet. In fact—" papers shuffled in the background "—you have yet to install a bottling line."

"How do you know that?" Now the hair on the back of Slade's neck rose for an entirely different reason.

"I'm prepared to offer your company a substantial sum of money for that bottling permit to be transferred to us. In return, we're prepared to offer—" He named an obscene sum. "And we'll bottle your small lots of wine every harvest for the next five years. No charge."

Slade gripped the chair tighter. "I'll have to get back to you."

"We'd like to meet."

"I'm sure you understand, Tom. We're a partnership. I'll have to get back to you."

With a refusal, right?

SLADE WAS IN JAIL.

He sat on the floor in the corner of the small, dusty cell in the sheriff's office.

Nate was sanding the rust off the cell bars. Flynn and Will were framing windows with wide rolls of painter's tape in preparation for painting. Will was struggling to tape in a straight line. The girls played hopscotch on the sidewalk with Truman.

"This will be the first of many offers we're going to receive." Slade knew what he had to do—advise his partners as to what was best for the firm. Based on what Christine said, he had a sinking suspicion that more offers would be forthcoming. Likely more lucrative offers and ones that extended to include not just the permits but the entire winery.

"Rose predicted this would happen, remember?" Will applied a strip of tape on the window's edge, examined his work, and peeled it up to try again. "We were just at the Lions Club meeting."

"That's right." Flynn unrolled a long strip of tape between his hands. "And we told them we wouldn't sell."

Slade couldn't believe that less than an hour ago he'd been happier than he'd been in years. He'd promised Christine they weren't interested in selling. But that was before he counted six zeroes behind a number. What they decided to do with the permit would either be seen as the savviest business move or the biggest miscalculation he'd ever made. It was no longer about personal promises—it was about a successful business venture.

"It's my job to advise you that this offer almost covers the cost of our investment here so far. The offers are likely going to increase, until as the partnership's CFO, I'll have to propose we sell." Two months ago, those words would have brought Slade relief. Now they sickened him. What would happen to Christine and the tentative balance they'd achieved? She'd have no reason to stay in Harmony Valley. And neither would he.

Too late, he realized he'd grown to love the quirky little town.

"I thought you were all gung ho on the winery." Nate stopped sanding, the unusually sharp tone in his voice reminding Slade that Nate's job hinged on the partnership's ability to attract people to town. "Of the three of you, you can't stop talking about it."

"The problem," Will said, "is that Slade likes to make money."

"Or prove to someone who doesn't believe in us that *we* can make money," Flynn added.

Slade smoothed his tie, his hand lingering over the knot, thinking of Christine's fingers on his silk and how they'd unraveled him. "What can I say? Some people get paid to swing a bat. I get paid to watch the bottom line." And despite the promise of Christine's wine-making skill, despite the high-tech equipment they'd invested in, despite the cache making money in the wine world would bring, Slade knew a check with at least seven zeroes behind an eye-popping number would be the safer investment.

"We gave our word." Will stopped trying to get his tape properly lined up on the window.

"Yep," Flynn seconded, eyeing Will's work with a frown.

When it came to programming, his partners were geniuses. When it came to money, not so much. "We have to be accountable for our bottom line."

"There are plenty of examples of people who didn't sell and held on to their investment only to see its value increase even more," Will pointed out.

"Why would you keep me in this partnership if you're going to ignore my advice?" There. He'd said out loud what he'd been worried about for months. It didn't make him feel better. His words agitated the anxiety that rode most days in his stomach.

"We're not going to buy you out just because we disagree with you." Will crossed his arms over his chest, a ping of annoyance in his voice. "What's going on with you?"

Slade noticed he didn't say they'd never buy him out.

"We came here to recharge," Will continued. "But we stayed to help revitalize the town."

"I never wanted to help." Slade spun his pinky ring. "You know I never wanted to help."

"But you have been helping," Will said quietly. "And it seems like you enjoy it."

What he was enjoying was Christine's company and striving toward the goal of making a name for them in the wine world. There'd

be great buzz in financial circles if they sold
their winery for a profit before they ever
bottled a drop, adding to their partnership's
worth. They'd be seen as golden boys who
could do no wrong. Let the next company that
came in deal with Mayor Larry. Their future
would be set. It was what he'd been working so hard to prove. He wasn't a fluke or a
failure. He could make his fortune again and
again. Overcome stress and odds and stand
tall while doing it.

Nate leaned down and tapped Slade's shoulder. "Look at the girls. They love it here."

Faith was giving Truman a piggyback ride.
Grace skipped alongside. They were planning
a campout in Flynn's yard tonight.

"But they aren't going to stay." The words
felt heavy and full of regret.

"I promised my grandfather." Flynn visibly
struggled to say more. "I promised him...this
winery would benefit Harmony Valley. I can't
sell out and just leave."

Every fiber of Slade's being returned to
that terrible November day eight years ago.
He felt again the debilitating grief.

"If an offer comes in that I think is perfect
and I'm outvoted on accepting it," Slade said
slowly, "I'm going to leave the partnership."

Because if they received an outrageously

large offer for every tank, forklift, and wine barrel, Slade could finally say he'd done it, he'd cleared his debt to his father.

He could sell the Death and Divorce House and move on.

Dinner tonight?

CHRISTINE LEFT SLADE'S text message unanswered. She listened to the installer go over how to operate the crusher and stem remover. Ryan filmed the man with his cell phone so they could review it again later.

Other than the bottling line, the main installations were complete. The winery was beautiful. Maybe not as luxurious as one of the showplaces in Napa, but no one could say that they'd cobbled together this winery. When the buyers came, as she knew they would no matter what assurances Slade had given her earlier, they'd be impressed.

Maybe she'd get a bigger termination bonus than her contract stipulated.

Christine hadn't thought she'd grow so attached to the winery, the town, or the man who'd brought her here, in so short a time. Leaving would be harder than the last time. In fact, every position she left was harder to leave than the last. She wanted to set down roots. She wanted the chance to extend herself and grow.

Cami's bitter words came back to her: *Your family isn't known for its loyalty.*

Was that who she'd become? A fair-weather winemaker? Moving on at the first sign of trouble like her dad, rather than sticking through the challenging times like her mom?

Her phone buzzed again: I understand.

Christine sighed and texted back: Busy. Wait.

Did she want to have dinner with Slade and the girls again?

Nana would speculate.

Heck, Christine would speculate. And what about the deal they'd made to respect each other's boundaries?

Boss-boss-boss. How hard could it be to remember Slade was her boss?

Pretty hard when she considered that gentle kiss on her forehead this afternoon, adding it to her memories, right next to the one of their first kiss.

She could take Nana along. Her grandmother was good with children. It probably helped that she was their size and had such an easygoing temperament.

She'd go if it was a working dinner. Was there any reason to call this a working dinner? She could take a couple of pictures of the new equipment with her phone and show them to Slade. She'd received new templates to review for the website. He hadn't seen any of them. And the problem of how to harvest the grapes without a crew remained.

Mentally, she could handle a business dinner. Emotionally, she wasn't so sure.

Her phone rang.

Her grandmother rarely raised her voice, but she practically shouted in her ear, "Why didn't you tell me Slade proposed?"

"What?"

Nana bulldozed right over her. "My friend Rose is always harping on about how Emma is marrying a millionaire. Well, now I can shove that right back at her. You should have told me first thing."

"He didn't—"

"What kind of ring did he get you? Emma's sporting a beautiful three-carat diamond surrounded by pink sapphires. But I'd like to see something bigger on your finger. You've got the taller body to carry off some bling."

"Nana!" Christine cut in when her grandmother took a breath. "We aren't getting married! Where did you hear this?"

"Everyone's talking about it. Mildred just called me." Nana's voice reflected her disappointment. "You mean you're not getting married to Slade?"

"No!"

"Could you consider it? Otherwise, I'm going to have to call Rose back with the news."

"Call Rose!" Christine hung up on her.

Her phone buzzed again.

Slade: Need to talk.

She texted back: Ya think?

Her phone buzzed again.

It was her dad: Word is your bottling permits are for sale. 80K cases? Don't let them push you around.

Gossip among the wine-making community was worse than here in Harmony Valley.

Christine wanted to yowl in frustration.

She answered back: Not for sale. Chill.

Not what I hear. Time to call it and get out.

Christine's stomach knotted tighter than one of Slade's ties. Her father wasn't going to stop badgering her. Not until she'd proven they weren't selling—which she wasn't even sure she believed—or she quit. Christine wanted to believe in Slade. She wanted to helm this winery. But if they did sell, when was the better time to jump ship? Before the sale or after? Her father was a firm believer in before.

Another text came in: You still employed?

She assured an old friend that she was, grumbling to herself about gossip, all the while feeling doubt weaken her knees, her backbone, her resolve.

This was supposed to be her dream job, the winery that solidified the platform of her reputation. Instead, her platform seemed ready to crumble and her dad's genes were telling her to run.

But there was more at stake here than merely a job. There were her grandmother's expectations and the partnership's promises that the winery would bring jobs to town. There were Ryan's expectations of a long-term job. There was Slade's expectations that she'd run away if she saw his scar.

He'd promised they weren't going to sell. She had to believe him, despite everything in her telling her otherwise.

"Everything okay?" Ryan asked.

"I need a shower and a drink." Christine's phone buzzed again. "And maybe another drink. Not necessarily in that order."

"You DIDN'T HAVE to pick me up," Christine said when she opened Slade's truck door.

Something was missing from both his expression and the truck. "Where are the girls?"

"They're over at Flynn's, having a sleepover with Truman. Best-case scenario, the kid won't wake up tomorrow morning with makeup on and his hair styled."

Christine shut the door and spun back toward the house, hurrying despite the heat.

He turned off the big black beast and ran after her. "Wait." He caught up to her on the front porch. "We need to talk."

"About what? How you're selling those bottling permits or the bottling permits *and* the winery? About your firing me?" Anger seeped into her fingers, wanting to grab on to something and shake. She gripped his arm.

"I told you we weren't selling." But unlike earlier in the day, his voice lacked conviction.

She gripped his arm harder, as if she could squeeze the truth out of him. "Then why have I gotten so many messages from other winemakers and my dad asking about the permits being on the market?" Her conscience fought with her anger. Anger won. She let go of his arm, thrusting it away. "Everyone's asking me if I need a job." The only way this could be worse was if her name was linked romantically to Slade's.

His expression darkened. "I can explain.

It's not what you think." But his eyes belied that statement.

Nana opened the front door. "You should be ashamed, practically leaving my granddaughter at the altar."

"Nana, I'm not interested in marrying him. Please close the door," Christine said.

"Marriage?" Slade reached for his burgundy tie, but her hand beat his there.

She stroked down the length, only to fist the ends in her hand and tug gently, not hard enough he'd choke, but hard enough to capture his attention. "We don't need to go to dinner. Explain why you won't sell. Now."

"Yes, I'd like to hear this, too," Nana said.

"This isn't about marriage. Close the door, Nana."

"But—"

"Close the door!" Granted, Christine was already one wineglass into her two-glass limit, but she'd been bombarded with too many text messages and emails from her Napa network of friends to have it completely together.

Nana closed the door but immediately went to stand at the window, a stubborn tilt to her delicate chin.

Christine knew she looked like the jilted lover, standing on the porch in a short denim skirt and fuchsia blouse, holding on to Slade's tie as if she owned him. But a girl had her limits.

Slade looked from Christine to Agnes and back. "I think I owe you a dinner."

Christine started shaking her head and couldn't seem to stop. It was the momentum of anger.

"Yes." He put an arm over her shoulder and guided her back to the truck. He didn't make her release her hold on his tie, not until he'd opened the truck door and she was about to step in. He covered her hand with his.

"Sorry," she mumbled, releasing his tie and buckling herself in, waiting to continue their conversation until Slade had done the same. His poor tie looked as if it had been stuffed into a gym bag. "Thirty minutes from now the entire town will think you're trying to dump me."

"Why would they think that?" He started the truck and pulled away from the curb.

"Because my grandmother—" Christine had to ungrit her teeth to continue "—bragged to everyone that I'd landed myself a millionaire."

"Ah, I think I know where that rumor started. At Phil's."

Christine narrowed her eyes as they drove past the barbershop. But Phil had gone home.

Slade cleared his throat. "It was…ah…the girls who planted the seed."

"What?" Christine squeaked.

"You left and they asked about you and said I should… That we should… That I…"

"You don't have to finish. I know how a girl's brain works." *First comes love, then comes marriage…*

Shoot.

"And then Phil started asking questions." Slade tried to smile. "He approves, by the way."

"I'm not amused."

Slade managed to look a tad hurt. How did this man manage to go through life keeping all his wounds hidden from others? She could read him as easily as she could a grapevine.

"After you came to the barbershop I got a phone call from a party interested in the permit."

"You sold out." The rumors were true. Her stomach roiled. "Stop the truck." She'd walk home.

"It's not like that. The partnership isn't selling."

"How much did they offer?"

"That's not relevant."

"How much?"

"I'd rather not say."

She reached for his tie, carefully, since he was driving. "How. Much?"

The figure he quoted had her dropping his tie and slumping against her door. "I am fired."

"Don't say that. The partnership will stick to its agreement."

But Christine knew better. She knew about balance sheets and profit and loss. A complete, newly constructed, top-of-the-line winery with this permit would be worth more than Slade and his partners paid for it and what they'd invested so far. Many times more.

"I want you to know that even though we haven't accepted any offers, I am going to recommend they sell at some point." Slade cast a quick glance in her direction, his face pinched as tight as a grape left on the vine too long. "I'm 99 percent sure they won't sell no matter what I recommend."

"I don't understand. Were you lying to me earlier at Phil's?"

"No. But you were right. We got an offer. It wasn't good enough to accept. But when an offer comes in we can't refuse and my partners don't sell, I'll have them buy me out. I won't compromise on my beliefs." His voice was dark and determined, as if he knew he was betraying the town but was convinced he had to do it. "I'll have made two fortunes in less than twelve months. I'll be free of Harmony Valley forever."

He's leaving?

She understood not wanting to compromise your beliefs. She hadn't realized making money was that important to him. She hadn't expected him to have values tied to big profits. She suspected his beliefs had to do with the scar around his neck and what happened the day his father died. Betrayal tangled with sympathy. There was no clear winner. Not her, not Slade, and certainly not the town.

Harmony Valley had seemed so idyllic. Other than Slade's ties, there was no posturing, no brand-name dropping, no battle to see who could buy the most expensive luxury vehicle.

If they did accept a buyout, Harmony Valley would change, and not in the way Slade and his partners were trying to change it. If only he knew what kind of people would move in to run the place, he'd see it wasn't best for his small town. He'd take that into account with his profit-and-loss columns.

"Take me to Tilda's," she said. It was an

exclusive seafood restaurant in Healdsburg, the bar to which many influential winemakers flocked for gossip and networking opportunities.

They parked on the street north of Healdsburg's plaza. Tilda's bar was crowded, more so than the main restaurant. Slade and his tie approached the maître d'. Christine marched past, elbowing her way through the crush of regulars.

"Back on the streets so soon, Christine?" A woman's voice, familiar, condescending.

Christine looked up at Cami Ippolito, her former boss and supposed best friend. She almost reached between her shoulder blades to check for the knife that Cami had left in her back. "What are you doing in Sonoma?"

"I'm interviewing winemakers." Cami in turn looked down on Christine's jean skirt, towering above her in trendy five-inch wedges. "That is, unless you want your job back. There's still time to reblend."

With effort, Christine kept her mouth closed, but her hands fisted. She felt Slade come up behind her, saw the flash of burgundy tie in her peripheral vision, watched as Cami's eyes connected with Slade's beautiful untrustworthy green ones.

"Although I'm beginning to see your job's

appeal. Is this one of your bosses?" Cami's smile was lipstick smooth, designed to rile women and entice men. She introduced herself to Slade.

Other winemakers looked with interest and recognition at Christine, making assumptions about who Slade was. Several nudged their buddies and inched closer. The crowd flowed around them as they jockeyed for position.

She would not feel sorry for Slade and what was about to happen—a winemaker's version of the Spanish Inquisition. They'd pry and prod and try to judge if Slade was an also-ran, a threat, or someone they should suck up to.

Let him see what he was bringing to Harmony Valley. Let him see.

Christine squeezed in at the end of the bar, composing her letter of resignation in her head, leaving Slade to deal with the swarm of sharks circling him.

Not that he was in any danger. Slade was a shark himself.

CHAPTER FOURTEEN

"WHAT CREATED YOUR interest in wine?"

"What style of winemaking do you favor for your reds—the French or the Californian?"

"How long can you hold out before you accept an offer on those permits or the winery itself?"

Each question asked with a smile as false as one of Evy's. Each question backloaded with subtle messages—*What, you think winemaking is easy? Yeah, you don't know a thing. Really, you think you can't be bought?*

Familiar frustration built as dark as a thundercloud on a stormy night. The winemakers swarming him thought he wasn't good enough—not to leap into making wine, not without years of experience and a pedigree. Those last few years, his father hadn't thought he could succeed at anything, either, including life.

Slade wanted to prove the crowd wrong. He could do this. He could make so much money that these jealous types would cluster around him for an entirely different reason.

But that would require him to turn down offers for the permits or the winery itself. It would require him to recommend to his partners they stay the course and make wine. It wouldn't free him from his past. From the house. From his scar.

Christine sat at the end of the bar, halfway through a glass of white wine. He imagined her slender arm reaching through the crowd, reaching for his tie, leading him away, as if he was hers.

She remained where she was.

Cami leaned in close, smelling of alcohol and musky perfume. "She'll leave you. At the first sign of trouble. It's what the Alexanders do. She's probably planning to leave you right now."

Something sizzled in his veins, hot and desperate.

He'd told Christine the partnership wasn't selling. It was practically a guarantee of employment. She'd be a fool to leave.

Her chin thrust out resolutely as she drank her wine, as if she was planning when she'd tell him, how she'd tell him.

He tugged at his collar.

Their eyes met across the crowded bar. The

buzz of conversation dulled, faded, receded, until it was just the two of them acknowledging they had no future.

She backed down first, her gaze dropping to the bottom of her wineglass.

Slade pushed through the crowd to reach her. He tossed a fifty on the bar and dragged her out of there and to his truck.

"Satisfied?" he said as he gripped the wheel, anger coursing through him. He felt ready to snap. "You knew those winemakers would be there. Did my performance disappoint?"

She didn't say anything, just plucked at the hem of her skirt as if she was unsure of her position in the truck, at their winery, in his life.

She was, he realized. For all her bravado and organized lists and invasion of his personal space, she was worried about her future.

"You risked a lot coming to work for us. Your livelihood. Your reputation." Maybe even her heart.

Like that's possible.

She was kindhearted. That didn't mean she could ever love him.

He started the truck, pulling out into traffic.

She kept looking out the window.

There was something else wrong. But what?

A snatch of conversation with her former employer returned. "What did Cami mean when she mentioned taking you back and re-blending?"

Nothing but road noise answered him.

He'd had enough silence to last him a life-time. "It's crap, isn't it? Your next release for Cami. Is that what you're worried about?"

Slowly, as if she was older than Old Man Takata, she turned to face him. "You saw what they're like. They enjoy the good life, like it's owed to them. But underneath there's a fear, and fear drives them to make bad choices."

Slade had a sinking suspicion that he wasn't going to like what she was about to say.

"Cami and Ippolito Cellars are a victim of their own success." She slid out of her shoes and tucked her feet beneath her, angling side-ways so her body faced his as he drove. "It happens sometimes. The stars align and a winery achieves unplanned-for success. You can't keep up with the demand. You sell out, and you wait patiently for the next vintage to mature."

"Cami doesn't strike me as a patient woman."

Christine finger combed a lock of blond hair along her neck. "No. She bypassed college to learn about wine making from her grandfather. She's got too much to prove to her father, not to mention the wine world. That'll drain your patience pretty quickly."

"And so…" He accelerated onto the freeway.

"And so, she pressured me for a short-term solution and I found one." Her fingers plucked at the skirt hem again. "Ippolito Cellars had been known for varietals, primarily Cabernet Sauvignon and Chardonnay. But blends are popular and you can make them with excess wine you or someone else has. We decided to make a red-wine blend, since I'd had some success with it at another winery. I blended several samples from bulk wine producers until I hit on a taste I liked. Then I arranged to buy three wine types we needed—Petite Sirah, Carignane, and Zinfandel. To be delivered when each type was properly aged three months later. At that time, they'd send new samples, I'd taste them, hopefully approve, and off we'd go to blending."

"Very smart." So like Christine.

"In theory. In the interim, I made the mistake of going on vacation with my family." She sighed, the weary sigh of the defeated.

"While I was gone, Cami ordered the wine delivered ten weeks early and started blending it herself. I got back and tasted her blend. It was undrinkable. Instead of mixing small batches, she mixed nearly two hundred thousand gallons of wine. It's sitting in tanks, ready for some poor soul to try to improve it so she can bottle it."

"Can it be fixed? Reblended, I think she said."

Christine shook her head. "Making a wine blend is like making spaghetti sauce. Once you have a strong negative note, it's nearly impossible to blend it out. Cami wasn't experienced enough to blend test batches in small quantities. She always thought I was too cautious, so she leaped right in."

"What a costly mistake."

"She's doing the damage-control dance. She hired someone to design a cute label. She'll bottle it and ship it out to some discount stores. She'll be lucky to break even and luckier still if some review sites don't associate her with the wine." She clenched her hands in her lap. "Or me."

All the arguments they'd had about committing to making too much wine before

Christine knew and approved of quality suddenly made sense.

Beside him, Christine gave another heavy sigh.

Of the two, she was normally the touchy-feely one. He surprised himself by reaching over and putting his hand over hers. "You know what you need?"

"To move to another country? I hear they're looking for winemakers in Chile." She managed a weak smile.

He shook his head. "French fries."

"WHY IS MAKING money so important to you?" Christine asked, after she'd demolished her small bag of fries and washed it down with a Diet Coke. "You already have a fat wallet."

"I told you that night we went bowling."

"I thought we were beyond lies." She gazed out the window.

He shouldn't have been surprised at how well she knew him. He'd already risked her respect by baring his scar. He wasn't going to tell her the grim details. Besides, she was most likely giving notice in the morning. No matter what he said, she didn't believe the partnership wouldn't sell.

They drove into Harmony Valley in silence. Slade stopped on Main Street in front of the old grocery store. "I need to text Flynn in case the girls are too much for him." Not that the town was large enough that it was an inconvenience to go back and get them, but a left here would put him quickly at Flynn's.

Are the girls all right?

Almost immediately a reply: All 3 fell asleep early watching a movie. No camping tonight.

Slade put the truck back in gear.

Straight ahead was the town square. Two turns right and he'd be at Agnes's house. A right, a left, and a right, and he'd be at the Death and Divorce House.

He wouldn't take Christine there. If he did, he'd tell her everything. Then she'd understand why he had to recommend selling. And why he was going to recommend she quit to find another job.

Life would be so much easier if she quit.

One less person to let down. He'd already let down too many.

Right. Left. Right.

Christine sat up straight and turned to him as he parked.

"You wanted to know about this." He gestured to his necktie. "Come inside."

He didn't wait to see if she'd follow. He didn't stop inside the front door, merely dropped his keys on the hall table as he passed, heading up the stairs. He didn't turn on any lights, stopping only when he reached the second-floor landing in front of the master-bedroom door.

She followed, climbing the stairs to the top with a steady tread.

"My father changed after my mother's fight with cancer." His voice sounded distant, as if the person speaking wasn't him, was far away and detached. "He became more cynical. Gone was the open, optimistic man who'd raised me, who was like my best friend. I thought he'd get over her death. But she'd barely passed when he was called in to help rescue his friends and coworkers at the mill fire." Slade swiped a hand down his tie. "He used to tell me I could do anything, be anything, if only I worked at it hard enough. But the loss of my mother and the deaths at the grain mill were too much for him. His glass became less than half-empty. It didn't matter that I earned a partial scholarship to Harvard. His view of my chances at a happy life turned grim."

Christine slipped her hand into his.

"He'd look at Evy and predict she'd leave me. He'd look at the twins and predict..." Slade swallowed, not wanting to recall the dire things he'd predicted. "He'd look at me and tell me not to reach for a goal or dream big, so I wouldn't be disappointed. Success, for me, became mandatory, the route to proving to my dad that life was worth living. I got a job on Wall Street. I bought an apartment in Manhattan. And still he foresaw the worst.

"Then the stock market collapsed, plunging me to ruin, just as my father had predicted. I lost my job, my salary, my savings, and my dad's retirement." He never should have talked his father into letting him manage his retirement, but he'd wanted to prove just how wrong his father was.

"We came here to tell Dad in person Thanksgiving weekend. I told Evy if I couldn't find a job soon, we might have to move back, at least until we got on our feet again. Evy told me she wasn't moving from New York. She said she'd been unhappy for a long time and wanted a divorce." Toddler twins and a cheating wife. His father had been right about Evy, at least.

"She dropped me off here, at the house, and drove back to Santa Rosa to spend the day shopping with money we didn't have." His hand drifted to his tie. "Talk about denial."

Christine gave the hand she held a small squeeze. It was an I-know-this-is-hard-but-keep-going bit of encouragement.

"Dad knew why I'd come. He'd seen the

news. And it was the day he'd always told me would arrive—*my failure.*" Slade drew a heavy breath. "But he didn't rub it in. He was different. Happy, almost. I apologized, expecting him to be heartbroken or upset. Instead, he talked about a trip we took to Yellowstone when I was a kid. He talked about how proud he was of me. He was like my dad again and I was relieved." Slade gasped, *"Relieved."*

He should have seen the signs. He should have known that no one could flip their attitude around like that.

"Dad suggested I take a walk and get some fresh air. I went down to the river park. I watched the river go by." He sniffed, fighting back the tears. "I actually felt better. Lucky. My life was crap, but I had my dad back." He tried to laugh, but laughter stuck in his throat. "Storm clouds were rolling in by then. It was one of those afternoons when the clouds got so thick it seemed like the sun had set."

Christine stroked his arm.

"He didn't answer when I got home. His door, this door, was pulled closed, but not latched. I pushed it open." Slade put his hand flat on the locked door. "He'd used a belt. On the closet rod." Slade's fingernails dug into the wood. "I can blur those minutes and forget the horror and whatever else the room looked like. But not his face." The eyes that stared calmly toward the door, as if he was finally at peace. "I'd lost everything then. My parents, my livelihood, my family." He dragged in air. "And then I saw the note."

Christine slipped an arm around his waist, closed the loop with her other arm, clasping her hands over his hip. He wanted to stay cocooned in her arms forever.

"He wrote, 'It's not worth waiting. Come with me.'" Slade tried to swallow. He couldn't manage, so he continued hoarsely, "In that moment, when I saw no hope, no point in going on, it was as if I'd been programmed to…end it. I saw the other belt at my father's feet."

Slade sank to the floor, taking Christine with him. "I started the process in a numb, dark fog, with silence roaring in my ears. Not knowing, not thinking. But then the sun broke through the clouds and I saw my mother's face. In a picture on the bureau. I realized I didn't want to die. Nothing was as hopeless as my dad made it seem."

Too late, his mind had crooned. It was the last thing he remembered before being saved by Evy, who hadn't been able to stop screaming.

He'd said enough to satisfy her curiosity. More and she'd know. She'd know and she'd leave.

"I was fortunate. I stared beyond the brink of death, but it left its mark on me." He kicked his legs out in front of him, letting the anger build, as it often did when he thought about the extremes his father had gone to, how fragile his own mental state had been. He'd never consider doing such a thing today. He'd seek professional help or a good listener, like Christine. "My dad is the reason I refuse to fail. He's the reason I'm a millionaire. Every dollar I make, every goal I achieve proves to him that life is worth living." That Slade could achieve his dreams. If only his father hadn't stopped believing. "That's why I have to sell the permit when the best bid comes in, to silence my father's voice forever."

He'd told her. He'd confessed. He waited to see if history would repeat itself, if Christine would leave. He had to brace himself for it, for the pain and the crumpling loss. They sat silently. He couldn't see her face in the shadows. Did she look upon him in disgust? In horror? With pity?

Christine got to her knees. But instead of leaving, she sat in his lap. Her hands loosened his tie, slid the silky fabric free. She set his tie aside and went to work on his buttons, spreading the cotton across his collarbones.

She smelled of vanilla and redemption. False redemption, since he hadn't told her the entire story. He gripped her wrists and held her hands still. "Do you think he forgave me?"

"For not going through with killing yourself? I'm certain he did." She curled her hands up around his neck and slid her palms down to rest within his shirt at the base of his neck. She traced his scar with one finger. "The question is…do you forgive yourself? After all, you didn't go through with it."

Her caring touch made him feel as though he'd been redeemed. But he hadn't earned it.

His hands traveled up her arms, down her shoulders, to rest on her hips. "I'll never forgive myself. It wasn't that I wanted to die. It was just that everything I'd taken for granted and worked so hard for were taken away. It was a moment of weakness. I learned the hard way that when things fall apart, you have to pick up the pieces and start over, not give up."

Tell her.

She leaned in and replaced her finger with her lips.

It was heaven.

It was madness.

Guilt made him stop. "I'm telling you this

so you know, so you realize the darkness I've faced. You don't have to pretend. I'm no one's Prince Charming. You can go."

"I was kissing your neck a second ago. Don't tell me you thought that was a pity kiss. Seriously, I was going to work on up to your lips, but now…" She removed herself from his lap and stood. "Now I'm just going to say that no one deserves to go through what you did or to be manipulated by a loved one." Her voice trembled. "Other than stopping me from kissing you, you seem pretty well balanced. Good night."

Slade listened to her go downstairs. The house creaked and groaned around him as if protesting Christine's leaving. Slade didn't protest.

It wasn't what he wanted, but it was how it should be.

Christine walking out of his life.

EACH STEP THAT took Christine away from Slade seemed like a mistake. He needed her. And somewhere deep inside, Christine needed him, too.

He took her seriously, even though she wore torn T-shirts and ratty shorts. He respected her opinion, even when he challenged her. His touch made her feel as if she could do anything she set her mind to.

She stumbled on the front steps.

I love him.

How could that be? They'd only known each other a few weeks.

She tested the idea again, her feet a slow cadence on the sidewalk. *I.* Step. *Love.* Step. *Slade.*

Of course, it was true. She loved how he laughed with her. She loved how he watched out for her and the girls. She loved the flash of insecurity when he touched his tie or tried to ignore how the girls ignored him. It made her want to hug him fiercely, tell him not to worry, and kiss his insecurities away.

Colossally bad timing.

He was her boss. This was her one clear shot at solidifying the name she'd been building for herself in the industry. Dating him would tinge her reputation with favoritism, dilute what she was trying to do here, make people judge her wine on gossip rather than quality alone.

He can't move on.

After all his talk about revitalizing the town, after all those days she'd seen or heard of Slade repairing and rebuilding houses and businesses, he still couldn't stop trying to medicate his feelings by making money. And there was his shame. The shame that kept him buttoned up and pushed everyone who would love him away. How could she possibly combat that?

"You're a good woman, going in that house. I've waited years for someone to realize he's a decent man."

The lone voice came from the porch at the corner house. A cigar glowed in the darkness. The aroma of cigar smoke lingered in the air.

Christine wasn't feeling like a good woman. She was a coward for letting Slade reject her.

Slade didn't think he deserved love, perhaps not even from his daughters. He kept himself buttoned up tight, both literally and figuratively. But he didn't seem to want understanding from her, at least not the understanding she'd wanted to give.

Christine went up the front walk until she could see part of the old man's face. "Weren't you at bowling the other night?"

"I was. My name's Hiro Takata."

Christine introduced herself and sat on his stoop, resting her chin in her hands to filter the strong cigar smoke. "You knew Slade's father?"

He nodded. "Daniel used to bowl with us, back before his wife died and the mill exploded. Kind of lost himself after that. Couldn't get him to bowl or come out for an evening smoke."

"Was that the first time he tried to kill himself?" Her question, a whisper, seemed to echo down the street.

"That I know of? Yep." He took a deep drag on the cigar and blew smoke toward the sky. "You planning on marrying that boy? He needs someone."

"He's… There's… It's not like that." What their relationship was, she didn't know. Just because she loved him didn't mean he felt the same depth of feeling or that there weren't still obstacles in their path. Loving Slade wouldn't be easy.

"I was put in a camp here in California during the Second World War. Saw a lot of hatred based on the shape of my eyes." Hiro's voice hollowed and hardened, until it was darker than the night. "Saw my mother shrivel up and die during four years of internment. Takes a lot out of a man to see death."

Christine reached out and gently squeezed his hand. It was no larger than hers, the skin a combination of smooth calluses and age-roughened wrinkles.

"I know how folks in town see me. I'm their mortician," he said. "They laugh about how I can look at a corpse and see dignity and beauty. They think it's morbid. But it's how I honor my mother. Of honoring the life someone lived, no matter how they died. Dwelling on the end—on how they died—means dwelling on guilt and sadness."

"Christine?" It was Slade, standing on the sidewalk, looking lost and alone. He'd buttoned up his shirt and put his tie back on.

"Good night, Hiro." She released his hand and stood.

"Ha, no one your age calls me that. To them, I'm Old Man Takata." He chuckled.

"Good night, Old Man Takata." She waved, sucking in fresh air.

"I heard voices." Slade said, falling into step with her. "Takata can talk your ear off if you let him."

"I enjoyed talking to him. He seems lonely." And he seemed to have some good insight about Slade.

Slade smoothed his tie. "I thought you'd be home by now."

"What? Crying into my pillow?" The jagged hurt that he'd let her leave resurfaced, only to be replaced by the gentler idea of loving him. "Were you coming to check up on me?"

"Yes." He slung his arm over her shoulder,

warm and tempting, tempting her to let things be, to ask no questions. "Don't get any ideas. I'm just walking *my friend* home."

"Right, because you don't deserve to be happy ever again." Before speaking with Slade's neighbor, she would've let the edge cut through her tone. Now the words were softened with love and understanding. She knew he wasn't the same man he'd been the day his father died. She knew he'd never give up on life again. But he'd given up on love.

"You're going to serve a life sentence living in that house alone," she said. "Wearing your ties and keeping everyone at arm's length. Someday the kids in this town are going to call you Old Man Jennings. You won't come out except at night when no one can see you and you'll yell out the window at anyone playing in your yard."

"I think you're confusing me with Takata. I don't plan on staying in Harmony Valley."

"Oh, no, I've got you pegged." She snuggled closer beneath his arm. "Faith and Grace will bring home the men they'll marry and you'll scare the crap out of them."

"You're assuming I'm letting them get married. I'm not going to let them date until they're thirty, if then."

"You wish." She stroked his tie. "Why are you making this so difficult?"

He sighed. "I could say the same for you. You told me in the park that we could handle being friends."

"I'm not the one who came out after I left."

They turned the corner onto Nana's street, the only sounds Christine's sandals and his hard-soled shoes on the sidewalk.

"Maybe I didn't like how you left."

They reached Nana's driveway.

"You, my friend—" she gently tugged his tie, as if that was the only thing keeping her from blurting out her true feelings and ruining everything "—don't know what you want."

"And you do?"

"I know I want a strong man by my side, someone I can come home to at night when my hands are stained purple from handling grapes all day, someone who won't mind those purple hands all over his body." She smoothed his tie. "I know I want to have kids and be a soccer mom, even though soccer season is during grape harvest. And I dream of one day owning my own vineyard with my own wine label. I'm a bit behind schedule, but I plan to have a long career, with at least one vintage of Harmony Valley Vineyards wines to my credit."

She hadn't realized until that moment that she wasn't going to give up on the winery. Or him.

He didn't say a word.

"I'll see you in the morning." Christine slipped from beneath his arm.

"Wait." He captured her hand.

She looked at their joined hands—his large and strong, hers seemingly delicate. But she was stronger than she looked. She could set aside blossoming love and wait for him to heal completely. "I've already put myself out there tonight. I'm not going to ask you for a good-night kiss and strike out completely. I like you." *I love you.* "But you hold my future in your hands." In so many ways.

When he would have spoken again, she cut him off. "I think there's something between us and I'd like to give it a chance, but you have to meet me halfway."

"What if I'm not ready?" His voice lacked the steady quality she'd become used to.

"Nobody with big career goals and dreams is ever ready. There's always a condition attached or another column to fill." She patted his stubbled cheek. "Good night."

She half expected him to pull her close, as

he'd done the other night, regardless of her protests. If he'd heard what Old Man Takata said perhaps something had sunk in, perhaps he'd realize that he needed to open up in order to move on.

But he didn't reach for her. He didn't press his body against hers. He didn't cover her lips with his.

Christine went inside, disappointed.

But there was also hope. Hope because she loved him and she'd seen something in his eyes that led her to believe that he felt something for her, too.

CHAPTER FIFTEEN

"DID YOU SEE that another Hollywood movie raised millions of dollars for production through crowdsourcing?" Ryan said, making himself a cup of green tea in the farmhouse kitchen.

"Crowdsourcing? That's where anyone can donate money to finance something? Don't they get a T-shirt for their ten-dollar investment?" Christine was on her second cup of coffee, trying to compensate for not sleeping well last night. She planned to use the dose of caffeine to tell Ryan this gig of theirs was in jeopardy.

Slade was wrong. He didn't need to prove to the ghost of his father that life was worth living by making tons of money. He needed to take off his tie and start trusting people again. His daughters. The town. Her.

But Slade was right, too. She knew the experience had made him strong, made him who he was today—strong enough to wear a tie in a far-flung valley during a hundred-degree hot spell. She couldn't overcome his beliefs about his scar and about money. He'd have to do that on his own.

Was she strong enough for a relationship with him?

"Each crowdsourcing project is different," Ryan was saying. "Some people are cheap, and they get a T-shirt. Some people get really excited and put up the big bucks. In return, they get to be an extra or go to the movie premiere." Ryan was only seven years younger than Christine, but sometimes she felt really old. Who could keep up with new developments like crowdsourcing?

"Ryan, what's your point?" This didn't sound like watercooler talk. And she had to check email before supervising the truck scale delivery and installation.

Ryan leaned against the counter, watching her add milk to her mug. "We still haven't found anyone to help us with the harvest, right?"

"Don't remind me." The image of grapes rotting on the vines kept her awake at night almost as much as her worry about her career and her feelings for Slade. It was a wonder she slept at all lately.

"But things like co-ops and crowdsourcing pool resources. We could, like, have the people of Harmony Valley help with the harvest and give them something—maybe a case of wine and a ticket to the vintage release party. Forty acres isn't huge. We can do it with ten or twenty people in a day or two."

"That's a great idea." Christine stared at the swirl of milk in her coffee. her mind turning along with it. "Except for one thing."

"What?" Ryan brushed his thick brown hair out of his eyes.

"Harvest is physically demanding. Everyone who lives here—and doesn't own or work for the winery—is old. Really old."

"I kind of worried about that." But clearly, he had hoped.

"We'll come up with something." Christine patted his arm, but she wasn't completely convinced they would.

Worse, if the partners sold the winery and she and Ryan were let go, they wouldn't need a solution. The grapes would rot on the vine, as they had for years.

"Listen, Ryan, I don't want to worry you, but you need to know…"

"GIRLS, EVERYONE'S DOWN at the sheriff's office ready to paint. We need to leave." Slade had on a shirt, pants, and tie he'd splattered paint on several months ago when they'd wielded brushes on a float for the Harmony Valley Spring Festival. He stood by the door and looked at his Rolex for the fifth time in thirty seconds, wondering what Christine was doing.

And chastising himself for wondering. And for not kissing her good-night the night before.

Footfalls heralded the twins.

Slade looked up. His jaw dropped and something that had been shut off inside his chest cracked open.

They weren't wearing matching outfits. They didn't have matching hairstyles. Even their shoes weren't alike. Faith wore jean shorts and a lavender T-shirt, with tennis shoes and sports socks, her jet-black hair in a high ponytail. Grace wore a hot-pink tank top over a blue cotton skirt with silver flats. Her hair was in a single low braid down her back. Both wore their gold baby bracelets.

"You two look beautiful." He'd finally broken through whatever barrier they'd erected, finally passed whatever test they'd given him. He couldn't stop grinning. "It's nice to see you express yourselves. You may be twins, but that doesn't mean you have to do or wear or like the same things."

"What do you think Mom will say?" Faith worried her lip.

"I'd hope she'd say what a great idea."

Grace looked at her sister. "See, I told you."

"Come on, everyone's already there." Slade shooed them out the door.

"Here's the town's next bridegroom," Flynn ribbed when Slade entered the sheriff's office.

"Dad, you're getting married?" Grace rushed in his path, looking up at him with bright green eyes that were so much more alive than the day she'd arrived in Harmony Valley. She hugged him.

Not to be outdone, Faith hugged him, as well. "Why didn't you tell us you asked Christine?"

Slade was so overjoyed at their first big display of affection toward him since they'd arrived that he almost couldn't deny it. Almost. "I didn't tell you because I didn't ask. Phil, the barber, told someone what you said yesterday about how I should consider marrying Christine, and by the time that tidbit made the rounds, it went from considering to actually asking."

"It's a good idea," Will said, not helping. "Christine's great."

"And she seems to like you," Flynn added,

winking at his nephew, who sat in the corner and mumbled, *"Girls."*

Nate was stirring paint, not saying a word.

"You don't want to get in on this?" Slade asked the sheriff.

"Nope. Whatever is or isn't going on isn't my concern."

"Finally." Slade picked up a drop cloth and covered one of the old metal desks behind the counter. "Someone who minds their own business."

His cell rang. Slade stepped outside to answer it. It was another representative of another company interested in buying their wine permits.

"We're not selling," Slade said before any figures could be mentioned. Best to avoid temptation.

Temptation happened anyway, higher than before.

He missed Christine's arms around him.

It took another few minutes for Slade to convince the man that they weren't accepting offers at this time.

The man told him he'd call back next week.

Slade returned to his friends and told them about the offer. "That was hard. The money covered the amount we've invested in the winery to date."

Will frowned. "I didn't believe you yester-day when you said we'd get more calls."

"This won't be the last one, either," Slade said as his phone rang again. "See?"

It went on like that all morning, until Slade dragged an office chair out to the sidewalk to take the calls. It was eerie how just a mention of what the last offer was caused the caller to say something like, *I'm authorized to up your last offer by 10 percent.*

Slade's hands started to sweat. What would his father say about him now?

Flynn came outside for some air and to stretch out his back. He stopped stretching when he looked at Slade. "The girls are happy now, but you're not."

"I'm not unhappy." And it was true. Faith and Grace gave him great joy. There was a peaceful rhythm to Harmony Valley. Some-thing always needed to be done, even if it wasn't the cut-throat, competitive pace he'd once thrived on.

Flynn took off his baseball cap, ran his fin-gers through his short hair, and resettled the cap on his head. "Dude, you've been unhappy for a long time. I thought the twins or maybe Christine would finally snap you out of your funk, but they haven't. You carry a weight on your shoulders. I don't know what it is, but if you need to, you know, like, talk about it—"

"No!" He refused to tell Flynn, or Will for that matter, how he'd tried to commit suicide.

Flynn shook his head. "We're your friends, man. You stood by me at my grandfather's deathbed. I think whatever is bothering you would bother you a whole lot less if you talked about it."

He'd look like a jerk if he didn't acknowledge something was wrong. "I'll think about it," he mumbled.

Flynn began stretching his back again. "Can you explain once more why these wine permits are so valuable?"

"Because they don't give out many. The state and the county want to limit the amount of wine bottled here, as well as control and prohibit people from trucking in wine grown elsewhere, bottling it in Sonoma, and then calling it Sonoma wine when it really isn't."

"People do that?"

"They have. And wineries that produce, ferment, and bottle wine here don't want their wine devalued or to have a bad reputation. So the permits have limits. If someone wants to bottle more wine, they have to apply for more permits."

"We're not selling. Grandpa Ed wouldn't

be happy." Flynn shook his finger at Slade exactly as his Grandpa Ed used to do.

"Flynn, at some point, we have to look at this without emotion. At some point, we aren't going to be able to say no."

"Not me." Flynn seemed so sure. He had no idea what was coming. "I'll say no."

"And I'll have to reiterate. If you don't take my advice, I'm leaving." Alone.

"Wow." Christine hung up the phone. "I wasn't expecting that."

"What?" Ryan looked up from his desk, where he was searching for articles about the vineyard's history.

Working in the second-story office was no longer an exercise in sweat. Nana's curtains helped the air-conditioning do its job. It would have been conducive to productivity if not for the constant buzz of text messages. Several of her friends, and those she wasn't so friendly with, texted with news that their winery was bidding to buy Christine's permits or the winery itself.

Footsteps sounded on the stairs. Slade arrived, looking attractively unperfect in paint-splattered clothing. His black hair was mussed, as if he'd thrust his hands into it and forgotten to smooth it back down.

"Oh, good. You're here." Christine sounded happy to see him, and she was, especially in this cute, disheveled state. Even millionaires had an off day, it seemed.

But that phone call… "That was the bottling-line manufacturer. They can start the install at the end of the month. It'll take a few weeks to set it up." She looked expectantly at Slade.

Here was where he proved she could trust him as a boss or prove she didn't have to rein in her feelings of love. Or both.

"That's good news." The neutrality in his voice proved nothing. He didn't even sit down.

"If you're not selling, yes, good news. I told them I'd call back to confirm the dates. I figured that bought you a day or two to make a decision. To sell or not to sell," she said with false cheer. "That is the question."

Ryan's face looked green, as if the unpredictable roll of the situation was making him seasick.

"I don't need a day or two." Slade's neutrality morphed into annoyance. "The partnership isn't selling."

Christine looked to Ryan. "Why don't I believe him?"

Ryan, bless his heart, tried to shrug nonchalantly. A valiant effort considering he was probably worried about his rent, his car payment, and his student loans. "He looks believable, but everybody has their price, I suppose."

"Good point." Christine mustered up the courage to look her boss in the eye. "What's your price?"

"More than anyone has yet to offer." Slade crossed his arms over his chest.

"Ah, but that means you have a price." She doodled on her pad.

"Christine..."

She waited for Slade to speak, but saying her name had apparently drained him of speech. "Well, I hear a truck rumbling down the driveway. Duty calls." She stood.

"I'll go." Ryan leaped up and raced passed Slade down the stairs.

Christine sat back down slowly. "You intimidate him."

"A hazard of first jobs. The fear of disappointing the boss and being fired." He glanced about the room, as if suddenly uncomfortable being alone with her.

"A very real fear, as it turns out." She waited for him to meet her gaze, trying to stop the mantra her heart crooned: *Talk to me, reassure me, love me.*

Without looking at her, Slade sat in the folding chair on the other side of her desk.

He shifted, trying to get comfortable. "We need to order better chairs. Maybe even go by that warehouse store you like so much."

Be still, my foolish, foolish heart.

She started straightening her desk. "I like the implication that we'll still be in business next month. What were you painting this morning?"

He looked absently at his black-splattered tie, as if he'd forgotten the paint. "The sheriff's office. The girls are still there, painting the bars with Truman."

"Let's hope that's the only time they know what it's like to be in a jail cell."

"They wore different outfits today." He used his papa-bear smile, the one that made her melt. The one that made her forget he was her boss.

She thought about snowcapped mountains in Chile and unemployment checks. "That's huge. Good for the girls. And good for you, too."

"And they hugged me." He stared at his hands. "I never thought they'd hug me."

"Two milestones in one day." A ding sounded, notifying Christine that she had an email. She glanced at her laptop screen and couldn't look away. "Excuse me."

Slade waited.

"It's from the human-resources department at Lalopolle Winery. They say if their offer for the bottling permits goes through, they'd like me to come in and interview for a position." Her world threatened to capsize. She gripped the seat of her chair. "What do they know that I don't?"

Slade scowled. "The partnership isn't selling."

"Says the man with a price. The man who told me he'd make the recommendation to sell." Self-preservation and childhood dreams elbowed fledgling love for Slade aside. Her father was right. It was time to jump ship. She lifted her hands to the keyboard. "I need to schedule an interview."

"Don't."

She waited for him to say she'd be the one to make this venture a success for the partnership. She waited for him to say he couldn't wait to taste their first vintage. She waited for him to say he didn't want her to go, that he needed her, that he couldn't live without her.

Heck, she didn't need to hold out for a declaration of love or a ring. She'd settle for some small sign. A gentle smile, a hand on her cheek, a kiss that said he couldn't live without her. Anything that explained his objection to her interviewing elsewhere.

His eyes flickered, shuttered. "Forget what I said. You should accept the interview." He was always releasing her, even when she could tell he didn't want to.

She knew then that it would take an earthquakelike act of nature for him to meet her halfway. She needed to stop listening to her heart. She needed to listen to her father. She needed to abandon ship.

One more day, her heart whispered, as if that would make a difference. *One more day.*

CHAPTER SIXTEEN

WHEN DINNER WAS ready that night, Slade couldn't find the girls. They weren't downstairs. They weren't upstairs. They weren't in the front or back yards. The house was empty, as it would be empty when they returned to New York. As the winery would be empty when Christine went on that interview and got the job.

He used to embrace the emptiness. He and the house had an understanding. But not anymore. He dreaded the forthcoming emptiness.

He stepped out the front door. "Faith! Grace!"

"Dad!" Grace was on Takata's front porch with Faith and the old man himself. She ran across the grass to their driveway.

Predictably, Takata yelled at her, "Keep off the grass!"

Instead of being cowed, Grace's grin widened. "Can Old Man Takata come over for dinner?"

It didn't escape Slade how the girls used

the nickname every kid in Harmony Valley had grown up using.

"Please," Faith seconded, jumping up and down next to Takata.

The last thing Slade wanted in his house was the man who wanted him to open up his dad's bedroom door. Slade was about to make some excuse, when Grace gave a pretty little pout and said, "Please."

"Sure, bring him over." Slade went back inside to set another place at the table.

The twins brought the old man through the front door, even though it was a shorter distance from his porch to the back door and the kitchen. But that would have required they walk across his lawn.

"Spaghetti. How nice." Takata hooked his cane on Slade's chair and sat in it. He put an empty plastic container next to his plate. "In case there's leftovers."

"You're welcome to them." The twins didn't care for leftovers. Slade set the bread bowl on the table. "I hope the girls weren't bothering you."

"Youth isn't a bother, unless they stray off the path. Sidewalks are there for a reason." Takata heaped food on his plate as if he hadn't eaten for days. As skinny as he was, that could very well be.

"You never had kids of your own, did you?" If Takata did, he'd have known kids don't like to stay on the beaten path.

"I married my Nancy too late in life." He leaned toward the girls. "It's hard to believe, but when I was younger, being a mortician wasn't seen as cutting-edge as it is today. It was very hard to get a date. Although, girls, you should know that the only thing guaranteed in life is death. That's why staking your career on death is so lucrative."

Slade choked on his water.

"When you consider a husband, you should consider his earning potential, too."

The twins giggled.

Slade twirled his fork in his spaghetti.

"Your father would be quite the catch, if it wasn't for this house." Takata glanced around the room. "I haven't been here in years. Same shabby cabinets. Outdated linoleum. What woman wants that? Is it still the same upstairs?"

Slade's spaghetti slipped off his fork. He didn't often think about the sky-blue apples and pears imprinted on the white Formica tabletop. He tried not to think about anything in the house. If...*when*...he left this place, he'd be leaving behind the things his mother loved.

"We have new bedspreads upstairs," Grace offered.

Faith sucked a spaghetti noodle into her mouth, leaving a tomato trail on her cheek. "Do you want to see?"

"I'd like that."

"I'm not sure that's a good idea," Slade said.

Three pairs of eyes turned to him.

"The stairs are steep." A lame excuse, but the only one he had.

"Are you implying I'm too old to climb those stairs?" Takata speared a cherry tomato. "I'll have you know I ride an exercise bike every morning while watching the news."

"No, I'm just… There's not much to see." Slade tried to regain control. "Two bedrooms and a bathroom."

"Three," Grace said.

"Three bedrooms," Faith clarified in a mock-helpful voice, sliding a glance toward their guest.

Which made no sense, unless…

Slade stabbed his fork into his spaghetti and glared at the old man. "Have you been talking to them?"

"Of course we've been talking. Your girls are very polite. Why wouldn't they talk to me?" So innocently spoken. So artfully delivered. Takata should have had a career on the stage.

"I mean—" Slade gripped his fork until the flatware made an impression in his fist "—have you been telling them things they're too young to hear?"

"No. Only that their grandparents died upstairs." Takata bit into garlic bread that hadn't been burned and salvaged.

Slade frowned.

"It used to scare us," Grace said. "But he explained how the body is like a car and the soul is like the driver. And when the soul leaves, there's just a car left here. So we shouldn't be afraid of their bedroom, because both the car and the driver are gone."

"Did our grandpa really hang himself upstairs?" Faith asked. "You'd never do that, would you, Dad?"

"No." He'd prayed they'd never ask him that. He'd prayed they'd never wonder what kind of man he was to have tried or worry if he'd try again. "You had no right," he rasped. He tugged at the collar of his shirt.

"Perhaps." Takata's gaze landed on Slade's tie, attempting to find more weaknesses in his defenses. "But I'm old and I don't have time to dance around issues, especially ones left dangling for too long."

"Dad?" Grace touched his forearm.

"I'm fine." He resisted the urge to touch the silk at his throat. He drew a deep breath and bared his teeth in an attempt to smile. "I'm fine. But there won't be any tours after dinner, okay?"

The girls nodded, exchanging conspiratorial glances with their guest.

They'd tried to outmaneuver him, those three. And they seemed proud of it, despite the fact they'd accomplished nothing.

No door would be unlocked. No tour of the upstairs given.

Takata kept talking through dinner—how to pick a good car, how to choose a proper bed, how to stay married. Their meal was over, the food cleared away, leftover spaghetti and green beans stored in Takata's container. He talked on, shuffling his feet beneath the table, occasionally rocking side to side.

The girls drifted out to the living room.

"It must be time for a smoke," Slade said, by way of encouragement. Takata had been there for two hours.

For once, the old guy seemed uncomfortable. "I'm working on it."

Slade blinked.

"Sometimes my joints freeze up and I can't

move. If I work them a bit, I can get moving again."

"Does this happen often?"

"Don't you worry about me. You have enough on your mind."

"I didn't say I was worried about you. I asked how frequently it happens." Slade recalled how often he'd seen Takata sitting alone—on benches, at El Rosal, on his front porch.

"I have rheumatoid arthritis." For once, he sounded defeated. "It happens every day, several times a day. Joints freeze up, hurts like hell for thirty minutes or so."

Slade felt a corresponding cold inside. "Is that why you sit outside at night? Because you can't move?"

Takata swelled up like a threatened puffer fish. "Why is it that just because a man is old, people think he can't take care of himself?"

Slade reached for the patience he knew his mother would recommend in this moment. He reached and reached, but it was hard to grasp when the old man had butted into his life and was scowling at Slade—*at Slade*—as if he'd done something wrong. "We aren't on the same wavelength. I haven't made any judgments about you. I'm just asking about your condition."

"Well, I'll tell you, it hurts," he stated flat-out. "How long and how many times a day it hurts is none of your business."

If Slade had been the kind of person to argue with senior citizens, now would have been the time.

"But I appreciate your concern. And I'm not too proud to accept help, as long as you don't rub it in or tell me I need to go live in a home."

Right. Slade stood. "Can I help you up?"

Takata grumbled his agreement.

Slade came to one side of the old man's chair, but nothing with Takata was ever straightforward and simple.

"Now, once I'm up, I'll take my cane in my right hand, and if you could steady me on the left side…"

Together, they got him to standing.

"Ah, still stiff. Could you walk me to the door?" And when they reached the door, he asked, "Could you walk me down the stairs?"

And so it went. Slade walked him slowly home and into his house, wondering how he was going to watch out for the old man and simultaneously keep his distance, worrying over who'd watch out for Takata when Slade finally left town.

"When was the last time you had the win-

dows open in here?" Now Slade knew how
Christine had felt coming into his house. The
shutters in Takata's one-story ranch were
closed, presumably to keep out the hot sun.
But the windows were shut tight, as well. The
house smelled of old man, soiled laundry, and
rotten garbage.

"I don't open the windows. Too much trouble."

And that explained why Takata was always
in cargo shorts and a tank top.

Slade and his partners had never come to
Takata's house to fix anything. The old man
had never asked. How long had it been since
someone had checked on him? Or helped him
with simple everyday chores? "I'm going to
open some windows."

"No." He scowled. "I'll just have to close
them again."

Slade hesitated only a moment before opening up the two front windows. Then he went
to the back of the house. The kitchen was a
mess. Dirty dishes everywhere. The stench
from the trash can nearly made him gag.

"Dad?" Grace stood behind him, holding
a hand over her nose. "What's that smell?"

"Get your sister. We need to clean house."

"Now?"

"Now."

THE TROOPS RALLIED at Old Man Takata's house the next morning—Slade, the twins, Truman, Flynn, Becca, Will, and Nate. There were squirrels in his attic, a rusted sink in the master bathroom, ants marching through his kitchen. And everywhere, dirty clothes and discarded trash.

Apparently, the only thing the elderly man took care of was his front lawn.

Takata complained the entire time. "I don't need any help. I can live alone just fine. Next thing you know, you'll be wanting to put me in a home." It became an easy refrain.

They listened, nodding until he was through, and then reassured the old man that they were only helping him get up to speed.

Becca, Flynn's wife, had the patience of a saint. She had Agnes and Mayor Larry drop by and explain that a little help was required from now on to keep him safe and living at home as long as he was capable.

"I'll add him to my client list." Becca dusted the mantel.

"I'll pay your fee, Becca," Slade offered, remembering she had debts she wouldn't let her husband pay. "Just don't tell Takata." Becca thanked him.

"How long have you gone without lights up here?" Flynn changed the burned-out light bulbs in the ceiling fixture while Slade steadied the ladder.

"You should all be next door opening up that bedroom on the second floor," Takata said instead of answering.

Flynn glanced down at Slade. "What do you think we'll find over there?"

"Cobwebs and old memories that need airing out," Takata replied.

Slade said nothing.

But later, as they were loading tools in Flynn's truck in the afternoon heat, his friend wouldn't let it go. "Old Man Takata's right. You need to air out that house and open the bedroom door."

Slade tugged at the knot in his tie. "Opening that door isn't going to do anything."

"Keeping it closed is holding you back, man. I can feel it."

Slade shrugged. "And now you're a therapist?"

"I'm observant and I'm your friend." Flynn stared him down. "You're afraid."

Exactly.

"At least let me look." Flynn made for Slade's front door. "I'll tell you if the boogeyman is still bedding down in there."

"No." Slade caught his arm.

"Dude." Flynn frowned at Slade's hand

until he released him. "It's just a room. You can sell the house and never look in there again. But you're letting it have some kind of power over you."

"The room doesn't have power. The memories do." And just like that, he felt the tightness around his neck.

"How bad can it be if I'm standing next to you?"

Slade tried to laugh.

When that didn't work, he let Flynn lead him into the house.

THE ROOM DIDN'T want to be disturbed.

The lock turned with a groan. Squealing hinges complained. Cobwebs stretched and broke as the door swung away from the frame.

The shades were up, the windows layered in a film of dirt. The bed was made, its blue-and-yellow star quilt covered in dust. The dust on the hardwood floors was undisturbed except for what looked like small trails made by adventuresome beetles. The bureau stood resolute, supporting pictures of Slade growing up, of his father as a boy, of his mother on her wedding day.

Flynn stepped into the room, looked around, and walked over to the closet, leaving a trail of footprints in the dust.

Slade stayed in the doorway, looking anywhere but the closet.

"His clothes are still all here."

"I closed this up the day he died." The room smelled like his father had been shut in a box for too long—Old Spice, sweat, and cigar smoke. Funny how he'd never associated the aroma of cigar smoke with his father before.

"Come inside."

Slade couldn't. He stroked his tie, staring out one of the windows. "Takata's got a few shingles missing."

"And not just on his roof." Flynn tapped his temple as he crossed into Slade's line of vision. He struggled to open a window.

"Don't," Slade said, taking a step backward. "Leave it alone."

"But—"

"I can't." Slade spun around and went downstairs.

He started walking and didn't stop for a long, long time.

CHAPTER SEVENTEEN

CHRISTINE CAME OUTSIDE to meet Slade on the front porch of the farmhouse. The heat shimmered off the gravel drive.

"Flynn called," she said.

Slade moved slowly up the porch steps and into her arms. He held on to her as if she was the best thing he'd seen in a long time.

Here was her proof. Her reason to be strong. Her reason to turn down that job interview.

She ran her fingers through his perfectly styled hair, murmuring soothing words. It felt so right to hold him. She could have done so all day, if not for the late-afternoon sun. "Come inside."

He hesitated.

She ran a hand down his mud-brown checked tie and gave a gentle tug, with an equally gentle smile. And then she led him inside to the blessed relief of the air conditioner, settled him in a chair, and sat next to him. "You were very brave this morning."

"I couldn't look at the closet." He couldn't seem to look anywhere now. His gaze drifted to a view of the river.

"It's a start."

"Flynn made me do it."

"I'm sure that's not true. You don't do anything you don't want to."

"I kissed you," he said raggedly.

"You must have wanted to do that." Her cheeks heated. "I wasn't the one who initiated that first kiss."

Slade's eyes turned dark, blustery green. "I didn't want to kiss you. You said—"

"Forget I thought we could get it out of our systems." It had worked with Johnny Harding when she was in the seventh grade. "Can we get back to the reason you're walking the valley when it's one hundred degrees outside?"

He nodded, slowly, deliberately, as if gathering up his control. "You're right. I could have stopped Flynn. I think I was…curious. Flynn went in and walked around. I couldn't. It was as if my father was there and telling me to stay out."

Would he have done that eight years ago?

She squeezed his hand.

"And the smell…I'd forgotten what he smelled like, but once we opened the door…"

His voice trailed off and he stared out a window.

"Flynn said all his clothes were there. That's all it is. Clothes."

His eyes. So haunted. "I'm a horrible father. My kids are living across the hall from... from..."

"Slade." She put her palm against his cheek, feeling the beginnings of stubble. "My grandmother sleeps in the same bed where my grandfather passed away. She loved him. And if you ask her, she'll tell you he wasn't perfect. But she loved him." Christine lowered her fingers, sliding them beneath his collar, beneath his tie. The backs of her fingers brushed the edges of his scar. "Your father had his flaws, and demons he couldn't deal with. But he loved you, or he wouldn't have wanted to go alone."

Slade drew her close, tucking her face into the crook of his neck. "In my head, I know I shouldn't blame myself. But in my heart..."

His heart had carried too much guilt for too long. "You can't change the past. You can only look to the future." Christine sat up, needing him to listen. "You have two bright, wonderful girls who need a dad in their life more than four weeks a year. They need someone who's going to be there for them when they make mistakes. Someone who knows what it's like to pick themselves up when things look irreparable."

"You think I should tell them what I tried to do?" He looked horrified.

"Yes."

"I've never even told Will or Flynn."

Christine scrunched up her nose. "But you lived with them. You mean they never saw your—"

"I wore a shirt and tie all the time."

"I guess I shouldn't be surprised." She stroked the brown silk. "Isn't it time to let these go?"

He put a hand over hers, holding it motionless. "No."

"At least think about it."

He stared out the window for far too long. And then he sighed. "Thank you. I've interrupted your work." His tender touch contradicted his dismissal.

"Don't thank me." Christine didn't want his thanks. She wanted his love. She should have expected the boundaries to return. She stood and walked toward the stairs to the office. Disappointment dragged her feet.

"Christine?"

She turned back to him.

"I lied." His mouth worked, as if trying to

stop him from saying anything else. Before she could ask what he lied about, he blurted, "I've wanted to kiss you since the day you showed up for work. I think about kissing you all the time. Even now, when I can't seem to lock the bad memories away where they belong, I want to kiss you. I want my arms around you and my lips on yours." His breath came in ragged gasps. His gaze pinned her, so full of wanting she couldn't move.

And yet, he did nothing about it.

FLYNN ROUNDED THE corner of his house. "I thought I saw someone out here."

Slade stopped watching the river drift past Flynn's back porch. He'd been there for hours. He couldn't stop thinking of Christine and how his heart ached to think he had to let her go. She deserved someone whole and unblemished. "Becca took the kids into Cloverdale for a pizza run. And I like the view from your porch better than the view from mine."

"It's not like you can't buy some property on the river. There's plenty of riverfront available." Flynn sat in a wicker chair next to his.

"I know it's weird," Slade said. "But that house is the last thing I have of my parents."

Flynn cleared his throat. "That's not exactly true. That room is filled with their things. And the twins showed me your family photo albums."

"Where'd they find those? You didn't let them in the bedroom, did you?" Unease clenched deep in his belly.

Flynn shook his head. "They said they found them in the hall closet. Baby pictures. Pictures of you as a basketball star, newspaper clippings, things like that."

"Everybody has memorabilia."

"Not me." He stretched his legs out in front of him. "Well, I had none until I came to live here with my grandfather when I was eight. But baby pictures? Nada."

"Your grandfather was a good man," Slade said.

They both looked out toward the river, remembering the man who'd raised Flynn and passed away less than two months earlier.

"It was fun to see your young, smiling mug." Flynn broke the silence first. "You were five years ahead of me in school. Back then, I looked up to you. Star athlete. Valedictorian. Scholarship winner."

"None of that mattered when..." Slade smoothed his tie.

"Your parents loved you, man. Your dad may not have had it together at the end, but he loved you." Flynn put a hand on Slade's shoulder. "Let him go. Let the bad stuff go and hold the good memories where you should." He tapped his chest with his other hand.

"And if I can't?"

"You can't? That's a first." Flynn stood, laughing, and then stared at him hard. "You don't remember, do you?"

Slade shook his head.

"Will and I were home visiting once. We were out on the patio at El Rosal, trying to figure out some impossibly unrealistic budget for the business so we could generate venture capital, when you sauntered by." Flynn fiddled with his ball cap. "I said something like, 'I can't do it,' and you stopped. You turned your head and flat-out told me, *'Can't* just means you won't.'" Flynn shook his head. "Will invited you for a drink. In a week, you'd worked out our finances, pitched our idea to several venture capitalists, got us funding for the app, and moved into our apartment. *Can't.*" He chuckled. "You were older than I was in school and you used to intimidate me. But that…that was the start of a beautiful partnership."

"I didn't get us much funding."

"Enough to pay for rent and an internet connection. It was enough, buddy. And you know what? Every time I look at some code and think I can't do it, I remember you saying what that meant. *I won't* doesn't get you to the place we are today. *I won't* doesn't clear out cobwebs or put the past to rest."

I can't kiss Christine.

How many times had Slade told himself that? The distance he kept between the two of them, which, granted, wasn't as much as it should have been, was like a sharp pain in his chest. The pain only eased when he was with her.

I can't date Christine.

She deserved better. He wouldn't allow her into the mess that was his scarred life. It didn't matter that she seemed willing to try, to meet him halfway—more than halfway when you considered the baggage he had to carry into a relationship.

Whenever times got tough, she'd wonder if he'd disappear and try to kill himself. Evy had told him that over and over again. Evy had told the judge and the lawyers that she couldn't trust him with their children because of that one moment of weakness. It had taken eight years of stability and success for the legal system to recognize that Slade was worth gambling on. He hadn't even known Christine eight weeks.

I can't love Christine.

Flynn was right. He was choosing not to explore the strong feelings from his past and stronger desires he had toward Christine. But it didn't matter if he said *I can't* or *I won't*.

It was better this way. For both of them.

"Is SOMEONE COMING to dinner?" When Christine got home from work, food covered her grandmother's pink kitchen counter. Tuna casserole. Corn-bread muffins. Steamed vegetables. Chocolate cake.

"We're bringing dinner over to Hiro Takata's house. It's community pot luck." Nana glanced at Christine's dirt-smeared shorts and tattered T-shirt. "I'll give you five minutes to wash up and change."

Christine snagged a corn-bread muffin, breaking it open. Steam rose. She popped a piece into her mouth. It was moist and sweet. "What's the occasion?"

"The fact that he'd let his place get out of hand. If Slade hadn't asked about his near-debilitating arthritis, we might have lost another member of our community."

"He's that sick?" Christine took another bite of muffin.

"He's old and frail. Rheumatoid arthritis can lock you up like a statue. The pain drains you. He's lost weight. Chances are he'd suffer an attack and go to sleep afterward from exhaustion." Nana tapped her watch face. "The man needs to rebuild his strength and the town needs to let him know we haven't forgotten about him."

"But you had," Christine pointed out.

"Because we're old and forgetful. We're lucky to have people like Slade and his friends around to keep an eye out for us. Now go! I need help carrying things over there."

Christine grinned. "That's all I am. An extra pair of hands." She sashayed down the hall.

"One of those hands would be a lot more attractive if you let that millionaire put a ring on it."

While Christine washed up, she debated what to wear. Capris and a cool blouse or a dress. A dress would be like throwing down a challenge to Slade, a test of his control. He'd stared at her with manly appreciation in her black feathered gown. Did she want to test his control and risk her heart again?

She knew the answer. She wasn't going to be a quitter anymore.

She changed into a simple green cotton sheath and a pair of low-heeled Grecian sandals out of her collection of shoes. It took her an extra five minutes to freshen her makeup, brush out her ponytail and pull up half her locks with a turquoise-and-silver comb at the back of her head.

These were final-countdown measures. It was easy to resist her in a torn T-shirt and dirty jean shorts. She was bringing out the big guns. And if this didn't work, tomorrow she'd send that email she'd drafted accepting a job interview at Lalopolle.

"That was worth the wait," Nana said when she met her in the hallway, smoothing her own simple blue cotton dress. "You look more like yourself."

She didn't feel like herself. She felt like one of the twins putting on an alter ego.

That was, until she arrived at Old Man Takata's house and saw how Slade looked at her, as if she was an ice-cream sundae he wanted to savor in slow, melting spoonfuls. He didn't come for a taste, but he came over to greet her.

"Wow," he said as he took the food from Nana's arms. "I mean…everything just looks… Wow."

It had been hot on the walk over. Under his gaze, Christine's temperature ratcheted up another few degrees.

"Young people nowadays," Nana huffed and left them in the foyer.

Christine didn't wait to hear if Slade had anything else to say. She carried the corn bread and cake toward the kitchen.

Hiro Takata's house smelled of wood polish and disinfectant. Every light was on, every window open. His furniture was classic 1970s. White velvet couch with big orange flowers and matching club chairs, all protected by a layer of plastic.

Old Man Takata alternated between smiling and grumbling. He joked with his bowling buddies and complained to the women about being fussed over.

Dodging canes and walkers, Christine reached the kitchen, which was already overflowing with food. The noise in the house was approaching raucous. Truman, Grace, and Faith ran by and out the back door.

"I'm sorry," Slade said softly, coming to stand beside her.

"Me, too." Christine touched his tie briefly. It was a beautiful red print.

She turned her back on him and helped set up the buffet, helped fill and carry plates for guests, helped satisfy the curious questions of residents about what was going on at the winery.

All the while, she felt Slade's eyes on her, making her skin tingle and her body feel energized, despite a small voice whispering in her head, *Don't hope.*

The meal and then dessert came and went. Some of the attendees looked tired and talked about leaving, moving toward the front door. Christine began picking up empty cups and plates. Slade appeared at her side with a trash bag, making things more efficient. He was, after all, all about efficiency.

Every time their glances collided, she let herself foolishly pretend that he was thinking, *The faster this goes, the sooner I can kiss you.* But he was good at control and she knew the lies she told herself would feel even more foolish tonight when she tried to fall asleep.

They finished cleaning up. It was time to collect Nana and head home.

He held her gaze too long and crooked his finger at her. Christine's heart pounded in her chest. She followed him to the kitchen, out the back, around to the driveway on the side of the house where Old Man Takata kept his garbage cans. Slade put the trash in the bin and turned to her, capturing her mouth with a kiss so full of pent-up longing that she felt like crying.

Someone opened Takata's front door and stepped outside. Several someones. Saying their goodbyes.

Before sadness had a chance to spear through her, Slade swept her into his arms and carried her across Takata's driveway to his, to the other side of a low fence, which was dripping in shadow.

He set her down and cradled her face in his hands. "I told myself we wouldn't do this. I told myself not to touch you. There're still things you don't know about me."

"I know enough about you here." She placed her palm over his heart.

Without warning he captured her mouth. He kissed and kissed and kissed her, until her lips were swollen and she couldn't think straight.

Her hands pushed against his rock-solid chest, giving her just enough space between them to reach the tie at his throat. She loosened the knot, unbuttoned the shirt beneath, slid her hands up to either side of his neck. The cords of muscle there were proof of his strength against the most severe of taboos, had probably helped to save his life.

Don't.

Because there was doubt, not about his ever attempting suicide again, but for her career and his commitment to her. Her mouth became rational, even if her hands didn't. "You're my boss."

He groaned, slowing his ardor only for a second. "You can report to Flynn from now on."

"Deal." A sham of a compromise. But the fire between them made her a fool.

He'd gone into the bedroom where it happened today. Maybe he hadn't fully faced his demons, but it was a start. And he was here, in her arms, no longer able to resist her.

Don't.

She wanted to argue, *You can't decide on a pair of shoes if you don't try them on.*

His hand slid around the curve of her waist.

She burned everywhere he touched. Her resolve went to ash, her common sense to cinders, her self-preservation incinerated.

This was where she belonged. He made her feel smart, capable, and confident. In his arms, she felt courageous. She could tackle anything life threw her way. She could take care of him and nurture his broken heart. Make him believe in himself and the power of love again. And she would, she would, she would. As long as he never stopped kissing her like this.

Christine tugged his tie free, wrapping the ends around her palm, rubbing the silk over his neck, his ear, his cheek. He was a precious gift to her, slightly scarred, in need of a gentle polish.

A car pulled into his driveway. The lights blinding.

Slade turned and shielded her behind him, giving Christine a moment to make sure everything was properly in place—it was—and smooth her hair.

"Slade? What are you doing?" A woman's voice. Horrified.

Christine stepped out of Slade's shadow, squinted, held up a hand.

A too-thin woman, in heels too high with dark, blunt-cut hair, walked into the glare of the headlights.

A familiar silhouette. She'd seen her... driving away the day she started work.

Slade's ex-wife.

CHAPTER EIGHTEEN

"SLADE, NO." EVY'S voice was surprisingly calm. "You know you can't do this to anyone else."

Christine had taken his hand when Evy got out of the SUV, standing side by side to face whatever his ex brought on. But Christine wasn't ready for this. Slade wasn't ready for this. Moments ago he'd been warm. Now his body felt frozen.

"Who's that?" An older woman's voice. It sounded like Agnes. And then Takata's screen door swung open. "Someone just pulled into Slade's driveway."

"I don't know who you are—" Evy was saying over the ruckus of walkers and octogenarians racing toward the door and fresh gossip. "—but you need to leave. For your own good."

"I'm Christine." His blonde warrior princess stepped in front of him, filling his heart with a bittersweet joy. Bittersweet because she didn't know Evy was about to crush whatever feelings she had for him. Crushing hopes was what Evy excelled at. "And I'm not going anywhere. I belong here."

Slade locked her claim deep in his heart, knowing he'd need it to comfort him later. "What are you doing here, Evy?"

"I didn't have cell-phone service in France. When we landed in New York and I turned on my cell, I got your messages. You were concerned for the girls. I tried calling, but I didn't get any answer, so I flew here."

He'd turned his cell phone off to avoid any more calls offering money for their bottling permits and he'd been at Takata's all day long. There was no answering machine at the house.

"Mom!" Faith ran across Takata's driveway, twigs in her hair. Something in Evy's expression stopped the girl from barreling into her mother for a hug.

Grace followed at a slower pace, surveying the situation. A splotch of ice cream had fallen onto her blouse.

Evy stared from one to the other. "Girls, get your things and bring them to the car. We're leaving."

"No," Grace replied calmly. She came to stand next to Slade, catching his free hand in her smaller one.

Now he had two defenders. But for how long? And at what risk to their hearts?

Faith stood between her two parents, clearly torn.

Christine switched the hand she held him with to the left and draped her right arm over Grace. "What's this about?"

Evy stormed forward, a lioness about to pounce on prey. "Girls, I told you not to listen to anything your dad said. I told you to use your defenses."

"What defenses?" Slade felt the first spiky stirrings of anger.

"And look at you. He got to you, didn't he? You talked!"

"You told them not to talk to me?" Anger solidified into a brittle, icy voice he barely recognized as his own.

"Of course I did. Don't look at him for permission." Evy snapped at Faith, who was staring apologetically at Slade. "I said get your things."

"Don't move, Faith." Slade had let his lawyer fight this battle for too long. Evy had instructed their girls to keep their distance? He'd instruct them to stay. "Your mother has some explaining to do."

"You want an explanation?" Evy's stance shifted toward a new target. Him. "I knew

I shouldn't have left them with you. I knew you'd brainwash them, just like your father did to you." She glared at their daughters. Her voice rose to operalike hysteria. "Did he try to make you hurt yourself? Did he?"

He'd made a tactical error, assuming she'd told the girls how to behave around him out of some vendetta. Evy thought she was protecting the girls. She viewed him as a threat to their safety. Slade saw what was coming, saw it playing out in grisly detail. "Evy, please."

But his ex was past the point of reason. She looked across the drive at Slade's friends, at his neighbors, and then back to Christine. "He's not who you think he is."

That got a shift in the crowd.

"Evy, don't." Slade felt Grace's grip and Christine's tighten on his hands, but his body was already starting to feel numb.

"Where did he tell you that scar came from? The one he hides? A mugger?" Evy laughed bitterly as she stalked toward them, her heels clicking on the pavement. "The day his father tried to kill himself, Slade tried to hang himself, too."

The crowd at Takata's was eerily silent.

Flynn broke away from the pack, shaking his head.

Christine squeezed Slade's hand tighter.

Faith and Grace? Faith looked as if she was going to cry. Grace stood her ground.

They know.

Those first few days when they got here, not talking, the wary looks. It wasn't just their mother telling them to give him the silent treatment to make him suffer. "You told them?" Slade felt as unstable as if the earth was shifting beneath his feet. "You told the girls what happened?"

"I wasn't going to leave them here with you unless they knew what you were capable of." Evy turned to play to the crowd. "His father left Slade a note, asking him to follow him. And Slade did. I came home just in time to save him from doing it."

The eyes of the Harmony Valley residents stared at him in wide-eyed disbelief.

"That's not true," Christine said. "You didn't save him. He saved himself."

He should have told Christine the entire truth instead of letting her believe...

"Is that what he told you?" Evy's lip curled.

Christine glanced over her shoulder at him. "Slade?" And then when he didn't say anything, she said more uncertainly, "Slade?"

"Christine...I..." Slade had trouble choking the words out. "The truth is I realized too late that I wanted to live. The truth is I would

have died if she hadn't found me." The words
cost him. Slade felt as if he was falling in on
himself, the same way he had that fateful day
in November. "I was lost. And I…"

Christine's mouth gaped open. Gone was
her fight, her compassion, her understanding.

He wanted to latch on to her and beg for
forgiveness. He wanted to wrap his arms
around her and Faith and Grace. He wanted
to swear on his mother's grave that they could
trust him.

But it was too late. The moment he omit-
ted the foundation of his horrendous mistake
to Christine, his chances had already slipped
away, like a twig drifting out of reach on the
current of the Harmony River. And with it,
the promise of love that was as soft and elu-
sive as the scent of vanilla when she was near.

"I told the judge," Evy was saying. "I told
the lawyers. I was afraid of what he might
do to my girls, of what he might convince
them to do."

Flynn swore. "Slade is more stable emotionally than you are."

Will stepped out of the crowd. "If you
were so worried about your girls, why did
you leave them here in the first place?"

"It was part of the revised child-support
agreement." Evy kept moving closer to Faith.

"I had to give them to him or risk everything."

"The money, you mean," Will said. "You wanted more money."

"The best schools cost money." Evy's huge diamond glinted in the headlights.

"So you made your ex-husband look like a monster to his daughters and then left them with him?" Flynn said too casually.

Evy didn't flinch. She'd convinced herself what she was doing was right.

If their roles were reversed, Slade couldn't say he wouldn't do the same, because he'd do anything to protect his kids.

"We're fine, Mom." Grace spoke up. "And Dad is fine, too. You were wrong. You don't have to worry. Go back to New York. We have nearly a week left."

"Grace, do as your mother says." Slade's quiet words seemed to stun the crowd. They stopped Flynn and Will from coming closer. They didn't understand the lengths Evy would go to. She'd make the twins suffer more than they were now. "Go get your things."

"I won't leave you, Dad." Grace jutted her chin out. "*We* won't leave you. Don't make us go."

Evy's bitter laughter filled the air. "Even your father knows that he can't be trusted with you. You can see the darkness in his eyes. His father still has the power to take him any time or he would have sold this house long ago."

Evy didn't know him at all, but Slade had no more fight left.

"Slade?" Christine stared at him. There was no sparkle in her eyes. No smile, either. He'd crushed her optimism and her defenses.

"Dad, say something." Grace tugged at his hand.

"Dude." Flynn came to stand next to him. "Tell her you *won't* let them go."

The house. The closed windows. The locked door. The bedroom upstairs that hadn't been touched in eight years. Eight years...

The closets. The belts. The ties. Eight years of seeing his father's face. Eight years and it was still as vivid in his mind as if it had happened yesterday.

He could tell himself ten ways from Tuesday that he wouldn't try to kill himself again, which was true, but he hadn't put the past behind him. And until he did, he didn't deserve to make anyone any promises.

"Pack your things, girls," Slade whispered, staring at Evy. And then stronger: "Pack your things and go."

Grace sobbed and ran into the house. Faith glared at him and ran after her.

"I told you before, Slade, you can't be close to anyone ever again." As if she hadn't done enough damage, Evy targeted Christine, closing the distance separating them. "You'd trust him? You'd trust him not to crack after a fight and finish himself this time? You'd trust him alone with your kids, when they're screaming for some toy he didn't buy them? You'd trust him not to lie to you when he can't even stop lying to himself?"

Christine hadn't taken her eyes off Slade, but still, she said nothing.

THE TWINS WERE GONE. Evy was gone. The old-timers were gone. The windows were shut.

Evy and the twins were headed to the airport. The potluck attendees were presumably spreading the good gossip they'd witnessed before tucking themselves into bed—*Remember when Daniel Jennings hung himself? It was nearly a double suicide.*

Slade's generation remained, having pow-wowed outside and said goodbye to the twins before following him into the house—Will and Emma, Flynn and Becca, Christine and Nate. Flynn had sent Truman home with Agnes.

Christine sat on the foyer floor, back to the wall, arms wrapped around herself. She hadn't stopped staring at him.

Nate stood a few feet from her, legs and arms akimbo, as if Slade were a suspect and Nate was ready to block any attempt Slade made to run.

Nate. Now, there was a man who'd do right by Christine. Tall, principled, and brave. Wouldn't catch Nate trying to off himself. Or lying about it. Wouldn't catch Nate choosing profit over promises.

The rest of his friends were wedged onto the couch beneath the front windows.

"I don't need an intervention." Slade sunk deeper into his father's chair, wishing they'd all go away, even Christine. Especially Christine.

"We disagree." Will's gaze was as firm as his grip on his fiancée's hand.

"Life doesn't hand out second chances just for them to be squandered," Emma said. Seeing as how she'd been in a car accident that almost killed Will's sister and had come away unscathed, Slade couldn't argue with her, much as he wanted to.

"You shared an apartment with us for five years and never said a word." Flynn sounded betrayed. "I gave you grief over those ties and…I would have understood if you had said something."

And sabotage their tentative relationship? Not likely. "It didn't concern you."

"It concerns me now." Flynn clenched his fists, pounding them on his thighs. "The way you let Evy walk all over you. The way you forced the twins to walk away. Your determination to sell and walk out of our lives. Yeah, it concerns me."

"And what was I supposed to do? You saw what happened when I opened the door upstairs. I couldn't go into the room. I haven't gotten past it." Slade dragged a hand over his face, watching Christine watch him. "Evy's right. They're safer with her."

"It's not a question of their safety." Becca placed a comforting hand on her husband's fist. "None of us here believe they'd ever be in danger with you. But those girls love you. And your ex-wife has suppressed that love for years. If you let them go now, she'll make sure you never get another chance with them."

"You don't understand."

"We do." Christine spoke, her voice as rusty and broken as the trust she'd placed in him. "We understand you're scared. The great and mighty Slade Jennings, who can stand up to conglomerates and legal teams and bargain for what he wants. The man who can meet any goal he sets. You're too scared to face this."

She stood and went upstairs.

A door opened.

He was afraid he knew which door.

"Whether you want to admit it to yourself or not, you've got some form of PTSD." Nate would know, being former military. "You hide it well. But hiding it means you'll never rid yourself of it. It's got a firm spot in your chest."

Christine came back downstairs. She was barefoot. Why hadn't he noticed that before? Had her shoes dropped on the driveway when he'd carried her across?

She didn't stop or say good-night. She just walked out.

Whatever it was inside Slade that had kept him going this long deflated. He slumped farther into his father's chair.

Flynn got up, tugging Becca with him. They went upstairs. After a few minutes, they came back down and left. Flynn didn't have his baseball cap on.

Will and Emma went next. A pilgrimage up the stairs, a few steps into the room, and then back down.

Nate pointed a finger at him. "Stay." And

then he, too, went up. This time a door closed before he returned.

"I haven't known you a long time, man, but I like you." Nate stood in the foyer.

Nate was perfect for Christine. Honest, steadfast.

"You don't need any of us here holding your hand. Only you can get yourself out of this. Just know we've got your back." And then Nate left.

Leaving Slade alone in a house that was quieter than he wanted it to be.

CHRISTINE COULDN'T SLEEP that night. She didn't believe that Slade was suicidal. She believed he was having trouble letting go of the guilt and the anger.

But that didn't stop a quiet voice in her head that kept repeating, *What if you're wrong?*

She'd wanted to stay with him until he believed he was worthy of love—hers, his daughters', his friends'. But Nate had convinced her that Slade wouldn't accept her love until he'd accepted the past as part of who he was.

What if she went to sleep and Slade tried something? What if Nate sent her a text message during the night that she was needed at Slade's and she didn't hear it? What if this crazy plan they'd come up with to help Slade heal didn't work?

Slade had been humiliated in front of his closest friends and a good portion of the small town. He'd let his daughters go without putting up a fight. He'd lied to her about what happened all those years ago.

Lied.

About something so important it shaped who he was today. How could Christine ever trust him again?

She wanted to erase Evy's words, because they'd created doubt where she'd had none before about Slade and his suicide attempt, and more importantly about the strength of the bond between them. She wanted to be with him, holding him and reassuring him things would be all right.

But he had to face this on his own. And come out stronger for it. Or they had no future.

At dawn, she dragged herself out of bed. She went into the garage and took out one of the high-heeled, red sequined ruby slippers. She put it on her window sill. It was a statement, of sorts, that only Slade would understand. She loved her shoes and wasn't giving them up. It was her equivalent of leaving the light on until he came home.

At work, she had several messages in her inbox requesting help getting in touch with Slade.

The sharks were circling, trying to find him, trying to find the partnership's weak spot. Who knew what they'd do with the information that he had a doozy of a weakness?

She had several serious texts, plus one voice mail from her father—all with the same message. *It's time to bail.*

She ignored the queries, ignored her father, and tried to book some meetings, review her schedule, process invoices. She was going to change the course of Alexander history and stay when things looked grim. Her decision went against the high standards of quality her family held so dear.

She wanted to do the right thing for herself and for the people she'd made a promise to by taking this job—people like Phil and Old Man Takata, like Mayor Larry and Nana. Like Flynn, Will, and, of course, Slade. She was choosing to be loyal and fight for a quality wine to be made here, even if she fought with new owners.

Flynn and Will had reassured her they weren't selling. She was embarrassed to admit that she had more readily believed them than when Slade tried to tell her the same thing.

Nate sent out a group text in the morning: Didn't go upstairs at all.

Meaning Slade hadn't ended the hold his father had over him.

Her cell phone vibrated. It was a text from Grace: Back in New York. Tell Dad we love him.

Grace wouldn't let her mother brainwash her that easily again. There was still time for Slade to salvage his relationship with his daughters.

Christine tucked her cell phone back in her pocket and kept working.

And braced herself for the next battle, as certain as a sunrise—her dad's arrival.

CHAPTER NINETEEN

SOMEBODY WAS KNOCKING on Slade's front door.

No one ever knocked on the Death and Divorce House door.

Disoriented, Slade sat up on the couch, fitting each shirt button through a hole before he stood. He gazed around the living room, but couldn't find his tie.

Christine must still have it from the night before.

"'Bout time you answered." Takata stood on his doorstep in cargo shorts that almost drooped off his nonexistent hips and an orange-and-blue Hawaiian shirt. He looked like a half-starved Macaw. He pounded his cane on the porch. "I need you to drive me somewhere."

"I thought that was Becca's job."

"That girl's too busy with people who need her help. Go get your keys." He shouldered his way across the threshold. "Why haven't you gotten rid of the chair Daniel hated?" He did the cane shuffle over to Slade's father's chair. "Your mother bought this for him. He hated it."

Slade let the screen door close. "My dad loved that chair."

"He loved your mother," Takata corrected, choosing to sit on the couch. "The chair he hated. Said it made him feel like he was driving a lowrider. Just look at it—it's not a chair for anyone over five feet. What does a tall man do with his legs in a chair like that?"

Slade did look. He did see. "I hate that chair."

"Most people, when they hate stuff, they get rid of it." Takata thumped his cane on the floor. "Hop to, boy. I have places to be."

"I'm not going anywhere without a shower and some coffee." He half wanted Takata to give up on him.

The old man didn't. He rested his hands on top of his cane. "I'll wait for the coffee."

Slade set the coffeepot brewing and went upstairs to shower, passing by the closed door to the master bedroom. He had no idea what his friends had done in his father's room last night. Curiosity had yet to beat anxiety, had yet to make him open the door.

Showered, fresh shirt, fresh slacks, fresh tie, and Slade was back downstairs.

"You didn't shave." Takata waved him back upstairs.

"I thought you were in a hurry."

"I am, but that doesn't mean I want to be seen with someone who looks like he was on *Miami Vice*."

"You watched that movie?"

"I'm talking about a television show in the '80s. Speedboat? Five-o'clock shadow? You look like you're out to bust somebody." Takata sighed. "Where's my coffee?"

Coffee wasn't all Takata wanted. He wanted eggs. And some of the cantaloupe Slade had yet to slice into, which was sitting on the kitchen counter.

An hour later, they were on the road.

"Are you going to tell me where we're going?" Slade asked.

"Get me to the 101 and head south" was all Takata would say.

They ended up in front of a very small shop in Healdsburg, tucked away on a back street.

"A tobacco shop?" Slade frowned. "Are you out of cigars?"

"I'm out of Cubans." Takata glanced furtively up and down the street. "They're illegal, you know. They only sell them on the down low. Cash." He handed Slade some bills. "If you go in there and they think you're a

cop and they don't sell me my Cubans, I'll…
I'll…"

"You'll what?" Slade almost smiled at the
idle threats of a man half his size.

Takata poked a finger in his direction. "I'll
make your life next door to me a living hell."

"Like it isn't already?"

That comment earned him a wrinkle-edged
glare.

Less than ten minutes later, Takata had his
precious underground Cuban cigars, and they
were back on the road to Harmony Valley. Before they took the highway exit home, Takata
made him stop at a grocery store, where he
bought a small bouquet of flowers.

"Take a right on Kennedy," Takata directed
as they came into town.

"Why?" That would take them directly past
the cemetery.

"Because I said so." Despite Takata never
having been a father, he had the lingo down.

Slade turned onto Kennedy. "We're not
stopping."

Takata huffed, "Then slow down as you
pass and I'll jump out. Just don't run me over
as you speed away with my Cubans."

Biting back a comment about ornery old
men, Slade turned into the iron gates of the Harmony Valley Cemetery. The air-conditioning in

the truck that had felt so comfortable moments before now blew out icicles that made every muscle in his body shiver.

"Head toward the back."

"I'm not going to his grave." Cold. Slade was so cold. Goose bumps blanketed his arms.

"Don't make everything about you," Takata muttered. "My mother and wife are entombed in the back. I haven't been out here in months. It's not as if Larry wants to drive me over every Sunday. And no one wants to come in the heat."

Slade shut up and drove to the rear of the small cemetery. He parked, planning to let Takata have a private visit with his family, but Takata said, "Bring the Cubans and the flowers."

Slade glanced toward the hill where his parents were buried. So close. Too close.

He got out of the truck. It was like stepping out of a meat freezer into a broiling oven. The temperature transition weakened his knees. It had nothing to do with the fact that he hadn't been this close to his parents since his father's funeral.

The heat didn't seem to bother the old man. He kept trundling along. Slade followed him up the shady path toward a grand tomb tucked in the back of the cemetery.

"When I owned this place, I wanted nothing but the best for my loved ones in their eternal rest." Takata paused to catch his breath halfway up the hill.

"You don't own it anymore? Who does?"

"Larry. He's bought up lots of property in town. Stands to make a fortune if your winery is successful. That's why he fights you over every penny. He's over-leveraged and short on cash."

They continued their slow ascent to the top of the small hill and sat on a bench in front of Takata's family tomb. The heat and surroundings were oppressive, despite a poplar that provided shade, and the occasional weak breeze that barely rustled its leaves.

Slade put the box of Cubans and the flowers on the bench between them. He stared at his loafers. "Nice view."

"Don't lie. Being here bothers you, doesn't it?" Takata removed a cigar from the box. "I take comfort that my loved ones are here, at my back. You probably don't think about your parents over there to the left, taking care of each other."

Slade pulled at his collar. "Mom wouldn't have approved of what Dad did."

"S'pose not." Takata lit the cigar with several quick puffs. "But she'd forgive him. That's what this place is all about. Forgiveness." He sat back on the bench. "My wife was very sick before she died. We tried everything—traditional treatments, new age medicine, prayer. But nothing I did could stop her from slipping away. In the end, she wanted relief from all the pain."

Takata took a big drag on his cigar. "For a long time, I had to live with my guilt. Why her and not me? I smoked. I drank. She'd done neither. One day, as I was sitting here, I realized the time of her passing wasn't up to me. I'd been left behind, alone, for a reason."

An idea put forth by Will's fiancée, Emma, last night. Too bad Slade wasn't a believer in fate. He couldn't see anything beyond proving to himself that he could atone for his father's loss by making money.

"I think the reason I'm still here is you." Takata's dark eyes drilled into Slade's.

It was Slade's turn to scoff.

"Laugh all you want. You're not getting rid of me." The old man gazed over the crosses and headstones marching down the hill.

As threats went, this one made Slade smile. "I could move."

Takata blew a smoke ring. "You'd have to deal with all your father's things."

A bird swooped to the grass nearby, hopping closer, as if to make sure they hadn't brought any food to share. It took flight with a disapproving chirp.

Slade wasn't willing to let the old man win that easily. "I could shut the house up and leave town."

"You'd leave an old man alone?" Takata tried his best to look forlorn, but Slade knew him too well. "Who knows? I may write you into my will. I've got no heirs."

Slade laughed. "You barely know me."

"I watched you grow up. You've done your parents proud."

Slade didn't know what to say. Takata's praise meant more than any write-up he'd gotten in business magazines.

"And now I want you to do me proud." Takata gestured downhill. "I want you to head down that slope and say some words to your parents. I'll wait here."

Slade's stomach wound up tighter than a slugger protecting home plate. "No."

"It's time to make your peace." Takata handed him the flowers and an unlit cigar. "These are for them."

Daisies. His mother loved daisies. Slade

rolled the cigar between his fingers. His gut unwound a smidgen.

"You're not alone in this world. You have a great many friends. A nontraditional family, if you will." Takata put a hand on Slade's shoulder and gave him a gentle push. "Your parents are here. And they've missed you."

Guilt, loneliness, and love propelled him to his feet. He made his way slowly down the hill to his parents' resting place.

There was no bench by their graves. There were just headstones.

Slade took the flowers out of their wrapping and set them in the too-long-empty vase attached to the side of his mother's headstone.

Jean Marie Jennings. Beloved wife and mother.

Slade laid the cigar at the base of his father's headstone.

Daniel Corbett Jennings. Beloved husband and father.

Nothing original on their grave markers. Nothing profound. No testament to how much they loved the Harmony River or the outdoors or…their son.

Slade knelt in the grass at their feet, feeling awkward and alone. But maybe not as alone as he had been.

Takata watched from the hill.

"It's been a while," Slade murmured, feeling like the inconsiderate son who hadn't called home regularly, even for birthdays and holidays. "I really messed up."

BRAD ALEXANDER CLIMBED the stairs to Christine's office with powerful steps that shook the entire farmhouse. "What's wrong with your phone?"

Christine looked up from the column of figures she'd unsuccessfully added three times.

Her dad stood at the head of the stairs, dusty, dirty, and obviously angry, as if he'd been busy and summoned out of the vineyards by an inconsiderate boss.

"Hey, Dad." She tucked the budget into a folder and introduced him to Ryan, who wisely mumbled something about taking sugar readings in the vineyard and escaped the office.

"You haven't answered me." Her father put his hands on his hips.

Christine had anticipated this conversation for a long time, possibly for years. She knew the only tactic to keep her dad from blowing up hinged on her remaining calm. Hard to do when she hadn't gone against her father's wishes since she was a spoiled, rebellious teenager.

She phrased her answer in nonconfrontational tones. "My phone is fine."

"Then why haven't you called me?" The volume of his demand was loud enough to shake Christine's resolve. Instead, it seemed to shake the dormer windows.

"Have a seat, Dad." Christine gestured to the folding chair on the other side of her desk. When he didn't move, she added, "Please sit down."

He reluctantly complied.

Christine met her father's gaze squarely, despite the nervous tic her leg seemed to have developed beneath her desk. "I haven't returned your calls or answered your messages because I'm not leaving."

"The big corporations are going to swoop in and you'll be obsolete. Alexanders don't make box wine." It was her father's familiar argument, delivered like a fire-and-brimstone sermon with a finger pointed to heaven, as if predicting a lightning strike if she didn't conform to his wishes. "The new owners will look at your salary and pink-slip you. I'm warning you now—"

"And I appreciate it." She cut him off, struggling to be gentle, but firm. "I couldn't have advanced my career this far without your advice and guidance."

That mollified him. He nodded his agreement.

"But it's time I made my own decisions and took responsibility for my own career risks."

His nod did a 90-degree flip to a headshake. "You don't understand what's looming over you."

"I do, Dad." And she told him, using her controlled, indoor voice. The one she used with investors and tour groups. The one a college professor had once told her made her more credible than her smile.

She told him how the partnership had convinced her they weren't going to sell. She told him how they had an aggressive five-year growth plan that would create a challenge unlike any she'd taken on before. She told him how no expense was being spared, even an unplanned makeshift wine cave.

She didn't tell him she'd fallen in love with her boss or that Slade had a less-than-pristine history. She'd let Nana torture him with that news.

"But, honey, are you sure?" Her father scratched the back of his neck. "You could be stuck here without a place to jump to if you don't make a move now."

Her leg had long since stopped shaking. Instead of falling into a shouting match with her dad, they'd had a very mature discussion. It would go down in Alexander history as a day to remember. "They're not lying to me. They're not selling."

He rubbed a hand over his sun-streaked hair, his eyes clouded with worry. "How do you know, honey? How do you know?"

Christine took a deep breath, knowing her smile wasn't confident enough to convince her father. "Sometimes you have to take a leap of faith."

Slade pulled into his driveway and asked Takata, "Do you need me to come inside and make you some lunch?"

"Don't baby me," Takata grumbled. "I'm a grown man. I'll make my own lunch."

"You have leftover tuna casserole, don't you?"

"Dang straight. Thanks for the ride."

Slade walked Takata to his back door, promising to check up on him later, which got him another groused protest.

Emotionally drained from his cemetery visit, Slade went into the house and sat in his father's chair. It really wasn't the right chair for someone his size. He wasn't that much taller than his dad.

Slade carried the chair out to the curb. If this was New York, that chair would be missing by morning, claimed by someone who'd appreciate it. As it was, Slade suspected the chair would be there a long time.

The house was strangely silent. Slade washed out his travel mug, put away dishes, opened the refrigerator door, and looked at all the food he'd stocked up for the girls. There were Grace's yogurts. There were Faith's blueberries.

The house was quiet. Empty. Sad.

Slade headed out, walking toward the river. He cut through the park where Mayor Larry did his morning yoga and found himself on the path that followed the river upstream. He'd always liked this part of the Harmony River best. There were fewer houses, fewer people, fewer distractions. He could think.

And he did. He thought about his daughters' smiles, their laughter, their hugs. The first time Evy took them away his heart had dragged behind his heels for nearly a year. This time, his heart might never recover. But…he would grow a callus because that was for the best. Children needed to trust their parents wouldn't let them down when life got rocky.

The land on either side of the river rose until forty-foot cliffs framed the river's progress instead of low, gentle banks. When he reached a bluff overlooking a bend in the river, he stopped. He could see a quarter mile each way. Empty pastures lined the river here, bordered by blackberry brambles, the fruit heavy on the vines. He sat beneath an oak tree and swung his legs over the edge of the rocky bluff. Below him, the river eased past several boulders, uncaring of Slade's emotional burdens.

The day was getting hotter. He rolled up his sleeves, grateful of the shade the oak provided. A breeze would be nice.

A small lizard scurried close, tilting his head this way and that, as if trying to find the best way to look at him.

Slade could relate. He was trying to find the best way to look at himself, too.

His friends and Christine thought he could just wave off his horrendous mistake and move on with his life. They didn't understand that he deserved to pay for his poor judgment every day for the rest of his life.

He brought to mind Christine's vivacious smile, the all-in approach she used to attack an overwhelming workload, the soft feel of her hands on his skin, the warmth of her lips on his scar.

In another life, he would have given his heart to her completely. He would've been down on his knees every day trying to prove to her how much he valued and treasured her. He would've been that man she wanted— lending her strength when she needed it, loving her despite vineyard-torn T-shirts and wine-stained hands. He'd love her for the talented, strong, optimistic woman she was and the beautiful woman she was on the inside. He'd—

The ground beneath him rumbled.

Earthquake.

The earth cracked and shifted without warning, crumbling his bird's-eye perch. For one heartbeat, Slade seemed to hang in midair. He lunged for a tree root as the rocks and dirt he'd been sitting on rained through the air, showering the boulders forty feet below him.

Christine.

She'd think he committed suicide. She'd think he didn't love her or the girls enough to live.

He clung to the rough wood, trying to find purchase with his feet, trying to ignore the panic-induced rush of adrenaline and the mind-numbing spike of fear.

The girls… Evy would win, tainting their memories of him.

I don't want to die.

CHAPTER TWENTY

By the time Slade got home, he was dirty, tired, and thirsty.

His friends were waiting for him on his front porch. The same usual suspects from the night before, minus Christine.

He hadn't thought her absence would hurt nearly as much as Grace's and Faith's. He felt as empty and sad as the house.

"There was an earthquake," Becca said.

Flynn came down the steps. "We couldn't get you on the phone."

They didn't fool Slade. They'd noticed he was missing and thought the worst. "Is everyone else in town okay?" Slade spun on Nate. "Or are you just checking up on me?"

"Everyone else is fine." Nate chewed on the inside of his cheek before adding, "We checked them first."

The anger and fight he should have felt last night finally made an appearance. "And then did you run upstairs to my dad's room to make sure I wasn't hanging there?"

No one spoke, a sure sign that they had.

"I'm not going to do anything stupid like that ever again." Not after inching to safety and staring down death. "You don't have to worry."

They looked at each other and then back at him.

"You haven't been in your dad's room," Will said.

"You have to face your demons," Emma said.

"Everyone seems to think my demons have been hanging out upstairs." Slade heaved a sigh. "And maybe they have, but that's not the only place to face them."

"You look like you've been rolling around the vineyard." Flynn grinned, perhaps sensing his friend was going to be okay, even if he hadn't opened the bedroom door upstairs.

Slade told them the condensed version of what happened. "All I could think about as I walked back here was what you would have thought if I'd fallen. You'd have assumed I jumped, right?"

No one said a word.

Indignation sent him charging up the porch steps. "I need a shower." He left them outside and went upstairs. At the landing, curiosity got the better of him. He opened the door to his dad's room, took a deep breath, and turned his head to look at the closet.

His dad's body wasn't hanging there. The specter of Slade wasn't hanging there.

His father's clothes were still shoved to either side of the closet, untouched since that fateful day, but there was a pile of stuff on the floor. A pile that hadn't been there all those years ago.

Slade entered the room. It didn't feel as if it rejected him. He didn't feel anything from the room but sadness.

He knelt before the pile. Flynn's baseball cap, the one his grandfather wore before he died, was upside down, cradled between the sandals Christine had been wearing last night—classy, expensive sandals as beautiful as the woman herself. Inside Flynn's ball cap was Emma's diamond-and-pink sapphire engagement ring, a wallet-size picture of Will's sister who'd almost died in a car crash, Becca's first husband's Purple Heart, Nate's handcuffs.

An odd collection of things. Each item carried special meaning to each of his friends about love. Their good karma to replace his bad.

Although… Slade fingered Nate's handcuffs. He wasn't sure the new sheriff was sending the same message as the rest of them. Did he think Slade needed to be locked up? Or that Slade was acting as if he was hand-cuffed to this house? This room? His memories?

Something glittered beneath Christine's shoes. He moved them aside and sucked in a breath. Beneath the pile were the girls' golden baby bracelets.

They'd come in here. Alone. Before they left.

Slade had to remind himself to breathe. He was incredibly lucky. His young daughters were so very brave. Even when their mother left them with him—practically a stranger, a man Evy had painted as unstable, dangerous—his little girls had been strong. They'd watched him. They'd been careful. They'd learned to love him.

And he'd let them go.

Knife blades couldn't have driven more pain into his chest.

He'd let his babies go.

He'd let fear and guilt and shame win.

Slade left the mementos on the floor and looked around the room, stopping at differ-ent items his parents had been fond of—the lilac afghan his mother had crocheted, the baseball his dad had caught from a homer at a

Giants game, his grandmother's small crystal bowl filled with quartz, his father's smile as he held up a huge rainbow trout. There was love in this room.

There were no ghosts. No demons. No shadows of his past.

It was just a room where something terrible had happened.

It had no hold on him anymore.

No hold.

Slade hurried out of the room, searching for his cell phone.

SLADE FOUND HIS friends later that afternoon on Flynn's back porch. He heard their voices before he saw them and hesitated only a moment. These people had changed his life. He didn't know how to thank them.

It was time to try.

He clutched a large cardboard box and ascended the porch steps.

He rounded the corner of the wraparound porch to find his friends in their usual spots— Becca in Flynn's lap on a chair, Will and Emma sitting close together on a bench, Nate leaning against the porch railing across from Will, and a new addition to their group— Christine. She leaned on the porch railing across from Flynn, much too close to Nate, who was *not* the right man for her.

There were gasps and exclamations when they saw him.

Slade walked into their midst, staking out a place against the railing between Nate and Christine.

No one spoke. They all stared at him.

Slade kept his head high. He wore khakis and a blue button-down without a tie. The shirt placket was open so that the sickle curve of his scar was clearly visible on his neck. He let them look their fill.

Only Christine didn't look. Her snub chilled him. Had she given up on him? Was he too late?

It seemed like a school year before Flynn spoke. "What took you so long?"

"I couldn't find what I was looking for. And I had to track down my legal counsel."

"Lawyers are never around when you need them to be," Will said. He and Flynn knew some of what Slade had done that day. They'd come up with a reason to assemble the rest of Slade's friends for him.

"I instructed my divorce lawyer to inform the judge of what Evy did—how she told the girls I was dangerous, not just to myself, but to them. I have a feeling they'll be on the next plane out."

"Why are you clutching that box?" Emma asked.

Slade awkwardly tucked the box beneath his arm. "Because I needed to return your things and I didn't want to lose your engagement ring." He found it and handed it carefully back to her. "I don't know many women who would leave a three-carat diamond on the floor of someone's house on purpose."

"Rings are replaceable." Emma smiled gently. "Friends are not."

"Or sisters." Slade rummaged in the box again and handed Will the picture of his sister.

Will touched his forehead to Emma's. Her finger stroked Amy's picture and then Will's face. She gave him a gentle kiss on the lips.

Beside Slade, Christine shifted against the railing, as if uncomfortable.

"Becca, you were the first person to show me how to let someone die with dignity and love. None of us, especially Flynn, could have stood vigil at his grandfather's bedside without your compassionate wisdom." He handed her the Purple Heart medal her first husband had earned. "I wish I'd known you years ago."

Things might have turned out differently for both himself and his father.

He reached for the baseball cap. "Flynn, I know you don't have to hide beneath this hat anymore trying to prove you don't look like your dad. I know you wear it to be closer to your grandfather." He handed the cap to his friend. "I hope you won't give me too much of a bad time when I show up to a business meeting wearing a tie. Some protocols still need to be honored." But Slade was done wearing one seven days a week. He finally felt as if he was free.

The handcuffs clanked together as Slade pulled them from the box. "Nate, given the emotional significance of everyone else's items, I don't want to know the truth behind these."

Everyone but Christine laughed as Slade handed them over. "I assumed you were trying to tell me to unshackle myself from the house."

"Close enough." Nate tucked the cuffs into his back pocket.

Christine was fidgeting now, no doubt realizing all the offerings but hers had been returned.

Holding the box with two hands, Slade looked inside. He winced. One hand loosened its grip and reflexively reached for the tie that no longer hung around his neck. He let his hand drop to his side, sliding it into his pocket before taking the box again with two hands.

"I brought back your shoes, Christine. I know you don't agree with how I spend money on myself or the girls, but life is short. People can be taken away from you, and people can take themselves away." He kept his gaze on her, hoping. "I realize now that my Dad died years before he committed suicide. Mental illness stole him from me. I know that I can't buy back those years or my innocence, no matter how much money I make. In the future, I want to spend more on making people happy than on the status and image that come with success."

He glanced down and saw she was wearing a cheap pair of flip-flops. "But, Christine, if you love high-quality shoes and they make you happy, you should wear them more often."

He knelt at her feet and placed his fingers lightly on her ankle. He could feel her pulse pound rapidly. He gave her a smile, equal parts gentle challenge and acceptance. He was ready to love her. "What do you say?

How about you wear this fine example of Italian workmanship?"

When she didn't move, he tried again. "I gave up my Italian ties. One of us has to represent." He lifted her foot up ever so slowly, nearly passing out with relief that she let him. And then he replaced her plastic flip-flop with Italian craftsmanship, first on one foot and then the other. He deposited her plastic sandals carefully in the box as if they were more expensive than the leather on her feet and set the box aside.

"I've let you down in so many ways, Christine. I didn't tell you the whole truth about the day my father died. I didn't stand up for myself against Evy or express my feelings for you. I haven't felt worthy of anyone's affection for years, much less been able to feel worthy of love when it's offered without expectation."

He still knelt at her feet, on one knee. "I was afraid. Not that I'd try to kill myself again, but that someone I loved wouldn't believe I wouldn't try. And so I locked myself away with expensive ties, trying to feel safe. Instead, I felt empty and lost and alone."

"This is better than when you proposed to Emma," Flynn whispered to Will.

Everyone shushed him. Everyone except Christine.

"I'll always have this crazy extended family." He paused. "Did you know Hiro Takata wants to adopt me? I don't understand how so many people find something to like about me, but I'm hoping you'll find many things to love about me."

He took off the engagement ring he'd slipped onto his pinky when he'd reached in his pocket and held it up to her. "I love you, Christine. I know we only met less than a month ago, but sometimes you just realize deep down in your heart that you want to spend the rest of your life with someone. I want to spoil you with great shoes and fancy dresses, even if they have feathers. I want to work as hard at loving you as you work in the vineyard. And I promise you that I will never leave you of my own free will. I'm yours from this day forward, from now until forever."

Tears in her eyes, Christine drew him to his feet. "How could I turn down an offer like that? Especially when I love you so very much."

"Maybe because he never popped the question," Flynn ribbed.

He'd been so nervous he'd forgotten to

actually ask her. "Will you marry me?" he blurted.

"Yes." Grinning, she slid her hands up to rest on either side of his neck. "I've been waiting for someone who deserves my love and loyalty."

Slade was so happy. There was only one thing missing. "The girls are going to be upset that they missed this."

"Not to worry." Nate waved his cell phone. "I recorded the whole thing."

LATER, WHEN THE champagne had been popped and toasts made, when family members, extended and otherwise, had been notified, when the sun had gone down over the mountains to the west, Slade leaned against the railing on Flynn's porch, his arm around Christine.

They were serenaded by frogs and crickets down by the river as Slade counted off how blessed he was with Faith, Grace, Christine, Hiro, Flynn, Will, Becca, Emma, Nate, Agnes... He was running out of fingers.

"This rock is huge." Christine turned her finger so the five-carat ring glittered in the porch light.

He caressed the finger that wore his ring

so well. "Does that mean you want to trade it in for something else? We could go smaller."

"No." She clutched her hand to her chest. "You said you wanted to spoil me, and you did just that. But it's not a ring I can wear every day in the vineyard, especially not during harvest."

"I could buy you an everyday wedding band."

"You don't have to."

"No, but I want to. Plain diamonds, channel set in platinum." Nothing but the best for his wife. She was the primary reason he was finally ridding himself of the shackles of the Death and Divorce House. The twins, his friends, Hiro. They had created a very strong supporting role, so that he'd finally learned that money couldn't wipe out mistakes.

"Oh, yeah." She nudged him playfully with her hip. "I won't worry about losing that, either."

"I have an early wedding gift for you."

She raised an eyebrow. "Seriously? You were that confident I'd accept?"

He pressed a kiss to her forehead, choosing not to tell her how lacking in confidence he'd been. "I made an offer on some property on the east side of town overlooking the river.

We'll need to build a house, but I know this great architect…"

"Have fun overseeing the plans. I think that should be a long-overdue birthday present for you." She snuggled closer, crooning softly, "And many more…"

"You don't want to help me design it?"

"I'm plenty busy working at the winery. Harvest is almost here. And I trust you." She rubbed a hand over his chest where his tie used to rest. "Ryan had this idea about crowdsourcing, which wasn't quite right. But then I realized Harmony Valley can call in a crowd—all the younger relatives of our residents. We can give them each a tie-dyed T-shirt made by Mayor Larry and a bottle of wine when it's ready. And Flynn wants to pitch moving here permanently to anyone who shows up to help."

Slade shifted until he held her at arm's length. "We were talking about building a home. The place we're going to raise our children. And you changed the subject to the winery?"

She laughed. "I know, I know. I get carried away with my work." She planted a gentle kiss on his jaw. "As long as you have a professional-grade kitchen and some kind of wine storage…and a fantastic bedroom, second story, overlooking the river…I'm in."

"You're a dedicated woman. And I wouldn't have you any other way." He wrapped his arms around her, pulling her close. "Now, my real early wedding gift to you is that I sent out a press release saying our permits and our winery are not for sale."

"That's so sweet."

"The reason being that our partnership has already sold—"

"You lied to me?" Christine tried to push away from him, but he held on tight.

"Let me finish." He waited until she stilled. "I bought the permits from the partnership and now I'm giving them to you." He did release her then. Or at least he let her step back. He kept his hands on her arms. He'd probably always be reluctant to let her go.

"What? But why?"

"Because I realized that personal promises should come before profit objectives. Because I'm not afraid to put my future in your hands." He grinned. "And because we're three beer guys who know nothing about growing or making wine. We need a fourth partner, someone who'll be in charge and have our best interests at heart. The partnership still owns the property and the winery, but you'll own the permit and control how much wine we make and when."

She stretched to her tiptoes to press a kiss to the scar on his neck. "You never have to buy me anything again."

That was nice to hear, but Slade doubted he'd be able to stop himself from spoiling her.

Life was too precious and love too fragile to take anything for granted.

* * * * *